ANDREA NEKIĆ

IS NOT FINE

VIOLETA MATIJEVIĆ-BAGIA

First published by Dragonfly Publishing, April 2025

© Text – Violeta Matijević-Bagia.

ISBN(sc): 978-1-7635525-9-3

A catalogue record for this work is available from the National Library of Australia

Fiction/YA fiction

Trigger Warning: This book contains references to sexual assault, self-harm, depression, anxiety, and suicide.

For those who were silenced. I hear you. I see you.

I believe you.

CHAPTER ONE

The Case of the Disillusioned Maths Professor

June 5th, 2006

My parents thought this hole of a school was a good idea. I did not.

I darted out of the way, narrowly missing the speeding twenty-cent coin. An outraged shriek sounded behind me.

I slid my arm out of the backpack loops and hugged the bag to my chest. I blame my primary school. They had held a future planning day in Grade Six and the teachers told my parents I would benefit from a smaller school to reach my full potential. But Dad knew best and decided he didn't need some pompous principal's advice, and I was sent elsewhere.

But in Year Ten, I had an encounter with a girl who slapped me for looking at her boyfriend, and after a stint in detention, which, by the way, never happens to me, Dad changed his mind.

Fast-forward a year and a half. Here I was at Deanell High School, which, according to the brochure, was *super* exclusive and *super* specialised. One look at the peeling paint on the shabby walls of the portables confirmed it was neither.

I'd managed to get through all of Year Eleven without incident, made a few new friends and kept my grades high on the shiny A+ scale.

But now the pressure was on. I was halfway through Year Twelve and desperate for this painful experience to end, and despite the angry teachers, snotty students, and snide remarks about being an emo (long story, don't ask), I'd kept my head down and grades up.

I smiled, I nodded, and I did whatever was asked of me. At home, at school, at piano classes and at tennis…

I sighed and stopped at the school's looming gates, looking up at the sign welcoming the "Leaders of Tomorrow".

'Andy!'

I looked up and smiled, waving my best friend over. Hailey was blonde, bubbly and loved all the same things I did. She welcomed me into her life when I found myself hyperventilating in the toilets one day during my first week at Deanell.

'Did you watch it?' she asked, raising her blonde brows.

'If Vaughn or Sydney die this season, I might die too.'

'Vaughn won't die. It's not even his real name. And there's no way Syd would die.'

'I hope you're right.' I shuddered, walking through the gates towards the locker bay.

Alias was our show. It was one of the things we both watched and talked about religiously, and it was kind of the only reason I got through every single week. The show was ending soon, which filled me with so much dread I could barely think about anything else. It was stupid. But every week for one hour, I wasn't Andrea Nekić. I wasn't a half-

Bosnian, half-Croatian girl living in a country where I felt like a massive outsider who did more extracurricular activities than all my classmates put together. I could be a *normal* teenager, dreaming about two characters' romance and then talking about it with her best friend.

'Want me to come over? We can watch reruns before the next episode,' Hailey asked.

'Ah, no,' I said, quickly trying to think of an excuse not to let Hailey come over.

She looked at me suspiciously, one blonde brow disappearing into her hairline.

I hated having people over. Embarrassment of the very ethnic way my family lived was just part of it.

'I could come to yours,' I suggested.

Hailey shook her head. 'Mum's got something on, and I have to be out of the house…'

She hated having people over too.

'What's on tonight?' she asked, changing the subject.

'Tennis first, then piano.'

'Oh, tennis and piano nights mean pizza, right?'

'Yep.'

It was the one time my dad allowed us junk food. He hated spending money on things he could make cheaper at home. The number of times I cringed when he brought out homemade ćevapi instead of pizza at my birthdays was another reason I stopped inviting friends over.

Reaching the portable locker bay, I took the rickety wooden steps two at a time and dodged two Year Eleven guys shooting spit balls at each other through straws.

I was wrong about this year. It wasn't just bad. It was hell.

'Six months until graduation.' Hailey opened her locker, revealing a poster of Tom Welling from some red carpet event promoting *Smallville*.

'Can't come quick enough,' I muttered, opening my locker.

There were no posters, no stickers, nothing that could possibly show anyone how nerdy I was.

I'd only ever once brought one of my pencil cases to school and that was in my first week. Daniel saw it and we bonded over *The Matrix*. He was nerdy too and liked most of the same things me and Hailey did.

Everyone else made fun of me all week. I never brought it back again.

It was hard to explain to my family why I didn't want to use any of the cool *Matrix* stationery they'd bought me. I lied and said it was too special to ruin, and my guilt ate away at me every time I pulled out the ugly tartan pencil case instead. But I'd learned early on that the only way I could survive was to blend in, be invisible. Be completely *normal*. Goodbye *Buffy*, goodbye UFO documentaries—at least in public.

I shoved my bag into the barely functioning top locker and rummaged into its depths searching for my pencil case.

The unlucky ones stuck with the bottom lockers had to get on their hands and knees and make peace with the squashed pieces of food from Home Ec on the floor just to get their books out.

I had a top locker this year, but I shared this set of lockers with a girl I'd seen maybe four times during term one and then never again. Elle Smith. She was pretty, well-liked by most people. She'd dated the hot guy from our year level, Julian Valesco, and I was eternally jealous and secretly relieved when she left. It meant he was single again—not that I'd ever have a chance with him.

'Hey, did you see your psych this week?' Hailey asked beside me.

I nodded, struggling to pull free the giant fifth-hand *Mathematics Methods* textbook.

'How has it been?'

'Same as always. He asks why I'm anxious or sad, and I tell him I don't know.'

'Is that the truth?'

'Yep. All I know for sure is that I hate my life.'

'Is it school?'

'Maybe… I don't know.'

She frowned at me. 'You do a lot. It could be catching up with you. Maybe you need a break?'

I laughed, and she scrunched up her brows.

'I don't think you understand how my family works. They'd probably rather see me dead than take a break.' I yanked the book harder, and it finally came free. I slapped it on top of the bright blue diary with the giant school emblem and looked across at her. She looked disappointed. A small crease in her brow deepened, and her lips formed a tight line.

'What?' I sighed.

'Nothing.'

'You're looking at me like my mum does.'

She shut her locker and repositioned all her things, so her

Harry Potter pencil case sat on top. She wasn't afraid of being singled out like me. I envied her.

'You shouldn't say things like that,' she said.

I rolled my eyes, shut my locker, and replaced the giant padlock on it.

'I have to go. Class is starting soon, and Mr. Proctor hates it when we're late,' I said.

'I'll see you later.'

I waved and waited for her to go.

Luckily, my class was in the adjoining portable. I made my way through the locker bay and back down the steps, falling in step behind a group of girls I knew from my class but didn't talk to.

When Erica Frost and her boyfriend, hot on her way-too-high-for-school heels, rain past me, I had to practically throw myself into the bushes to evade them. Wearing a uniform was just a *recommendation* here. No one paid attention to the required polished look the school brochure stipulated. Well, some of us did. I continued weaving through the bodies, all while making sure my skirt was to code, my socks evenly drawn up at my knees, and my shirt tucked in neatly beneath my wool vest and blazer.

On the surface, everyone looked happy, smiling faces surrounded by native trees and a decent main building. Sure, they'd whacked a new coat of paint on the Performing Arts Centre, if you could even call it that. But they only did that because last week, a kid from Year Eight spray-painted a giant dick on it.

Kind of perfectly described Deanell High. Behind a

rudimentary façade and fresh licks of paint, there were dicks everywhere.

There had been assaults committed by students from our school and the rivalry one that were swept under the rug, physical and verbal altercations that were hushed, and mental breakdowns the counsellors ignored. Teachers resigned without a word, and students just stopped coming to school. Whenever someone asked where they were, the response would be a sinister "they're gone".

It was safe to say that Deanell High was not what the shiny brochure stated. It was the last stop for kids who messed up at their previous schools, the kind who probably should have ended up in juvie.

My previous school was completely opposite to this one. Students lazed comfortably on perfectly manicured lawns with equally perfect grounds spanning the equivalent of two city blocks. We wore blazers and hats, played polo at school and tennis on the weekends (that's where I picked up yet another one of my extracurricular activities), watched classic movies, and learned about music. The teachers were passionate, and the students cooperated.

A loud screech from the PA system announced the beginning of period one. I glanced at the clock loosely nailed to the faded yellow walls and sighed.

Proctor was going to be pissed. It was five to nine, and if you weren't in class already, you were late and likely to be a victim of flying coin attacks and duster throws. The school board should have made it an interschool athletics event.

And as if the universe wanted to confirm it, he appeared

at the door to his classroom, red, heaving, and totally unimpressed.

'Three minutes!' he shouted, slapping his wooden ruler against the glass partitions that were installed a few months ago when a group of science students snuck in to make drugs with school equipment. Rumour has it they had a lucrative MDMA business. But now, the wooden walls only went three-quarters of the way up, and the top had glass panels running all the way around—privacy without too much privacy.

'Two minutes!' Another vein bulged out of his forehead. When no one heeded his warnings, the vein doubled.

'Hurry up!' Proctor shouted from the room at the end of the four-classroom portable, which was only meant to be a temporary shed until the government gave the school enough funding to build something new. Guess the budget was spent elsewhere. Probably painting over all the dicks.

Finally, people started moving with some urgency, the flimsy, hollow floor screeching and groaning underneath the weight of thirty Year Twelve students rushing to class before Proctor finally lost it. He had a sack of coins ready to throw. Just as I reached the classroom door, he threw one.

The coin clanged against a window in the back held together by grey duct tape and sheer will. This was nothing, though. Last week in science, he threw a duster at Gareth Haddish, who sat in front of me. He ducked, and the duster hit my shoulder. Proctor spent all afternoon apologising, and I spent all night telling my sister about it. She actually asked Mum if she could go to Deanell, too.

'Get inside, now!' Proctor yelled again. 'You're getting on every last nerve.'

It couldn't be healthy, being this high-strung at his age. His face puffed with anger and turned redder. I shielded a grin as I filed in after the infamous twins, Anna and Anthony Walters. They were the bane of every teacher's existence, and they knew it.

Last week, Anna threw a bag of flour in Proctor's car vents, and it took him three whole days to stop coming to class with white patches in his hair. The week before, Anthony and a few of his friends stole his keys and hid them in the tree out front. When I say hid, I actually mean they punted them like a footy. It took two tradies from the construction site next door an hour to find them.

I found my seat up front and pulled my jumper over my nose, hoping to block out as much mould and Lynx Africa as I could. Josh sat down beside me, and Daniel followed suit. We were the three most law-abiding students in the class. Most people came and went as they chose. Not us, though. We stayed, listened, and participated like the good kids our parents knew us to be. The only addition missing from our quartet was Hailey. She didn't see the point in suffering through this hell for some unguaranteed extra marks.

'Did you and Hailey decide when we're all going to the movies?' Josh asked.

'Not yet.' I shook my head.

'Unacceptable. We never miss a fortnightly catch-up,' Josh muttered.

With all the extra classes and part time job I'd taken on

this year, it had totally slipped my mind. On top of that, my little sister Jelena was now old enough to start hanging out with her friends, so I was taking her out and picking her up when my parents worked. Given that I didn't have my license yet, it meant I had to walk her everywhere.

'I'm free on Sunday,' Daniel whispered.

Before I could reply, a loud bang up the front made all three of us jump. Proctor was throwing stuff again. He needed a chill pill, something strong like I'd been taking.

Mood stabilisers, the psychiatrist called them. To control even the toughest anxiety attacks. The only thing they did was make me a zombie, but even then, I still couldn't stop thinking about all the ways I'd disappointed my parents.

Proctor slapped his ruler against the dusty old blackboard again, setting off a puff of dust. That, combined with the sprinkling of plasterboard from the ceiling coming down with each turn of the overhead fan, was enough to make a girl wish she was anywhere but here. Every night, I had to brush the powder from my hair, and every night, I'd have the same complaints to Mum. She said it was just going to take some getting used to. But I didn't want to get *used* to asbestos poisoning.

Eventually, she stopped asking how school was, and I stopped complaining. Instead, I just gave her the updates of the standard As and A+s. She was content. Dad was content. We were all content. I took my pills. I cried in bed and repeated it all the next day with a smile on my face.

'Test results are in,' Proctor said. 'Some of you should be proud. Others very disappointed.'

I shrunk into my seat while the twins sniggered like they couldn't care less. Sometimes, I wished I could be like that, but I was too hung up on pleasing my parents to get anything below 80 per cent. If I did, I would probably never hear the end of it—from Proctor *and* Mum and Dad.

I couldn't wait for the year to be over so I could start a new life. Maybe I could move to the city in a super cute apartment and have a housemate, buy loads of plants, and maybe have a cat—a weird, naked-looking one you had to dress in jumpers because they were skittish and delicate.

Proctor handed back the tests from last week. I watched as each student's reaction matched exactly what I'd pictured their results to be.

Kayla Singh, the typical teacher's pet, beamed and triumphantly showed her 87 per cent mark to her friend Simina, holding the paper up so we could all get a peek. Josh, the sports star, shrugged beside me. He did okay, but it could have been better. He grinned at me.

Daniel, the class clown and all-around nice guy, frowned. I caught a glimpse of the bright red 75 per cent on his paper. His dad was a hard ass and expected everything from him. I could relate.

'It's good,' I whispered, nodding down at the mark.

His eyes flicked to mine, and a flush of pink reddened his cheeks. 'I guess.'

He looked away, but I had already caught the small glimmer of sadness creeping across his eyes. His parents had been separated for almost a decade, but it didn't mean his father wasn't in his life. Daniel spoke highly of him even though he was always on his case about school. But Daniel never complained; he took it in his stride. He was the only person at this school I felt like I could talk to openly, aside from Josh and Hailey. We'd all kind of bonded over similar interests. Daniel and I, though, had a little more in common. He was born here, but his family was Romanian, so he understood all my ethnic family nuances that many others didn't. It made whining to him about curfews or having to leave the movies before the film even finished to pick Jelena up so much easier. He just got it.

When my family moved to Australia twelve years ago, I was placed in ESL, an English as a second language class, where I was meant to learn English at a slow, steady pace. A few weeks in, the tutors decided it was too easy for me, and I was moved into advanced English. I picked up piano as a hobby and then tennis. By the time I was seven, I'd mastered three languages and basic math.

'Andrea.'

My head shot up. Proctor was standing at my desk, the paper held closely to his chest, gripped by long, bony fingers.

'Yes, sir.'

I couldn't make out the number, but I didn't have to. I already knew what it said.

'Could have been better,' he said, laying the test on my desk. My eyes travelled down to the top right corner. Eighty-two per cent circled in obnoxious red pen. 'Could you stay after class, please?'

'Okay,' I said quietly, keeping my eyes downcast.

I slid the paper into my giant binder, which was full of

scribbles and dawdles of poetry and short stories. I wanted to be a writer—not a tennis player, not a piano teacher, not a math professor. I drew in a deep breath and returned my attention to the front of the class.

It didn't matter what I wanted. It never would.

Proctor handed out another quiz, and before too long, the class dipped into stress-fuelled silence. Everyone here was pulled out of Foundations and encouraged to join because their teachers had identified skills that needed nurturing. While I enjoyed the challenge, I missed the simplicity of Foundations—the simple tasks and tests I could do without thinking too much.

Not like here. In Methods, if you weren't nailing at least eighty per cent on each test, parents would be called, and meetings would be held. I finished the quiz and closed my book, remaining in my seat as the bell rang.

Usually, the hot flushes and the slight tremble in my left hand alerted me to the onset of an "episode" and it usually only came when I was worried about a test. Considering I'd done well and had no reason to worry, I frowned. Why was I stressing now?

I focused on the fan spinning lazily above us: one, two, three... I looked over at the chaotic stampede of people rushing to get out of the small, wooden door blocking their freedom. Inhale and exhale, one breath after the other... Then, I collected my things and met Proctor at his desk.

'You wanted to see me?'

'I did. Have a seat,' he gestured while tidying the pile of quizzes he'd just collected.

I dragged over the heavily graffitied chair Daniel had been sitting on and tentatively positioned myself on the edge. I hated butt-warmed chairs.

'Do you want to tell me about that test result, Andrea?'

'Nothing to tell. I had an off day.'

Proctor's wrinkled forehead scrunched as he watched me through squinted eyes. There had definitely been a spark of passion in there somewhere.

'Why haven't you applied for the math program yet?' he asked.

'I didn't think it was mandatory.'

'It isn't. However, it would be beneficial for you.'

'I've got too much on.'

'I think you're selling yourself short. I've already spoken to your father.'

My chest rose and fell with that stupid onset of an anxiety attack. 'Why?'

'Because you're in Year Twelve. It's crunch time. You can still earn extra points toward your enTER.'

'But I enjoy this class.'

He chuckled. 'I may be old, Andrea, but I'm not senile. Enjoyable is not the adjective I'd use to describe your opinion on this class.'

I frowned.

'Now, when I recommended that you join my math program, your father was thrilled.'

'So, it's done then.'

'Well, no.' His brows furrowed, looking down at me through thin-rimmed glasses. 'It's your decision.'

I almost laughed but quickly stopped myself. He clearly didn't know how Balkan parents worked. I did what Dad said. When he suggested this school, I started this school. When he suggested starting tennis, I started tennis. When he wanted pizza, we ate pizza. There was no discussion, no asking, no *choice*.

'Andrea?'

'Sorry.'

His expression hardened. 'Is everything alright?'

'It's fine, sign me up.'

'You don't have to if you don't want—'

'I do,' I lied. 'It'll help me get into Uni.'

'Alright then.'

Before he could say anything else, I curtly nodded and excused myself.

'I'll email over the details for the class,' he said as I closed the door behind me.

Next week, I'd be joining the math program for losers like me, designed to showcase my skill front and centre.

Perfect. Just what I wanted.

CHAPTER TWO

Looking for Andrea Nekić

I reached into my locker and rummaged around until I found the folder I was looking for. As I pulled it out, a bunch of loose paper fell and fluttered behind me.

'You'd fall to pieces without me,' Hailey chuckled, collecting them all and shoving them back inside my locker.

'Thanks, Mum,' I said sarcastically.

She grinned and linked her arm through mine.

'What are we doing for your birthday?' she asked.

'My birthday isn't for a few more months.'

'It's June now, and October will come around before you know it.'

'Don't remind me.'

'But it's your eighteenth.'

'I know.'

'So, we're celebrating, right?' she tried. 'You've got your P's then, too?'

'Yeah. October thirteenth.'

'Spooky! We definitely need to celebrate then!'

'Yeah, like I need Freaky Friday to make my life any freakier.'

'Come on, it'll be fun.'

'Maybe, if I don't fail my test.'

I still hadn't clocked up all the hours needed to get my license, and Mum was too busy to take me out more than once or twice a week, which usually was a short drive to and from work. I did not want to be at the mercy of public transport and asking for lifts for the rest of the year, so I had to get my butt into gear and make sure Mum took me out more often.

On top of that, it meant that the rest of the year would come upon us quickly, too. Exams would start in October. We'd graduate in November, and that was it. A hot flush spread through me. It was too quick.

I followed Hailey, and we hurried through the courtyard, which meant cutting across the oval to get to our next class. This was always a risk because the boys who played footy thought it was hilarious to punt a ball at any group of giggling, pretty girls who walked past in hopes of smacking one in the head. And that usually resulted in make-out sessions. I would never understand it. My eyes did coast today, though. That impossibly cute guy, Julian Valesco, was playing.

Hailey caught me looking. Unfortunately, so did he. I cringed and quickly turned back to the front, hurrying off the grass, but not before I was sure I caught him smiling. At *me*? Impossible. Probably smirking at how stupid I looked.

'Spill.'

'What?' I shot back.

'Who're you perving on?'

'You're a loser. I'm not perving on anyone. Keep walking, we'll be late.'

She looked back over my shoulder, and I chanced another

glance. Nope. I hadn't imagined it; he was still looking and smiling. I whipped back around, shrinking into myself. He must have taken too many hits to the head when the ball missed the girls.

'Maybe we could go bowling,' I said quickly.

'Oh, you are not changing the subject.'

'Totally am, and oh look, the bell is about to ring.' I pulled my arm free as the bell rang and grinned at her. 'Too late.'

'This conversation is not over, Nekić.'

I smirked and led her down the busy hall to English. 'Kind of looks like it is.'

'Why're you so eager to get to class anyway?'

'Mr. Benson is awesome.'

'And you're not an English nerd at all.'

'Nope, not even a little bit,' I laughed.

Mr. Benson was already at the front furiously scribbling. Hailey and I grinned at each other as he continued jotting down instructions.

He was a stocky man with a short, full beard like a singer from an eighties rock band but long after their glory days, like when they had to get a day job in accounting or something regular like that. He was also fun, which made the banter even better.

'Movie report time, everyone!' he said, tapping the notes he'd made on the board.

'Any movie?' Kayla asked from the back.

'Yes. Any movie, any era.'

I flicked my diary open to today's date and jotted down a few movies I'd been dying to write about. Beside me, Hailey did the same. Aside from one or two different ones, we had the same list. We grinned at each other.

'Let's get started. There are only a few weeks until your SAC, and this will be good practice,' Mr. Benson said.

'I'm going to write about *Romeo and Juliet*. The original, though,' Kayla announced.

I rolled my eyes.

'The original was a play. *Not* a movie,' Hailey muttered.

Benson chuckled, turning to Hailey. 'You're right. Be sure to reference the written material as well. You don't want to rely on bastardised versions of classics.'

Kayla stiffened and hung her head. I shielded a smirk. I didn't know why she irked me as much as she did.

'So, if I do *Romeo and Juliet,* I can use the Leo film?' Kayla asked.

Hailey stifled a snort before mimicking the way Kayla spoke—kind of stiff in her seat and head high, always running her long fingers through her hair. She was so pretentious.

'Reckon she knows who actually wrote Romeo and Juliet?' Hailey whispered.

'She's actually really smart. Maybe even smarter than me,' I grinned.

Hailey rolled her eyes. 'You're no fun. Speaking of Shakespeare and plays, you're coming to my rehearsals in a couple of weeks, right?'

'When have I ever missed them?'

She grinned and returned her attention to the front.

'Daniel, what's your movie of choice?' Benson asked.

'Oh, this will be good. I bet it's something romantic. Something he can watch with you,' Hailey whispered.

'What are you talking about?' I hissed.

'I see how he looks at you.'

'He does not.'

'He so does, and you do too.'

'I don't look at him like that, believe me.'

'Oh, my ass.'

'Trust me, there's someone else on my mind like that,' I snapped back in a hushed tone. Someone who should have been in this class but, for some reason, wasn't here today.

'Oh, would that be the oval guy?'

'Shh!' I said, ignoring the burning in my cheeks as Daniel looked over at us.

He didn't catch a word, though if he did, he didn't show it.

On the first day of school, he'd introduced himself to me, and by lunch, we'd practically learned about each other's entire lives. The girls here looked at him with hopeful anticipation, and I felt protective of him. He was cute, ridiculously cute, actually, but that wasn't why I was staring with anticipation. Our minds worked the same way. It was nice. It was easy.

He turned, his eyes meeting mine as circles of heat spread across my cheeks. Thankfully, no one saw it, not even Hailey.

'*Mean Girls*,' said Daniel. 'The *original*.'

Laughter broke out across the classroom. Hailey clapped him on the back.

'Interesting choice,' Benson mused. 'And why, may I ask,

did you choose it?'

Daniel turned to the class and flashed a bright, white smile before he leaned back in his chair. 'Well, sir, you might not realise this, but *Mean Girls,* directed by Mark Waters, is the most iconic movie of the decade.'

Kayla chortled. 'You're going to have to explain that one.'

'Well, Kayla,' Daniel said in a sickly-sweet tone I knew was a million volts of fake. '*Mean Girls* is a teen movie about social dynamics, self-sabotage and social currency all wrapped into one neat, plastic bubble.'

My cheeks flushed again. *Was I living the Mean Girls life?* Minus the hot plastics, the guy who was into me, and, well, everything else that kind of came with it.

'I'm a little too keen to read your paper now, Daniel,' Benson chuckled. 'What about you, Josh?'

'*Gangs of New York.*'

Kayla sniggered.

Josh's shoulders sagged.

'Enough!' Mr. Benson looked at Josh, then back at Kayla. 'I won't tolerate that kind of rudeness in my class, especially if it is aimed at someone else, Miss Singh. Do you understand?'

She turned in her seat as though she was searching for someone to back her up but when no one did, she scrunched up her perfect little nose, before turning back to the front.

'We're all here to learn, and we all have strengths in different areas,' Benson explained sternly looking around from face to face before settling on Kayla's. 'And shooting down people while they're trying is about the worst thing someone can do in my class.'

'Josh,' Benson said after a little while. 'I look forward to reading your essay.'

'Thank you, sir.'

After a full period discussing interesting movie choices, the bell went, and everyone shot to their feet and darted for the door. As always, I was the last to pack my stuff up since I always took everything out of my bag at the start of class: diary, notebook, textbook, novel, folder, paper…

'You're such a dork!' Hailey chuckled.

'I like to be organised.'

'There's organised, and then there's *you*.'

I smirked, nudging her out of the way. 'At least all my stuff fits in my bag. You carry two.'

'Well, I also like to be prepared.'

'For what?' I looked down at the library bag hanging on for dear life. 'An entire movie marathon?'

She shot her middle finger up at me with a grin, hauled her massive collection of movies, books and comics into her arms and waved before leaving with the other students.

I grinned to myself and finally zipped everything up.

Daniel was with Benson at the front talking, so I hurried past, hoping I'd get out in time and catch Julian walking home. He was hands down the hottest guy in school. He'd never even looked in my direction until he smiled not once but twice at me today.

'See you next class, Andrea! Good work on the practice essay,' Benson called out.

'See you!'

'Oh wait. I'm coming with you.' Daniel followed me.

I raised a brow at the grin on his face.

'Got something for your birthday,' Daniel said.

'Why?'

'Why? That's not the response I was hoping for.'

I grinned. 'What did you expect, a kiss?'

'Uh, no, but I wouldn't be opposed to it.'

'Keep dreaming,' I said pushing past him. 'You know my birthday isn't for another four months, right?'

'I know, but everyone is going to be busy with exam prep and all that. I didn't want this to get lost in all the other crap.'

'That's true,' I sighed.

I gestured to the back gate, and we started down the path littered with lunch order bags and Samboy cartons. Daniel followed behind me, waving at the football coach, jogging with a few of the school's big hitters. They'd played inter-school games and won more times than not. Some of the Deanell guys had a chance to go onto the AFL someday. Daniel was sadly not one of those guys. He was a great player with loads of promise, but last season, he broke his leg, and since then, his knee has never been the same. He still played friendlies, though, which reminded me that there was a game this weekend and practice tonight, which meant Julian would be there and not walking home…

'Don't you want to know what I got you?'

'Ah, sure,' I said, pulling my mind away from the way Julian looked in the Deanell High sports uniform.

'A little more enthusiasm, please.'

I cocked my brows again.

'Come on, Nekić, I know there's a smile in there somewhere.'

I felt my lips curl into a smile.

'There it is,' he laughed, handing me a small parcel. 'And this is for you.'

'What is it?'

'Open it and see!'

'Now?'

He shrugged. 'If you want. Or you can open it at home and tell me what you think.'

'Miss Nekić?'

I turned to the voice and saw the petite Mrs. Hayes trying to make her way down the path toward us.

'I guess I'll wait for your call tonight,' Daniel chuckled, waving me off.

Damn it! I tucked the parcel into my giant binder and forced a smile.

Hayes reached me and, with a flustered breath, said, 'Are you still attending the book club?'

'Is that tonight?'

'Yes, is that a problem?'

I sighed. Yes, it was a problem. A HUGE problem. I had tennis and piano tonight, the third lesson this week because I had a recital coming up and needed the extra practice.

'Miss Nekić?'

'Sorry, no… that's fine. I'll shift tennis but can't cancel piano, so I might be a bit late.'

'Oh, that's fine if you're late. Are you certain your parents won't mind?'

'Believe me, they're wondering why I'm not doing more.'

She tittered and disappeared back into the crowd.

Yay, another busy night to look forward to.

Taking a shortcut behind the adjoining school, I stopped abruptly when I saw Julian Valesco standing beside the small gate that separated the schools. His jumper was slung over the gate behind him, and his white school shirt was only tucked in on one side with his tie haphazardly hung around his neck. His dark blond hair was casually swept to the side, not styled how he normally wore it. He must have just finished practice.

I noticed his school bag was overflowing with a change of clothes, a pair of football boots and a footy jammed neatly on top.

I drew in a sharp breath and swallowed the nerves that had been lingering all day and approached him.

He smiled, and I literally stumbled over a tuft of grass that hadn't been cut properly. *What were they paying the landscapers for?*

Julian chuckled when I muttered under my breath.

'Not going to practice tonight?' I asked coolly.

He had footy practice every Wednesday night and sometimes on Thursdays. *Wow, I sounded like a stalker.*

'Just finished.'

'Heard the team is doing well this season.'

'I didn't know you were a fan?'

'Sometimes.'

I hated football—in all forms. But I liked watching them

play, and I liked seeing him.

He chuckled, causing all sorts of gooey emotions to flutter inside me again.

Julian pushed away from the gate, collected his jumper, and stepped closer to me, 'Well, there's still a lot of time to fuck it up.'

'I guess there is,' I said, hyperaware of how close he was now. His eyes were a much richer shade of hazel than I'd thought, closer to brown. His jaw was speckled with a dusting of hair that had grown back between the mandatory clean-shaven look the school demanded.

When he moved beside me, I noticed that he smelled great, too. Not Lynx, but something more grown-up.

'The coach thinks we have a shot if everyone puts in a few more training sessions before the big game,' he said. 'Unless we fuck up during the scout match.'

'When is the big game?'

'July twenty-seventh. Scouts come out on the twelfth.'

'Bit more time to get ready, then?'

'Coach thinks so,' he said.

'And what do you think?'

'I think we lost a great asset when we lost Daniel last year.'

Daniel. Right. That's how I knew Julian. Not because I was a weirdo who skimmed the term class breakdowns searching for his name. I spotted him when Daniel made me come and watch the game once, and I was immediately intrigued.

'Do you guys still play together, or...?'

'Not really.'

'Why? I thought sports bonding or whatever was a thing?'

He laughed again. 'Well, I guess sitting on the bench isn't much fun. Plus, he can't even hang with Josh since he's always busy with the captain stuff.'

'True. I thought Josh wanted to play soccer, though?'

'He's gunning for Melbourne Victory but hedging his bets.'

'That's fair.' I scanned the surrounding area of the oval. There were a few stragglers, and a few, like Julian and me, just hanging out and talking.

'What are you doing tonight?' he asked.

'Study, piano, bed. Oh, and book club.'

'Book club? Any good?'

'I guess so if you're into that sort of thing. It's helpful if you want extra practice or credits.'

One side of his full lips quirked into a half smile. 'And you go to nail the extra creds, right?'

'Right,' I agreed. 'But how would you know that?'

'I'm not completely oblivious. I know you're really smart.'

'Really lame, more like.'

'Hardly. I heard you play piano last week in music. I was wagging, so I had to sneak around.'

'So, you snuck into the music room?' I cocked my brows.

'No one checks there.'

'That's a good point.'

He picked up his bag and slung it over one shoulder. 'I'll walk with you.'

'You don't have to.'

'I want to.'

'Why?' I challenged.

'Why not?'

I snapped my mouth shut, stuck for anything smart to say.

He started walking beside me as if my silence was my acceptance. My heart ricocheted against my ribs, and the onset of anxiety slowly crept up and settled between my bones.

We walked side-by-side in silence until he turned to face me. 'Are you happy with your classes this term?'

'I guess,' I shrugged. 'Didn't have much choice.'

'Heard you got sucked into the math program?'

Heard? From whom? Why was he interested?

'Yeah. Apparently, I'm selling myself short,' I muttered.

I knew it was true. I was advanced for most of these classes. But here I was, self-sabotaging again. Damn *Mean Girls*.

'I think it's cool. Especially so late in the year.'

'Cool?'

'You don't want to blend in with the plastics. You're better than that.'

Okay. Wow.

'Besides, Proctor needs someone who gives a shit about what he's teaching. Maths gives him life.'

He continued talking about his classes and mine as my brain kind of floated away alongside my logic. Whatever. I was allowed a few moments of feeling giddy around a super-hot guy.

'So, tomorrow night's training is meant to be good. We're taking on the rival school.'

'Sounds interesting.'

He laughed. 'Yeah, you seem really interested.'

'Sorry,' I laughed. 'I'm not that into footy.'

'More of a soccer girl?'

'More of a single-player sport kind of girl.'

'Ah,' he said, nudging me. He was flirting; he was *definitely* flirting. 'Sports where other people can't take the credit?'

'Sports where other people can't mess up my game.'

'Deep. I like it.'

'Uh-huh, sure. This is me,' I said, nodding to the bus at the stop. 'Might catch you tomorrow.'

'You might,' he winked.

CHAPTER THREE

Life is Not Black and White Like a Piano...

The bus dropped me off at home just before four, which gave me ten minutes to strip out of my uniform, check I wasn't sweaty, and pull on something comfortable that I could wear to piano then book club. Luckily for me, both venues were close to each other.

But tonight, Dad was my chaperone. It meant I had less than five minutes to be dressed and downstairs with my sheet music and book club notes.

He was already in the car, drumming the steering wheel to AC/DC, which was blaring too loudly to be legal.

'Ready?' he asked me.

'I think so,' I nodded, checking over everything twice to make sure I hadn't forgotten something important.

'Book club finishes at seven thirty tonight?'

'Yep. Should I catch a taxi home?'

'No, Mum will get you.'

'Okay,' I nodded and pulled out my book club notes, hoping to get in as much cramming as I could.

'You seem stressed,' he said as we stopped at the lights.

'Do I?' I turned to face him and noticed his furrowed brows.

'Yes.'

I huffed, dropping my chin as I folded then unfolded the note paper.

He closed his hand over mine.

'Sorry.'

'Something is wrong?'

'No, Dad, I'm fine,' I said, forcing a smile. 'Just school.'

'Okay.' He let go of my hands and turned back to the road when the light turned green. 'You tell me if something is wrong.'

'Always,' I lied.

'Good. You know I will listen.'

'I know, Dad.'

He was a shit liar, so was I. Neither of us knew how to be honest with each other, and it had everything to do with the fact that we were basically the same person. Proud, private, and carrying the weight of everyone's problems on our shoulders.

It didn't matter how deep I had sunk into the barren earth beneath my feet. I would continue to carry Mum, Dad, and Jelena on my shoulders to spare them the horrors around us. The snide remarks about being outsiders, the taunts about broken English and laughter behind our backs.

'We are here,' he announced, pulling into the dimly illuminated lot at the back of the music school.

I reached across the console and hugged him, lingering for a moment. When he returned the hug, I smiled to myself.

'Dad,' I started. 'I get why you want me to do well in school and piano.'

'You do?'

'Yeah. You want a better life for me.'

'That's all I wanted.'

We looked at each other for a moment, silence hanging between us. I considered telling him there was too much pressure, too much stress, but when he smiled, I knew I couldn't. He was the one person I knew would tell it to me straight when it came to certain things. Emotions, not so much. Every conversation, as strained as it was, carried weight behind it that I could equate to gold. He and Mum left Bosnia and everything they knew and loved to come here so I could be safe and thrive. If he told me to do something, I knew it was for my benefit.

'Have fun,' he said with a smile.

'I don't know if piano practice counts as fun, but sure.'

He shook his head, smirking, and waved me off.

I stopped outside Helen's door and listened to the music coming from inside. She had been my piano tutor for the last eight years and had a stern, don't waste my time attitude but she was incredibly talented. The door to her room opened just as I approached, and her previous student, a young kid with spiked hair who looked like he would rather be pulling his own teeth than playing classical music, stormed past me.

I darted out of the way and repositioned the sheet music under my arm.

Helen gave me a well-practiced smile, the one every teacher at Deanell presented when the students were wasting their time.

'How are you, Andrea?' she asked.

'Busy. You?'

'Same as always.'

The conversation died out, and I sat upright at the piano when she closed the door.

'Let's begin.' She nodded, setting the metronome.

I began to play, and the second I did, I checked out. My brain was not in it today. My heart wasn't either.

Helen stopped the metronome and sighed, pulling her glasses down to rub her eyes.

'You either get this right or you don't,' Helen said. 'It's up to you, Andrea. You're the one who's going to be up there in front of everyone.'

'No pressure,' I muttered.

'Your recital is in September. I know that sounds far away, but it'll come around before you know it. Not to mention the scholarship you've applied for at the music academy.'

'I get it. Fail this, no scholarship.'

'What's the issue?'

'No issue. I'm just tired.'

'Luckily, piano doesn't exert any physical energy.'

I sighed. I should have stayed at school and worked on my assignments.

'Again,' she said, resetting the metronome.

The melody once again filled the room, drowning out the fragmented, clumsy tunes from the other students filtering in through the thin walls.

'You're not concentrating.'

Biting my tongue, I started from the top.

There was a small chance that I would see Julian

tomorrow; he had a biology class right before mine, which meant that we could bump into each other…

'Andrea!' she snapped, catching the metronome. It made a grinding sound beneath her palm. 'You're not here.'

'I'm here.'

She glanced up at the clock, a simple white and black analogue design, something Art Deco from a seventies store. Probably genuine too.

'We've been playing the same page over and over for almost the entire lesson.'

'It sounds fine to me.'

She took a long breath, leaned in the high back stool, which groaned under the pressure, and looked around the dimly lit, mahogany-clad room.

'You're my finest student, Andrea. The most naturally gifted I've seen in years, but you're acting like you couldn't care less.'

I couldn't care less. It wasn't an act. But I didn't say that. I never said anything I wanted to. Never turned down a project, an extra class, an invitation to do more activities.

'I'm sorry, there's just been a lot on at school and home.'

'Anything you want to talk about?' Her tone softened.

'No,' I said and started the metronome again.

Once the lesson was done, I collected my sheet music and carefully slid it into my bag.

Helen didn't have any parting words, just a courteous nod and a slight frown, which hurt more than if she just said she was disappointed. Was I on the same level as the spikey-haired kid?

As she walked me outside and into my waiting taxi, I found myself wondering why I'd agreed to go to book club tonight.

You love books, that's why.

It didn't matter now. I had a schedule to stick to, which didn't include an existential crisis. That would have to wait until the weekend.

The taxi dropped me off just outside the school gate, and once I'd paid the driver with a wad of cash Mum made sure I always had on me, I gathered myself and walked back to school for the second time today.

Mrs. Hayes was waiting by the door to the library's after-hours entry as she did every book club. She smiled and bounced a little on her heel as I approached. I plastered a wide smile on my face and presented the polite, well-mannered Andrea everyone knew.

'Sorry I'm late.'

'Not at all. We're still waiting for one more person.'

'Great.' I smiled and made my way inside.

Emina Simoski, a girl from English class, was already seated next to Ronnie Patel, her best friend who never left her side. Right beside her, Josh was grinding his teeth, looking as miserable as I felt. He was only here for extra credits since his English class results were pretty dire. His scowl was only matched by the white-knuckled grip he had on his copy of *Looking for Alibrandi*.

I smirked at him. Thankfully, he reciprocated, and I plopped myself on the beanbag next to him.

'Enjoying it that much, huh?' I nodded at the book.

'Don't get me started. I'd rather do Proctor's math quiz again.'

'That's a huge call.'

'It's the truth,' he sighed.

'It's okay, I've got your back,' I said. 'I know the book well enough to make us both look like lit mavens.'

'That'll take a lot more effort.'

'I'm prepared for the hard work.'

He grinned, and we both looked up as Hayes walked in with Julian.

Holy shit. Why was he here? He was meant to be doing something more exciting, not here reading Looking for Alibrandi.

His russet eyes scanned the room, stopping on the empty spot to my left.

He smirked as our eyes met, making a flush spread all the way from my cheeks up to my roots. Then, when he gazed beyond my shoulder the playful look on his face vanished. A cold expression I couldn't decipher replaced it. I looked behind me. Josh had the same look.

I frowned and turned my attention back to Hayes, ignoring the fact that Julian was about to sit beside me. As the air shifted, I caught a full whiff of his cologne. It was definitely something more mature than what the other guys here wore.

'Now that we're all here, let's extend a warm welcome to Julian, who's here for some extra credits, and I hope you'll all help him out,' Hayes said, rubbing her palms together with a spring in her step. 'Now to the fun stuff, let's discuss the text.'

'I found it difficult to read,' Emina started off, oblivious to the weird tension.

'Why was that?' Hayes encouraged.

'Aside from the suicide and the implied abuse, it's full of angsty topics.'

'That's a good point, but do you think the text encourages difficult conversations?'

'Yes,' Emina nodded quickly. 'I think it's important today, more than ever, that people aren't afraid to speak up. Especially girls.'

Hayes nodded. 'What about you, Josh?'

I heard a rapid intake of breath, but then Josh straightened and gave me a determined look before glaring over at Julian.

He spoke without tearing his gaze away. 'There's a real sense of douchebaggery in the book. I think the men in the story think they own the women like property and treat them badly.'

'Yes, there's a very strong sense of misogyny in this narrative. Why do you think that is?' Hayes looked around, stopping on me. 'Andrea, do you think there are external factors that come into play?

I felt Julian's gaze on me and when I chanced a quick look, I was stunned to find my assessment correct. I tore my eyes away from him and looked back to the front.

'Definitely. The whole book challenges cultural and societal perceptions,' I said, ignoring Julian's gaze on me. 'Especially the expectations on women to stay home, raise kids and be housewives.'

'Good. How else is this demonstrated?'

'Well, the popular girls, who are Anglo, by the way, are happy enough being the token girlfriends. But Josie, being a *wog*, doesn't stand for things being the way they are, especially because she's seen how her mother was expected to behave by the men in her life. She wants to rise above that,' I answered.

'Good. Anyone else?' Hayes asked.

'She's a strong woman,' Julian said, his deep voice gliding over me. 'She's indomitable, which means that she's unique, and the other girls feel threatened.'

My heart fluttered, and the knot lingering in my stomach, tightened.

'And what do you think that does for her character?' Hayes looked at Josh.

'It makes her more desirable,' he answered.

Hayes nodded. 'For whom?'

'Everyone,' Emina added. 'Boys like her because they're getting sick of the bimbos.'

'And why is that?' Hayes asked.

'Because they're easy, and boys like a challenge,' Julian added.

Hayes's brows disappeared into her hair line as she shot Julian a look. Josh scowled beside me. I felt my cheeks getting hotter.

'Right… well, that's…' Hayes fumbled.

I cleared my throat, then quickly said, 'I think Josie is different because she doesn't care that she's not liked. She just wants to be herself.'

'And do you think that helps her in her life?'

'I think it keeps her safe.'

'How so?' Hayes asked gently.

I looked at Josh and Julian and then back at the girls in the circle.

'Andrea?' Hayes encouraged.

'She's smart. She thinks for herself. So she's not about to make stupid decisions. It keeps her safe.'

'Good,' Hayes smiled. 'Now, if you were to tell me a trait that makes Josie unattractive, what would you say?'

She nodded to Emina first.

'Her lack of staying true to herself,' Emina replied.

'How so? Andy?'

'She wants to be an Australian so badly that sometimes she hides who she really is,' I said, feeling the truth of those words bury themselves deep into my core and claw through me like a rabid dog. 'She wants to pretend she's like all the other girls with normal lives. Non-ethnic lives. But she contradicts herself a lot.'

'Josh?'

He ground his jaw. 'Her fear of telling people who care about her what's going on in her life.'

Tension was building. Everyone dipped into uncharacteristic silence. Josh was edging closer to the seam on the beanbag, and a quick glance across at Julian confirmed that he was staring Josh down with a scowl on his face.

'Julian?' Hayes said.

'Her fear of letting loose.'

'You would say that, wouldn't you?' Josh shot.

'What is that supposed to mean?'

'Oh, I'm sure you don't need me to elaborate, mate.'

'I think I might.'

'Enough,' Hayes snapped, holding her hands up.

Her tiny frame shook as her pale eyes darted between the two guys. I didn't dare breathe as they stared each other down.

When Julian remained glued to the beanbag, Josh shook his head and erupted to his feet. He stormed out of the small discussion circle and dropped the book on Hayes' side table as he left the room, slamming the after-hours door behind him.

I flinched, and the movement off to my side told me everyone else had had the same reaction, everyone except Julian. He simply reclined into the beanbag and got comfortable.

'Well, that was interesting,' Ronnie said, closing her book.

'Guess he didn't like the book,' Julian chuckled, making everyone else laugh—even Hayes.

But when he looked over at me and smiled, I retreated into my beanbag and frowned.

What did Josh mean? And why did Julian seem bothered? It all left a strange feeling roiling inside me. I'd heard rumours that there had been some rivalry on the team between him and Julian. Apparently, Julian got the ruck position, which Josh had been gunning for, and when Josh was made captain, the tension between the two grew.

'Okay, people.' Hayes returned her attention to us and

continued. 'Would you say the story is black and white in the message it conveys?'

'It's not black and white at all. The subtext is as important as the main story,' I argued. 'There's a whole turbulent world beneath it all.'

Just like right here, I wanted to say.

She nodded. 'What kind of world?'

'Fear and family, social status and expectations,' Emina added.

'And how do you think these societal expectations mold Josie?'

'She's afraid of not fitting in, and while she wants to rise above it, ultimately, she's on the same page as those she's working so hard against,' I said.

Hayes nodded again. 'These are all valid points, which I'm sure you can use for the final piece due at the end of the month.' The discussion continued for another fifteen minutes or so until Hayes called it a night.

'Andrea?' she called me over. 'Could you make sure Josh knows the deadline?'

'Yeah, of course.'

'Thank you.'

Once Hayes left to tidy up the beanbags, I waved goodbye to Ronnie and Emina, leaving Julian and me to walk to the kerb together. Julian waved down a cab.

'We can share?'

'No, thank you,' I smiled. 'Mum's there.'

He glanced over at the green sedan coming down the road.

'Catch you tomorrow?'

'Yeah, sure.' I found myself nodding.

I waited until he left before I said goodbye to Hayes, who always waited until everyone had gone home safely.

Mum pulled over and stopped a few metres away.

'Who is that boy?'

'That's Julian. We have a couple of classes together.'

Mum paused, processing the information before pulling out into the street. But before she could question me anymore, I changed the subject.

'I heard that Mister Željko invited us over for dinner this weekend.'

She glared at me like I'd asked her about some secret date she planned on lying about.

'Yes. Ruža is celebrating promotion at work.'

'Oh cool, so we're going?'

'No.'

'Why not?'

She frowned. 'We're not going.'

'I got that, but why?'

'You know Dad doesn't like going anywhere.'

'What about you?'

'What about me?'

'You like going out. You like dressing up and seeing your friends.'

She smiled. She gently squeezed my knee and returned her attention to the road ahead. 'I like spending time with my girls.'

'You're getting shitty at lying too.'

She frowned but didn't correct me.

It's not like she didn't enjoy spending time with us, but I couldn't remember the last time we went out as a family let alone to a friend's house. Sometimes, I felt like we were pariahs. The ethnics who weren't Australian enough to fit in but too different to belong with our own people. So, we sat on the outskirts, watching two worlds, neither of which we belonged to.

'This sucks.'

'What does?' she asked.

'Us.'

'How do you mean?'

'I mean, look at us,' I groaned, gesturing to the space between us. 'You hate that Dad never goes anywhere. You hate that you have no say or that whatever you do say doesn't mean shit because Dad dictates everything.'

'Andrea. *Dosta.*'

Mum always reverted to Croatian when she was stressed. *Dosta* was her word of choice for me. *Stop*. Stop talking. Stop having an opinion. Stop being anything other than the dutiful daughter I was meant to be.

'No, Mum. I'm sick of it. Do you know how shit it's been growing up being the nobody ethnic?'

'You know how hard we worked to live here.'

'Why can't we be like Zeljko? Why can't we go to parties or restaurants or have plans? Any plans!'

'Because…'

'Because Dad doesn't like going out, right?'

Mum let out an exasperated breath and ground her jaw.

'I hate it. I hate who we are.'

'You don't mean that.'

'I really do.' I put my headphones on and zoned out.

CHAPTER FOUR

Sharing is Caring

The morning came swiftly after I practically passed out after dinner.

Mum's customary response to conflict was to forget it ever happened and move on. I couldn't say I shared the sentiment. I was still bitter and angry, and the anger only simmered as the months and years went on.

'You're working too hard, ljubavi,' Mum said the second I appeared in the kitchen.

I rolled my eyes. 'I'm fine.'

'You don't look fine.'

'How does fine even look?' I took a clean glass from the dishwasher, set it under the coffee machine, and turned it on.

'What are your plans tonight?' she asked, resting a hand on her hip.

She had been working a laborious job for almost fifteen years, and it showed. She went to bed, drank way too much coffee, and still fell asleep during every movie night we had. She'd given up on makeup and jewellery years ago, although she did go to the hairdresser occasionally. She was a natural brunette, but she tried to keep fresh highlights all year round.

We looked similar, but my cheeks and lips were fuller, and I was shorter. She said it made me cute. I loved that until

I came to Deanell. Cute was for kids, not for girls who were competing against the likes of Rachel Murdoch and Jess Bennett. They were tall, strawberry blonde, with blue eyes, and *sexy*.

They were the kind of girls that the boys here liked.

Not ethnic girls. Not girls like me.

'So?'

'So, what?' I cocked my brows, dipping my spoon into the sugar pot.

'What are you doing tonight?'

'Homework, Mum. What else?'

She frowned. 'You need to take some time for yourself.'

'That's why I asked if we were going to Željko's.'

'Not this again.'

'Whatever.'

'You can be a lot of work, you know that?'

I smirked. 'Sure do.'

'Dad is proud of you.'

My hand froze over the cup, spilling some of the sugar.

'I'm proud of you too,' she added.

'I'm glad, Mum.' I walked over to her and carefully threw one arm around her body, balancing my coffee on the other.

'What are you two doing?' Jelena's voice sounded down the hall.

Jelena was a carbon copy of my dad and equally opinionated.

'Secretly discussing how to disown you.'

She stuck her finger up at me before darting out of the way of my hand.

'Get your stuff ready. I'm walking you to Maya's.'

'Okay.' She grabbed a juice from the fridge and disappeared back down the hall.

'I'm watching Daniel train today, but I'll be back later on.'

She gave me a sly smile before lowering her gaze to the sandwich she was packing.

At my old school, there was a guy I liked: Rory Thomas. He was on the rugby team. He got a bit frisky, but I handled it. Then there was Evan Davidson, a polo player. He was sweet and polite but completely immature. It didn't last. Finally, Luke Concetta. I was obsessed with him in drama class, but he liked boys. I evidently had terrible taste in men, and I was only seventeen.

'He is sweet,' Mum said.

Yep. Sweet. That was the word I'd use for Daniel. Not like Julian. He was something else. Intense. Full-bodied. Mysterious. And he was starting to sound like a description on the back of my coffee.

'I'll see you later.' I kissed her on the cheek and slung my crossbody bag over my shoulder. 'Jelena!' I shouted down the hall. 'Hurry up!'

'Coming!'

Jelena presented herself and followed me out.

We walked out onto the street, giving the sad, engine-less car in the drive a longing look. I hoped that my part-time job at the jeweller would allow me to save up enough money to get that done some time this century.

'There's this new game I want to get when we go

shopping,' Jelena said.

'Oh yeah?' I asked, remaining somewhat fixated on the fact that I needed to do something about the car. 'What's the game?'

Had I not bought this ridiculous bag, I might have had enough money to fix the engine. As if right on cue, the dangly gold tassel on my bag jingled offensively against the stillness of the Saturday breeze, reminding me how much I sold out.

Dad said my grades were so good last year that he'd buy me whatever I wanted as a present. I remembered seeing the bag in Chadstone, and I absolutely had to have it. It was sparkly, just the right size, and it matched almost everything I wore.

Deep down, though, this trackie-wearing, bike-riding girl was trying to break free, and I kept shoving her back into the darkness and suffocating her with labels I couldn't afford and clothes I didn't belong in.

Girls here didn't dress in Adidas or Puma. They wore nice clothes, and they had nice things.

'*Guitar Hero 2*!' Jelena proclaimed.

'You're going to deafen us.'

'You could play with me.'

'Maybe.'

'That's what you always say!' She stuck her tongue out.

When I tousled her hair in response, she slapped my hand away with an exaggerated gasp and disappeared from the room. She spent hours in the bathroom trying to learn how to use a straightener. It never worked, but I didn't tell her that. Maybe it was because I was a shitty sister, but deeper inside,

I knew that wasn't true. I wanted her to stay young and stay a kid for as long as she could, something I wasn't afforded because of the war that took everything from us.

'I'll play with you,' I decided.

'I'll believe it when I see it.'

'You drive a hard bargain.'

We cut across the neighbour's yard and through their back gate, which led straight to the park. When we moved here, their son helped my dad set up all the tools in the garage and even helped him out when we got occasional clients. Dad started this whole custom-built furniture thing, which embarrassed the hell out of me. Everything in the house was homemade, all the chairs, all the tables, every damn shelf. He listened to music entirely too loudly and watched random movies that no one had heard of, which made me hate having friends visit. Eventually, I started making excuses about not being allowed to have people over, and eventually, they stopped asking.

It was easier that way. I had books and TV. I threw all my energy into them and finally started writing. By the time I was fourteen, I had won a few competitions. I even got paid for one piece I wrote. That officially made me a published writer, and I've let it drive me ever since. Someday, I was going to be an author. That's why I was working so hard. I wanted to graduate top of the class, get into a good uni and maybe be good enough to do my masters.

'Hey, kid!' Daniel's cheery voice sounded from across the street.

Jelena waved and hugged him when he jogged over.

'Coming to hang?'

'Nah, going to Maya's.'

'Aww, okay, that's cool.' He covered his heart with his palm, giving her a huge frown.

I laughed. 'You're a loser. As if you enjoy hanging out with my sister more than me.'

'Your sister doesn't hang shit on me, Nekić Senior.'

Jelena punched me in the shoulder, practically throwing me off balance as she laughed and ran toward Maya's house.

'Bye, Nekić Senior!' she teased.

When she was safely inside with the promise of a sleepover, thanks to her mum calling my mum late last night, Daniel and I continued.

'You've started something.' I rolled my eyes.

'Well, don't leave yourself so open next time.' He gestured down the path toward the back way to the school. 'Did you open the present?'

'Oh shit, no. I'm so sorry. Last night got busy and I–'

'That's cool. No stress.'

'I really am sorry. I'll open it tonight.'

'Just message me when you do.' He smiled and nodded towards the pitch.

'Not training today?' I sat, surprised to see the field empty.

'Not today. Josh wants to rest, make sure he doesn't break a leg before the big game. But he said we could play some hockey, though. Keen?'

'Josh is here?'

'Yeah, why?'

'No reason.'

The whole thing with Josh at book club had been so bizarre. When he spotted us, he jogged over.

'Hey, you good?'

'Was going to ask you the same thing, why?'

'Just asking.' He sat beside me, dropping the hockey stick.

'You have a reason to be asking, or are you just being weird?' I challenged.

'You're both being weird.' Daniel frowned. 'What's going on?'

'Nothing,' Josh shrugged.

'Why'd you freak last night?' I asked.

'Last night?' Daniel shot back, his eyes darting between me and Josh. 'What happened last night?'

'Book club got kind of heated,' I said, then turned to Josh. 'You bailed halfway through. What happened?'

'I was bored.'

'You looked angry.'

'Disinterested.'

'My ass. The second Julian walked in, you flipped.'

Daniel turned. 'Valesco was there? Really?'

'Yes,' I felt my cheeks heating up. 'Extra credits.'

'Extra credits? He's smashing all of us in class, except maybe you,' Daniel baulked.

'I don't know. I'm not his teacher. That's just what Hayes said.'

He pursed his lips and tossed Josh a knowing look. My cheeks flushed with heat.

'This is getting stupid.'

'Look, I've just heard that he's shifty, okay?' Josh replied.

'Shifty, how?' I demanded.

'He's a player, and I don't want you to be—'

'Oh, my God!' I shot to my feet. 'We're not—and I don't—uh, no. Just no.'

'Someone explain,' Daniel barked.

'He was getting cosy with her after school, and then he conveniently turned up to book club,' Josh muttered. 'It just looked shifty.'

'I can't believe this!' I threw my hands up.

'Valesco was trying to hook up with you?' Daniel asked quietly.

'No, he wasn't,' I said quickly, then turned to Josh. 'And you, were you spying on me?'

'Yes, he was. And no, I wasn't spying. I was walking home. It was kind of hard to miss.'

Daniel inched back on the bench, remaining uncharacteristically quiet.

'Even if he was trying to flirt with me, why is it shifty? Because I'm not good enough for him?'

'Do you even hear yourself? This is stupid,' Josh muttered.

'So I'm stupid now too?'

'No, you're not stupid, and no, it's not that *you're* not good enough for *him*. You can do so much better because he's genuinely a shit person.'

'And still, no one has told me why.'

'I already did.'

'Because he's shifty. That's dumb.'

'You're right. It's dumb. I don't know why I brought it up. Do what you want.' Josh picked up his hockey stick, turning to Daniel. 'You coming?'

'In a sec,' Daniel said, looking across at me.

'Fine.' Josh shook his head and sprinted to the middle of the field.

'God, that was intense,' I muttered.

'He's not wrong.'

'Not you too!'

'Come on, Andy, we're just looking out for you.'

'There's nothing going on. It was literally one conversation after school.'

'Okay, but you know how guys can be.'

'And you think I'm stupid enough to get into a shit situation?'

'You're not stupid, but you're kind. Sometimes too kind.'

'What does that mean?'

'It means that people take advantage of you,' he said, looking down at the space between our hands on the bench. 'And guys like Valesco know how to play.'

'I'm not going to be the victim of some player, and he's not even like that. He's nice.'

'Word gets around. He's not good news, Andy.' Daniel's eyes found mine again. 'When he left his old school, it wasn't because he wanted to. He was expelled.'

'What?'

Daniel nodded. 'Got into some pretty bad fights, nearly knocked a guy unconscious, and they booted him. His dad is loaded, and word is that he paid off the other kid's family so they didn't press charges.'

'I had no idea,' I said quietly. 'He's nice to me.'

'Of course he is. You're a pretty girl with a golden heart.'

The compliment was lost between the insinuation that my naiveté would be responsible for some heinous thing.

I ground my teeth and stared up at Daniel. His sage green eyes were locked onto something on the horizon. Was he annoyed that Julian was interested in me? Is that why they were ganging up on me now?

'Andy…'

'Don't worry, I'll stay away from Mister Shifty.'

'It's not a joke,' he said, his tone stern.

'I didn't say it was, it's just… intense.'

'Yeah, well. It's an intense kind of situation. Anyway, I didn't ask you here to fight.'

'Good, because for a moment, I thought this was a roasting.'

He cracked a smile and handed me a hockey stick. 'Let's see what you've got, Nekić.'

~

After a solid hour of sweating it out on the oval and being told I would have a chance on a kid's team, we were done.

Josh packed everything up and hauled the bag over his shoulders.

'You two hanging back?' he asked.

Daniel, who was still struggling to get his laces tied after I'd accidentally smacked him across his hand with the hockey stick, gave me a sheepish grin and shrugged.

'Happy to hang back if you are?'

'Yeah, that sounds good. I don't have anything else on tonight.'

'Okay, I'll see you both on Monday,' Josh said, shaking Daniel's hand before giving me a quick hug goodbye.

Crouching in front of Daniel, I shook my head and took his laces tying them for him.

'Thanks.'

'Least I could do after I almost broke your hand.'

He laughed, holding his hand out to me. When our skin touched, my breath hitched sending a frenzy of butterflies to surge inside me.

For a moment, we stood quietly on the oval, face-to-face and holding hands. I almost forgot how to breathe, and Daniel looked like he was drawing in rapid breaths. But then my critical thinking kicked in, and I freed my hand.

He gave me another sheepish grin before looking down at the space between our feet.

'We should walk.'

'Yep, good idea.'

'Where do you want to go?' he asked.

'We could get a coffee?'

'Anywhere in mind?'

'What's close?'

'I drove, so whatever you feel like. You just say the word, and I'll take you.'

'Oh...' I slowed, looking across at him. 'Is—is this a date?'

'It can be.'

I flushed. My cheeks heated up quicker than I could turn my face away.

'Or, it doesn't have to be,' Daniel said quickly.

'Can it be a maybe… for now?'

He scanned my face for a moment before he nodded with a smile. 'Of course.'

I let out a long breath and followed him across the oval toward the street parking. His car was the only one left. When he unlocked it, he whipped around to my side and pulled the door open.

'You're a nerd,' I teased when he got in.

'You call me a nerd. I call me a gentleman.' He wiggled his brows and turned the engine on.

'Such a nerd.'

'One day, you'll appreciate it.'

'Oh, I'm sure,' I laughed.

He returned the gesture and pulled out onto the main road that led to the freeway. 'Where to?'

'Let's go to Chapel Street.'

'Love your style,' he grinned.

I relaxed as we settled into the drive. He glanced across at me every few minutes with a smile while I marvelled at the skill with which he shifted gears, making the sportscar's engine rumble like a purring lioness.

I'd never been into cars, but suddenly, I wanted to know everything, and as Daniel explained the specifics of the engine, effortlessly taking the car from gear to gear, I found myself captivated by this *cute* guy.

Maybe Daniel meant more to me than I knew. Maybe I

needed to listen to him about Julian, and maybe I needed to focus on my priorities.   .

That would be a Monday problem. Today, I was going to enjoy my time with Daniel.

CHAPTER FIVE

Anonymous Messages are Never Cool

The holidays were over and we were back at school. I already missed the random drives and coffee dates with Daniel and wondered if they would continue. Part of me also wondered whether I wanted more with him. On the other side of that coin, I was looking forward to walking home from school with Julian which also felt right. I was confused.

Hailey was waiting by the gate, frowning.

I tightened my backpack straps and pushed on toward her.

'Have another lazy night, did you?'

'I guess. Nothing special. Why?'

'Why?' she replied, deadpan.

My brain was full of Pythagoras, scales, and books, and a dull thrumming that was getting worse. Then it hit me.

'Oh, Hailey. I'm so sorry!' I threw my arms around her. 'I am so, so sorry!'

'You didn't even call, you bitch.'

'I'll make it up to you, I swear.'

'Don't worry, there are still a few rehearsals left, but if you miss the show, I will stab you.'

'I believe you, sheesh. And who even does rehearsals on holidays?'

'Who knows?' she snorted through a laugh and nudged me forward. 'So how come you didn't make it?'

'Honestly, my brain was fuzzy from all the SAC prep. I totally forgot.'

'And that's all?'

I flushed, and she caught it right away.

'Was there a boy involved?' she teased.

'I had coffee with Daniel.'

'Again?'

'Again.'

'Sounds like that's becoming a regular thing?'

I grinned, 'Maybe.'

'Did you hang out all holidays?'

'No, just a few times. Coffee and drives.'

'Oh, drives?' She grinned again. 'Starting to like cars, are we?'

'Oh, you know, maybe.'

'You really should start keeping a diary, though.'

'I have a diary and a calendar.'

She glared at me, and we both burst out laughing. 'You need Jesus, then.'

Hailey smirked and went off to drama while I continued to my locker. Julian was there. I scratched the back of my neck, reminding myself that I had school, piano, math club, job, and everything else to focus on. I was already forgetting my best friend's rehearsals.

And then there was Daniel.

'Morning,' Julian said casually.

'Morning.' My knees knocked.

'I watched a good doco last night.'

'Oh yeah?' I rummaged through my bag, finally picking out what I needed and shoved everything else into my locker.

As I leaned my knee against the bottom locker door, Julian's eyes coasted down to Elle Smith's small, faded label.

'You good?' I asked him, catching the way his jaw clenched.

'Yeah, fine.'

He made a small sound, shifting from one leg to the other while his gaze remained glued to the peeling name. His blond hair fell over his eyes, but I didn't mistake the crease in his brow.

'What's your deal?' I shut the door and double-checked to make sure the lock was sound.

'Nothing, we're going to be late to class.'

My brows tugged up. 'Since when do you care about being late to class?'

'Since now, come on.'

I dropped it and followed him through the hall. He kept his eyes ahead and shoulders tensed. Usually, he'd nod or greet anyone that looked his way but not today.

'Now, I know some of you are worried about the workload, so I'm happy to hand out a week's extension. Any takers?' Mr. Benson announced as the rest of us filed into the classroom.

A few hands shot up. Josh, his good friend Andrew, a few others from the football team… and Julian. *I guess that's why he was eager to get to class.*

'Use this hour to work on your essays and ask me any

questions you have,' Benson said, plunging the class into silence.

I looked over at Daniel. He'd already opened his notebook, grinning at me when he caught me looking.

'Smartass,' I mouthed with a smirk.

He gave me an exaggerated bow and leaned back in his seat, making the plastic groan under the pressure.

Beside me, Julian shifted, catching my attention. His eyes were hooded, and the intense smile on his face made me quite literally drop my pen. A hot flush instantaneously consumed me, and I couldn't help the dumb grin on my face.

Holy hell.

I tore my gaze away. Daniel hadn't missed the exchange. He turned his face from me and remained fixated on the task for the remainder of the class.

My good mood quickly fizzled out. Once I finished the last paragraph, I shut my notebook and kept my eyes down.

Pens scratched against the paper for the next thirty minutes until the bell rang, and everyone dispersed to their next periods. Julian said a quick goodbye.

Daniel stood beside my desk while I packed my things. 'Andy—'

'Please don't start.'

'Okay,' he said, then shifted to his other foot. 'Let's get a coffee. I drove again.'

'I can't.'

'You have a free period, right?'

The pleading in his eyes cut through me. I chewed my bottom lip but stood my ground. I couldn't do this right now.

'I do, but I have to study.'

'Can I help at all?'

'Sadly, no,' I smiled.

'Can we do coffee another day?'

'I'd like that.'

'Really?' he beamed.

'Really.'

He smiled and packed his things with a quick nod.

Good. Situation defused.

~

Hailey let out a long groan as she struggled up the stairs to the art building hauling a huge ass canvas and easel.

'Did you do anything new to your painting?' I asked, watching her unfold it at her station.

'A few tweaks. You?'

'No, I didn't get a chance to.'

'Is everything okay?'

'Can't a girl miss out on one homework assignment?'

'Ah, not when the girl is you.'

I laughed and shook my head. 'I'll catch up, don't stress.'

'Not stressed. Worried.'

'Don't be. I just had to prioritise Proctor's classwork last night. He's gotten me on a math program too. There is *so* much math.'

'Math is a little more important than this,' she laughed as Mrs. McKenna walked in.

'Since most of you lovely people have a bit of work left on your paintings, I will give you the full hour to work on them. Music choice today?'

Several hands went up, and after a few suggestions, we settled on 80s rock and got to work.

Hailey worked furiously on her painting while I perfected the small snakeheads on my Medusa. The hour went by in a flash, and I was packing up and getting ready to go home before I knew it.

'What's on for tonight?' Hailey asked as we packed her huge easel and canvas up and started down the hallway toward our locker bay.

'Not much. Going to play *Guitar Hero* with Jelena. She's practising for the new one she wants to buy.'

'I love that game. When you get decent, let me know, and I'll show you how it's done.'

'Deal.'

We collected everything we needed and finally left the school. I slowed down when we both spotted Julian as we reached the pathway leading to the back gate.

'Wanna catch the bus together?' Hailey asked.

'Nah, we usually walk together.'

'Oh, sweet. Let me know when you get home.'

'I will.' I gave her a quick hug.

Hailey had her issues with Julian, but over the last few weeks, she dropped them. She didn't like him, but she didn't give me any more shit.

The one-time chat after school had become a regular walk from the gate to the end of the street where he caught the bus and I continued home.

'Didn't know if I was going to see you today.' Julian smiled and walked over to me, pulling me into a hug.

I was ashamed to admit it felt really good, and I eagerly hugged him back.

'Sorry, got held up in art. You know you don't have to wait for me?'

'I wanted to,' he said, gesturing to the footpath. 'Did you have a good day?'

'I did. Got heaps done on my painting,' I said, ignoring the flushing in my cheeks. 'Also, the essay for book club. How's yours coming along?'

'You'll have to show me when you finish. And the essay is done.'

'Really? Did you get the essay done for Benson, too?'

'Yeah, finally.'

'Never knew you to fall behind.'

'You and me both. Mum nearly died. Dad threatened to pull my inheritance.'

'It happens, right?' I sighed, falling into a comfortable stride. 'Would your dad do that?'

'Nah, he wants me to be a lawyer like him. So, I guess he keeps taunting me with money, and I keep playing into it.'

'Doesn't it annoy you?'

'It used to. Now I know the money will be a huge help in the future, so if I play my cards right, I can make sure I appease him and help my mum and myself.'

'You've got it all planned out, then.'

'I bet you do too, right?'

'I do. Kick-ass enTER, then uni and writing.'

'What're you going to be when you're older?'

'A writer, maybe a journo.' I chuckled.

Julian was sweet and misunderstood. The girls who were usually chasing him had no idea what he was like, what his interests were or anything that didn't involve sex. I knew all those things. He had a younger brother. They lived with his mum. She raised them mostly alone since his dad was a bigshot lawyer in the city and always away for work. Eventually, they separated. His mum was Australian, his dad Italian. They caught up as a family once a month to sign cheques, hand over documents and whatever else they had to tend to. Despite it all, he remained optimistic. Most of the time, he coasted through being envied by the guys and adored by the girls.

'Can I ask you something?' I bumped his shoulder with mine.

He smiled, biting his bottom lip. 'Whatever you want.'

'Is it true you were expelled from your old school?'

'Yep,' he said quietly. 'Punched a guy in the face.'

'Can I ask why?'

'He said some shit, and I just lost it. Something about Dad protecting some shady people attracting other shady people.'

'He's a criminal lawyer?'

'Yeah, works on some rough cases. Never talks about them, obviously, but it doesn't stop the fallout.'

'I'm sorry.'

'Yeah, I was too. They said I was lucky his family didn't press charges, but whatever. He deserved it. Came here, and Dad made the rest go away.'

'How?'

'Well, they weren't exactly saints, so if they expose me

by pressing charges, they expose themselves. Don't think anyone would risk ruining their life and career for something that will prove their guilt too.'

'You already sound like a lawyer.'

'Someone who knows how to work the system.'

A chill settled over me.

'Sorry, I shouldn't make light of it,' he said quickly. 'But it's something I learned early on from Dad.'

'What?'

'How to frame things the way you want them to be seen.'

I frowned.

'You're looking at me differently,' he said seriously. 'Do I scare you?'

'You terrify me.'

He frowned and slowed as we neared the edge of the park leading to my house. 'That's not good.'

'I get why you did it. I just don't like violence.'

'I'm not a violent person.'

I turned, drawing in a deep breath, and peered up at him. He watched me for a moment before he threaded his fingers through mine and giving me a goofy grin. My insides melted, and I tried to remind myself that the conversation with Josh about him being *shifty* was just Josh's way of looking out for me.

Guys could be weird, but Julian wasn't like that. He was unlike anyone I'd ever dated, not that we were dating or anything. But he seemed a lot more mature, more *experienced.*

'I watched a really great episode of *Ghost Hunters* last

night,' said Julian.

'Which one?'

'The one where they go to St. Augustine.'

'Oh yeah. That lighthouse is terrifying. Even in the daylight, it looks scary.'

'It's still a maritime museum, isn't it?'

'Yeah, it is. It's open to the public, but most of the action happens at night.'

He chuckled and walked us over to a set of park benches. Trees stretched as far as the eye could see, and only tiny glimpses of roofs were visible every few kilometres or so. Up in the park, there were gazebos where I sometimes had barbeques with my dad and sister when Mum was at work.

'You watch a lot of docos.'

'Bit lame, isn't it?' he laughed.

'Not at all. Well, maybe a little. But I'm the same, so it's totally cool in my books.'

He nudged me and smiled. 'This has been really nice.'

'What has?'

'Walking together.'

'Yeah, it has.' I forced the butterflies to settle down by taking a deep, calculated breath before releasing it.

This was getting too much. Every time his hand would brush mine, I flinched, Josh's stern warning on repeat in my mind.

I pulled my hand free and gave him a tight smile.

'You okay?' He cocked his head.

'Yep.'

'I should get you home. It's actually pretty cold tonight.'

I shivered in response.

He chuckled and wrapped his coat around me, then as he moved to sit back, I turned my face at the exact right moment when he did and drew in a sharp breath as his lips brushed my cheek, close to my ear.

He froze. So did I.

Then, after an eternal moment, he brought a hand to my cheek and I closed my eyes, feeling my breath catch in my throat.

I turned my face, knowing that if I moved just a fraction, my lips would meet his. Did I want to kiss him?

Yes. The answer was yes.

But higher reasoning told me that wasn't what I *should* be doing. What I should be doing is getting home. I needed to finish my essays. I needed to study for Methods, and I needed to…

'We should get you home,' he said again, stopping my rambling thoughts.

My eyes snapped open. For a moment, neither of us moved, then Julian's thumb brushed my cheek before he pressed a kiss to the spot just beside the corner of my lips. The rich fragrance of his cologne lingered in the air between us, and it took everything inside me to control myself and move.

When my legs felt like they wouldn't melt beneath me, I managed to get up and then laugh when he looked across at me with a chuckle. We hurried our pace, hoping to catch the last of the daylight before the streetlamps came on.

I gave his coat back and we parted ways at the end of my

street.

I slipped past my front door and took a moment to check the mirror by the entry to make sure my cheeks weren't bright red.

'You're home late,' Mum said from the kitchen. 'Did you have a good time?'

'I just walked home from school.'

'With a boy?'

'Yes,' I muttered under my breath.

'Daniel?'

'No, Mum.'

'When can I meet him?'

'Never,' I smirked. 'It's nothing serious anyway, just someone from class.'

First lie.

'The boy from book club?' she tried.

'Yes, Julian.'

She nodded. 'Okay, well, you don't need me to tell you to be careful.'

'I know, Mum.'

'And you don't need me to tell you how much your recital is counting on your focus.'

'I know, don't worry.'

'Are you feeling confident?'

'Absolutely.'

Second lie.

Two more months until I either embarrassed myself beyond redemption or wowed everyone in the audience.

'You'll do great, ljubavi.'

'I will,' I nodded without much more thought and retreated up the stairs. I was going to have a shower, watch a movie, binge-eat a block of chocolate, and not feel bad about it. But first, I had to message Hailey.

Home. Safe and sound.

Good. See you tomorrow! She messaged back.

I shut the door behind me, tossed my phone on the bed, and turned the computer on. Several notifications came in all at once on Myspace and MSN.

I opened the first message. It was from an account with no display picture, no friends, or contacts.

I clicked into it and felt the blood drain from my face.

Watch ur back, bitch. U don't know who ur playing with.

The next was even worse.

He's going to chew u up and spit u out. You'll wish u were dead.

Tears sprung from my eyes. Shallow breaths came and went in quick succession, making my throat tighten.

Reckon u can handle the player? U don't even know the game.

CHAPTER SIX

Cartoon Heroes

*B*reathe *in and out. One, two, three...*
I closed my eyes, turned the screen off and took another deep breath.

Once my heart was beating right, I opened MSN again. The messages stared me in the face.

I needed to talk to someone. I turned on the webcam, hit connect and waited.

A few seconds later, the call connected, and Daniel's face popped up on the screen. The second he saw me, his expression hardened. When I looked up at the small box with my face in it, I saw why. My skin was pale, and my eyes bloodshot. I looked like I hadn't slept for days.

'What's going on?' he asked.

'I got some really awful messages.'

'What did they say?'

'I'll forward them.'

Daniel waited a moment for the texts to come through, and as soon as they did, his eyes snapped up to mine.

'Who sent them?' he asked.

'No idea, blank profiles.'

'Fake accounts?'

'Clearly.'

'What's on your mind?' he cocked his head. 'I can see your brain working overtime there. You have a theory, so share it.'

'There's no theory, just…'

'Just what?'

'I've been hanging out with Julian.'

'Andy,' he sighed, his gaze dropping from the screen before his hand shot up and brushed away the long part of his fringe that had fallen over his eyes. I'd told him once that it looked like Beckham's hairstyle, and he styled it like that for the rest of the month.

'I know,' I snapped back. 'But he's just been so nice, and he listens and I—'

'I listen. I'm your friend. He's bad news.'

'I haven't done anything with him, Daniel.'

'And keep it that way. I mean it.'

'Like I said, nothing is going on. Why do you even care?'

A frown tugged at his lips. 'The fact that you even have to ask really sucks.'

Not knowing how to respond, I looked away from the screen.

'What are you doing now?'

I looked down at my pjs. 'About to go to sleep.'

'Want me to come over? We can watch a movie?'

'You know what, yes, that would be great.' I had to make this better between us. 'I miss you.'

'We hung out at school.'

'You know what I mean.'

He dropped his gaze before nodding. 'I'll see you in a bit.'

The last thing I wanted was for Julian to come between our friendship.

He disconnected the call, and I dropped into the fluffy doona. This was good. I needed this. Mum would be overjoyed; she loved Daniel, and she'd already sworn that the boy would be welcome here at any time.

Funny, I thought. The idea of having him over didn't send me into a frenzy like it did whenever anyone else asked to come here…

While waiting for Daniel, I took the opportunity to make myself presentable. I wasn't going to dress up for him, but I would do him the courtesy of not wearing ripped socks and paint-stained leggings. Last year, Dad and I decided it would be a good idea to repaint the entire house. Neither of us knew what we were doing, and it showed. The cornices were hideous, the paint colour was a bit gross. To be honest, we probably made the house look worse, but it was the best weekend ever.

I changed into some fresh trackies and tied my hair back just as Daniel arrived with two large bags full of soft drink, chips, and lollies.

Mum welcomed him with open arms and then promptly started pulling out bowls and glasses for our night.

'Not too late, okay?' Mum said, and we both nodded.

Jelena appeared behind Mum.

'Can I watch movies with you?' she asked, reaching around Mum to steal a handful of the sour worms Daniel brought over.

'Not tonight. Next time, though,' I said.

She sulked, but Daniel offered her a block of caramel chocolate.

'Andy and I need to talk about some important things. We'll play *Guitar Hero* together soon, though. Cool?'

She nodded and eagerly snatched the block.

Daniel and I retreated upstairs to my room.

'Thanks for that. Sometimes she's a lot.'

'She just loves her sister.'

'I know.' I hated being a bitch, but all I wanted was some peace and quiet, a nice night in with my best friend, and no anxiety attacks.

I shut the door as Daniel plopped himself down on the far end of my bed, which was pressed against the wall creating a nice nook to lean against.

I turned the stereo on and put in a mix I'd made a while back. Then I sat down beside him.

'Pillow?' he asked.

'Yes, please.'

He threw it over, and I wasted no time face-planting into it.

As I got comfortable, I heard him fish out his phone and keys from his navy shorts and set them on my bedside table. He was born for the preppy look. I had no idea how he always managed to look so stylish. A lot of it had to do with the fact that he shopped at Chadstone all the time.

'How do you feel about these messages?' he said, craning his neck.

'Shithouse.'

'Understandable.'

'What do I do about it?'

'You could report it.'

'Who am I going to report it to?' I groaned into the doona. 'There's no profile.'

'The email they set the account up with has to be legit, so maybe that.'

'Well, yes and no, they could have also made a fake email.'

'That's a lot of effort.'

'So is sending anonymous hate messages.'

This was all so complicated and messy.

Why was being seventeen so freaking hard?

Daniel picked up the remote and started flicking through the Foxtel catalogue. After searching through the documentary section for more than fifteen minutes, we settled on one about one of the most famous UFO sightings ever, the "Battle of Los Angeles".

'Should I turn the music off?' I asked.

'Nah, keep it on.'

I settled into the comfort of my bed.

'Did you know that the cops and politicians who'd witnessed the whole thing were ridiculed for years?'

'No shit?'

'Yeah, they were called liars, psychos, you name it. But the worst part was that there was all this evidence from all these news stations covering the story, and it was still put down to mass hysteria.'

He laughed.

'What?' I craned my neck up to meet his gaze.

'You are one cool chick.'

I snorted and dropped my head back on the pillow. 'Cool isn't the word I'd use.'

'Well, I will. Tell me more about this battle.'

'The military started shooting the sky where they saw this object blacking out the stars.'

'Seriously?'

'Yep, they had these good, solid photographs, proving there was something in the sky that their missiles were hitting. They still tried to say it was mass hysteria.'

'Yeah, funny how people can shun someone even when there's literal proof, right?'

'It's scary. Imagine having gone through something so terrifying, so big, even though there's proof, but no one believes you because a bunch of other people say it's just hysteria?'

'But you believe them.'

'I do. I would always believe someone if they told me something awful happened.'

I craned my neck again and saw him smiling. My heartbeat kicked up instantly, making a shiver roll up my spine in a way I hadn't really felt before. I mean, this was Daniel. My *best* friend. The one I wore daggy clothes around. The one I could tell anything to. I raised myself on my elbows and watched him curiously as he dropped his hand to my waist to maneuverer us so that I was lying flat on my bed, and he fit right beside me.

As I made a move to smooth the wayward strands of hair from my face, he caught my arm and slowly slid my sleeve down.

I watched his gaze leave my face and land on the scar from years ago. He traced it with his thumb.

'What happened here?'

'Cut myself.' I shrugged, biting my bottom lip.

'Why?'

We'd never spoken about that part of my life. Actually, I'd never spoken about it to *anyone*. But I didn't feel like I had to lie to him or hide.

His fingers remained wrapped around my wrist.

I would have normally snatched my arm back and made some lame excuse about breaking a bottle accidentally, but I decided instead to tell him everything.

'I was overwhelmed. There was a lot of pressure at school, at tennis, piano… Whenever it got too much, I did this. Usually only a little, and it helped.'

'How did it help?' he asked gently.

'It felt like the cut opened a tiny hole for all the pressure to escape safely without blowing.'

'But this time was different?' he looked at the scar, which was a jagged, deep cut that had long since turned shiny.

'Yes. There was so much rage inside me, and I had no idea why I was feeling so much. I didn't know what else to do.'

'Have you done it since?'

'No, never again. This was the last time.'

He drew my arm up to his lips and kissed the scar. My breath slowed until I could no longer breathe. And then, when he gently lowered my arm to my stomach, my brain scattered into a million pieces.

'Hey,' he said, tipping my chin up. 'You're shivering.'

'I'm freezing. You know my dad doesn't believe in the heater.'

'Oh.' He looked around, grabbed the throw at the end of my bed, and wrapped it over me. 'Better?'

'Much.' I snuggled into the soft fabric, feeling the heat from my cheeks spread all over my body.

'Good, because you look like the cutest little burrito that has ever lived.' He tightened the blanket up under my chin, making me laugh.

His expression seemed pensive and almost thoughtful, and I would have given anything to know what he was thinking.

The documentary was long forgotten as the narrator droned on about the misinformation agents running the UFO community. Daniel's lips slightly parted, and when he moved closer, I felt the pressure of his leg against mine and a whole new sensation came over me.

Daniel took my hand, threading his fingers through mine. The heat spread through me, but so did panic. I pulled my hand back and ripped the blanket off moving to the edge of the bed. I released a long breath and drew my knees to my chest.

'Andy?'

'Yeah?' I said, my voice kind of squeaking at the end.

'You're really cute,' he chuckled, then ran his fingertips along my shoulders where my hair sat messily. 'Actually, not cute, you're incredibly beautiful.'

The gentleness in the gesture did all sorts of things to my

insides. My stomach fired up like a million tiny fireflies fluttering, and my palms tingled, quickly growing hot.

As his other hand fell to my shoulder and he turned me toward him, my hands moved on their own. I didn't care how stupid I looked. I knew what I wanted. Plus, I'd read enough trashy romance novels to know what to do. I carefully lifted my hand to his cheek and stopped, waiting to see what he would do.

When his eyes found mine, his face lit up into a wide smile, immediately causing a flurry of joy to rise to the surface. Most of my days were filled with study and piano and the general sense of anxiety with a sprinkling of dread— when was the next assignment due, when was the next text coming, what was my next task? This was new, this was nice, like *really* nice.

Although, a part of me kept wondering whether this was what I wanted with Daniel. I knew these kinds of things ruined friendships; I'd heard about it all the time. Elizabeth, the only girl I still spoke to from my old school, told me how sleeping with her best friend ruined their friendship to the point where they couldn't even be in the same room.

But the second Daniel leaned in, I pushed Elizabeth and her ruined friendship to the back of my mind and met Daniel halfway.

As Aqua continued filling the room with lyrics about cartoon heroes, I melted into his touch. He was gentle. Every move was a careful one. Every time we parted for air, he'd smile and search my eyes as though each touch following the previous one was given only with my permission.

His hands dropped to my hips and gently lowered me down into the soft sheets, causing several of the dozen pillows I used to build my own nighttime fort to fall onto the floor. Then he pressed his elbow into the pillow beside my head and kissed me again. His hand slipped from my waist down over my thigh.

I clasped my hand over his.

His eyes opened, flicking down to mine.

'I feel like I should make you take me out to dinner first or something,' I chuckled.

He let out a relieved breath and slid his hand back up to my hip. 'I want to take you out for dinner, Andy, but not just because I want this with you.'

'Really?'

'Damn straight. Though I won't lie, you're making this really hard for me.'

I smirked against his lips and kissed him again, hoping to hide the now obvious flush on my cheeks.

'I was going to ask you. Totally cool if you don't want to,' I began, then pulled back.

'Spit it out, Nekić.'

'My final piano recital is on the eighth of September.'

'I'll be there.'

'Really?'

'I mean, yeah, if you were about to invite me.'

'Ah, yeah. I was.'

'Good, because that would have been so awkward.'

I grinned. 'I'll tell Mum to get another ticket.'

'Can't wait.'

I chewed my lip, shielding my smile. Daniel drew my face to his again and kissed me.

When he pulled back and looked at the clock on my table, he lowered his forehead to mine and sighed. 'I think this is where I need to say goodnight,' he said gently.

'You have to go?'

He reached over for his phone on my side table and then pulled his arm free and sat up. 'Yep, I definitely have to go.'

'You're sure you're not upset?'

'Definitely not upset.'

'Daniel?'

'Everything is all good, Nekić. I promise. But if I don't go home now, I won't have a home to go to.'

He kissed me, harder this time, and I had to stop myself from demanding he stay the night.

'You really meant it about the dinner?'

He frowned and tilted his head to the side. 'Dinners and lunches and breakfasts. Why?'

'I know how boys can be, and I know they hate waiting for—well, they hate waiting around for that.'

'I want all of this with you, but only when we're both ready for it. And when we are, it'll be perfect.'

With another *very* heated kiss, Daniel said goodbye and saw himself out.

CHAPTER SEVEN

Rudimentary

I did my best to avoid my mum's wide grin as I walked back into the kitchen. Half her face and grin were shielded by the giant mug I'd gotten her ten years ago for Mother's Day. The pink "World's Best Mum" text was discoloured and chipping in most places. I didn't know why she still kept it.

'I'm going to bed, Mum. Do you need help with anything?'

'No, ljubavi, you go to bed.' She washed out her mug. 'Still going shopping tomorrow?'

'Absolutely.'

We'd planned a shopping trip weeks ago, but Mum decided we'd make a day of it rather than cramming it in after school, so we changed it to a Saturday, which meant I was now going to miss out on seeing Daniel.

'We'll be back by five,' Mum grinned as though she'd sensed my dilemma. 'Tata and I have a date.'

'Oh? What are you two doing?'

'We going to go to Željko's.'

I baulked in surprise. 'That's awesome.'

I hugged her goodnight and smiled when I saw the small collection of new makeup still in their wrappers on the counter, and a cute little bangle. I really hoped Dad would make more effort for the both of them.

I climbed the stairs feeling elated, and when I snuggled into bed, thoughts of Daniel lingered with me. When the time was right for both of us, it would be perfect, just like Daniel said.

~

'Andrea!'

The sound of my mum's high-pitched voice jolted me awake.

I shot up in the bed, looked around, and then relaxed. Daniel hadn't accidentally stayed over, and I hadn't accidentally done anything wrong. And it was most definitely Saturday, so I hadn't slept in and missed school.

'Andrea!' she screamed again.

Jesus. Whatever it was, it wasn't good.

'Coming!' I yelled back.

I slid out of the bed, stuffed my feet into a pair of fake Uggs and jogged down the stairs. She stood at the counter with arms folded over her chest and a stern look, shooting daggers at me.

'What?'

'*What?*' she shot back. 'I have taught you never to lie to me. What is this?'

'What's what?' I padded over to the fridge, eager to get some juice in before she had a conniption.

She slapped an envelope down onto the counter, and my heart leapt into my throat when I saw the music academy emblem on top.

'You declined scholarship for piano?'

'Mum, I don't want to play piano professionally. I don't want to play at all.'

When our eyes finally met, I felt like a small part of her soul had chipped away and floated into the ether. She dropped onto the stool at the bench, shoulders slumped. 'Why?'

'Because I don't. It doesn't make me happy anymore. It just stresses me out.'

'You never say anything.'

'Of course not. Look at your reaction, Mum. I can't tell you anything.'

'That's not true.'

'Isn't it?' I sighed. 'Look at you, you're about to cry, and this is just about a stupid piano school. God forbid, I have to tell you anything important.'

'You know you can.'

'And while we're talking, I know you're busy, and you're stressed, and you hate your job, but I'm stressed too, Mum. Did you even know that I'd been taking extra math and English classes just to get a better enTER?'

She frowned. 'You could tell me.'

'No, Mum, I can't. Because it's too much for you, so keeping it in is better.'

'Is not better, Andrea.'

'I'll keep playing this year because I'm choosing to, but next year, I'm out.'

'Have you spoken to Dad about this?'

'No.' I took a long sip of the juice. 'And I'm not going to.

I'm almost eighteen. I want to make my own choices and decide what I want to do.'

'Andrea…'

'Can we just go shopping and be a normal family?'

'What does that mean?'

'It means I always have to think about how you two feel before myself, Mum,' I frowned. 'I haven't felt like myself in years. I'm looking after Jelena. I'm making sure she eats in the morning and gets to school. I get it. You *have* to work; we need the money, but I'm tired, Mum.'

'Well, since we talking truth,' she said and stood up. 'You know how much your father and I have given to be here. We left everything back in Yugoslavia. We came here with clothes on our bodies and few toys.'

I snapped my mouth shut.

'You think it is easy for your father, who is mathematician, to be working in factory?'

I sat down.

'And I'm a qualified engineer, Andrea. I don't enjoy being covered in crap from the factory and pretending to be happy every single day while people treat me like idiot and talk down because I don't understand their language well.'

Tears filled my eyes, reflecting my mother's green ones.

'No, ljubavi, you don't think about these things because we don't want you to. We want you to go to school, wear your bags and wear nice clothes so you can fit in.'

Mum gathered herself before getting up.

'I don't fit in, not even with all that. I'm still just me.'

'You're not helping yourself at all when you act like this.'

'I'm sorry.'

'I know you are,' she said. 'Now get your sister. We should leave soon.'

~

As we walked through the shopping centre, I couldn't change the heaviness now hanging between us.

Jelena was oblivious. While she ranted on and on about the sale price of the game she wanted, Mum kept giving her one-word answers, and I kept counting down the time until we could end this shopping trip.

I sighed as we made yet another loop of the lower floor before deciding on a café so Jelena and Mum could make a note of the shops we'd come back to.

'Find us a spot, and I'll order,' she said, speaking more than one syllable for the first time since the argument.

While I waited for Mum, I thought about the way Mum and I fought and how different my relationship with my family had become.

Where did it change? Had I become a selfish brat? Maybe. Probably.

But I was going to stand my ground, and the piano school thing was the first step of many I was taking for myself. I grinned to myself. Tonight, I would see Daniel and maybe I wouldn't be opposed to seeing what could happen with him.

'What're you smiling about?' Mum sat in the oversized armchair opposite me and crossed her legs.

'Nothing.'

'Well, you know people who grin to themselves look batshit crazy,' Jelena muttered.

'Gee, thanks.' I snapped.

Mum laughed. 'She's right.'

The best thing about Mum was her ability to defuse situations covertly. It wasn't the first time. A few years back at my old school, I had a full-on meltdown, and a week later, I was taken to hospital for cutting my wrists. I had no idea why I'd done it, but when Mum saw it, she lost her shit, and Dad drove me to emergency. They sat with me for two hours while the doctors stitched me up, and then we never spoke about it again. Now, every time I exhibited sadness, or mood swings of any kind, I caught their eyes scanning my arms. So, I learned to hide it better. Winter was easy—long-sleeved jumpers and long coats did the trick. Summer was harder; I started wearing more bangles, beaded bracelets and even tennis sweatbands like they were a fashion statement.

'So?'

'Just thinking about the school year, it's nearly all over.'

'It's just the end of one part, ljubavi, then you have uni.'

She smiled, showing off her pretty face. Watching her sip her coffee and gaze at the sights around us, I thought about the girl she was, sitting with the doctor and her mum when they told her she was pregnant. Was she scared? Excited? Did she plan it, or was it all a surprise?

She told me that as a kid, she always wanted to have a big wedding and have babies. The big wedding part didn't happen; money was tight, and her parents were conservative. But the baby part did.

Then, the war in Yugoslavia broke out.

Whistles in the night of the impending attack missiles

rang through the air for days. It didn't matter that the dust didn't settle; they didn't wait to fire again. I remembered the smell of embers and the way my mum's salty tears tasted while we ran through the rubble. She'd pressed my cheek to hers and covered my eyes with her hand so I wouldn't see anything around us.

They didn't know that I remembered any of this, because while they were trying to be strong for me, I was doing the same for them.

I didn't tell them how much the kids in primary school bullied me or why I didn't receive any birthday party invitations. Then I learned the meaning of ignorance. What they didn't know couldn't hurt them. They both had so much to carry already, so I kept it to myself, vetted what they saw and heard, and everyone was happy.

'How is school going?' Mum asked, breaking me from my thoughts.

'Usual.'

She nodded. 'How are your classes?'

'They're good too, getting the grades I want.'

'And what about Daniel?'

There it was, the question she was leading up to. I rolled my eyes. Jelena seemed to have been waiting for this moment too. She grinned and immediately chimed in. 'Is he your boyfriend?'

Both Mum and I ignored her.

'I like him,' Mum said.

'Me too.'

'He went home late,' Mum continued, a hint of a smile

bursting to come out.

'The documentary was long.'

She looked at me, her bright green eyes narrowing, almost disappearing under the scrutinising gaze.

'He had to go home,' I added. 'Because we are both responsible adults.'

'Good, because babies are a lot of work—'

'Oh my God, Mum!' Both Jelena and I blurted out.

She held her hand up. 'I'm just saying it's all well when you're young and having fun, but things happen.'

'Nothing happened, nothing will happen. Relax.'

'I'm relaxed,' she shrugged with a laugh. 'But don't you be too relaxed.'

'I'm not, believe me.'

For a moment, we enjoyed the quiet stillness. I leaned back in the armchair and took another sip of coffee. But then Jelena shot to her feet, scaring the crap out of me.

'Mum, there's Maya!'

I caught sight of Jelena's friend waving at us as she walked along with her dad.

'Can I go?' Jelena bounced in her spot.

'Yes, go, go, but we meet later.'

'Yes, I promise!'

She disappeared in a split second, and I could have sworn she left behind a dust cloud like in the cartoons.

'Andrea,' Mum said, her voice suddenly serious.

My stomach churned; that tone was always reserved for something I didn't want to talk about. The last time she sounded like that and had the furrowed brow thing going on, it was to tell me that her sister had died back in Germany. I cried for days. I'd been meaning to call my aunt for weeks, but study and piano always got in the way, and then the opportunity was gone forever.

'Miš,' she began. 'You know that you choose what you want to do in life?'

'Of course.'

Her lips pursed into a straight line.

'If you don't want to do something, you say so. Don't be afraid to say no.'

'I know, Mum.'

'I know you do, but if someone pressures you into something you don't want, don't feel you must say yes. It might be simple to know, but things can change quickly. Especially with boys.'

'Mum, Daniel isn't like that.'

'I didn't say he is, but sometimes life doesn't go to plan.'

I released a relieved breath and reached over, squeezing her hand.

'I'm my own woman, Mum. You and Dad taught me that. I'm strong because of you.'

She chuckled and leaned over the small circular table to kiss my cheek. 'Good, I've done a good job then. Now let's go and buy you a dress.'

CHAPTER EIGHT

MIA

The second Mum and I got home, I got her to help me into the dress and take a million photos. I sent a couple to Daniel hoping he would like it.

Nothing.

I tried sending a few more texts.

Still nothing.

I thought we were hanging out tonight. I sent.

I waited, and when no response came back, I tried again.

It's cool if you're busy. Just let me know.

When he didn't reply to that either, I shook my head and tried to push him out of my mind. Maybe he was busy or out with his dad. I know they went hiking heaps, and there was usually no reception where they went.

'Andrea?'

'Yeah?'

Dad came in with a large bag and two water bottles.

'Hike?'

'Right now?'

'Obviously not.'

I laughed.

'Tomorrow. Early.'

'Okay, I'll be up.'

I didn't look at my phone again and tried to forget Daniel. I picked out some hiking clothes, the new boots Dad bought me as an early birthday present and went to bed.

~

Monday rolled around with no contact from Daniel.

So did Tuesday. He also didn't show up to school. I waited until second period and then texted him again.

> *You didn't have to pretend to be sick just to avoid seeing me.*

When he didn't reply, I rethought my approach. Maybe he thought I was being serious.

> *I'm kidding. Hope you're okay, message me. I really enjoyed spending time with you, and I hope we can organise that dinner soon.*

Followed by:

> *PS. Dad and I went hiking Saturday. Maybe we could do that together one day. I know some good trails.*

I looked at the phone for a good five minutes, but there was no reply. I frowned and replaced my phone in my blazer. Under normal circumstances, I wouldn't have dared disobey the school's rules. Phones were meant to be stowed away in our lockers. But today, I carefully secured the phone inside my inner pocket and made sure no one saw.

If Daniel messaged, I needed to know.

Period three and four went by quickly. I only went to the bathroom twice each period to check my phone, and by the time lunch neared, I felt my heart rate spiking.

Daniel *still* hadn't replied.

Maybe he didn't want to talk, maybe he was nervous, or worse, regretful. Maybe he decided I wasn't worth the time since I wasn't ready to give it up when he tried, and that whole excuse about getting home was made up. Had he really lashed on me? Surely not. That wasn't possible.

Of course it was, the annoying voice in my head said.

The nagging feeling that he just had no idea how to break it to me that he wasn't interested anymore kept dragging me down into a pit I couldn't get out of.

The bell signalling the end of the fourth period rang, and I packed up my books, shoved my pencil case into the binder and made a beeline straight for the locker bay. Lunch time.

My getaway was cut short when Hailey stopped me. 'I got you something.'

'Why?' I chuckled.

'Well, I saw this and thought it was perfect for your birthday.'

'But it's ages away.'

'I know, but we have SACs this week and next, and then I know you're busy as with your recital, then it's holidays, and then you'll be busy with your parents and—'

'I get it,' I laughed. 'But you didn't have to get me anything.'

'I know, but I wanted to. So, open it.'

I looked at the clumsily wrapped gift, which was half the size of her and adorned with a big, pink bow and what I assumed was glitter spray that had mostly fallen off.

I grinned and took it from her.

When I finally peeled off the first layer of brown paper,

my fingers traced across the edges of what felt like cool glass and a wooden frame.

I ripped off the last of the sticky tape and turned the frame around.

Sarah Michelle Gellar was posing with a stake, her perfect blonde hair falling over her shoulders, and she was wearing Angel's large cross around her neck.

'It's the Buffy season one poster!' Hailey exclaimed.

'This is my favourite one!'

'I know!' she chuckled, throwing her arms around me. 'Do you like it?'

'I love it!'

She laughed and hugged me again. 'I'm glad.'

When I pulled away and tucked the huge frame under my arm, her eyes narrowed. 'What is it?'

'Nothing.'

'You're not seriously lying to me, are you?'

'Just had a tough class.'

'Sure it's nothing to do with Julian?' she raised one brow.

'No, nothing to do with him.'

'You're sure? Because you can always talk to me if something is going on. I'm a good listener for boy troubles.'

'Nothing is going on. Least of all boy troubles. Promise.'

'Okay, but I mean it.'

She gave me another quick hug and disappeared into the sea of bodies leaving me to wrangle my books, bag, and giant ass Buffy poster. As I neared my locker, I drew in a deep breath when I spotted Julian standing beside it. He had one shoulder resting lazily along the edge of my door and a foot pressed on the bottom locker.

My cheeks caught fire as his gaze travelled across my face, dipping to my lips and then back to my eyes. I probably looked like a total loser carrying this huge ass poster. I tried to angle it away just so that he couldn't see what was on it. The corner of his top lip crept up into a smirk. Too late. He saw it. I sucked in a long breath and kept walking.

Holy mother of God. The nonchalant attitude, the dark hazel eyes, the perfectly messy hair, and undeniably perfect olive skin drove me mad. Did he model for a surf magazine? If he didn't, he should have.

'Hi, Julian.' Jess Bennett walked past him, swinging her hips.

He didn't even look at her. She shot a nasty look my way. A prick of sheer, petty joy raced through me.

My eyes drifted back to Julian. I wet my lips as a flush spread through me, and a little voice in the back of my head that sounded an awful lot like Daniel asked what I was doing. I frowned before I could stop it.

'You don't look happy to see me?'

'Conflicted,' I said truthfully.

'Conflicted?'

'Yep.' I reached for the lock.

After three failed attempts and growing nerves heating my cheeks, I finally got the door open. Once I was sure everything was secure, including the giant poster which I had to stash behind the lockers, I followed him outside and we made our way to the oval.

'Why are we going this way?' I asked.

'I wagged last class, and I don't want to risk being seen by the teacher.'

'Fair enough.'

The footy team were training again; their big scout game was tonight.

'Why aren't you training for the game tonight?' I asked, scanning the players, desperately trying to see whether Josh was there.

'I'm resting. So are some of the other boys.'

'Who?' I looked back, spotting Josh running across the field.

He was running for a mark, but as Julian and I walked behind the goalposts, Josh's eyes shot to me, and he missed the huge player running at him. The spectators on the sidelines broke into a fit of laughter.

'Nick and Illya, to name a few. They're terrified of injuries, so they don't train on game days.'

'Right.' I looked away.

Julian walked close beside me making me hyperaware of Josh's gaze on us.

'Do you want to talk about it?' Julian asked.

'Talk about what?'

We sat at a free bench and when Julian reached over and took my hand, I flinched so hard I almost jarred my shoulder.

He laughed, 'The fact that you look like you're going to freak?'

'It's been really hectic at home. Then there's piano—my mum freaked out about me quitting. Dad's never home because he's so busy. Then there's all this book club shit and

English, and you—wow, I just gave you my whole life story.'
I slumped back.

'Isn't that what you usually deal with?' he said, his brows rising. 'So, what else is bothering you?'

Julian leaned in, head tilted like a puppy trying to understand. His gaze was deep, full of need and urgency. Did he want to… kiss me?

'Daniel and I had a thing, and I thought he wanted more but now he's literally rejected me.'

'I'm really sorry,' he said gently, taking my hand again.

I looked at his fingers intertwined with mine and realised what was really bothering me.

'I really like you,' I blurted out.

I liked Daniel. I liked Julian. But here we were. Julian's brows rose again, and for the longest time, he sat in complete silence. A group of Year Ten girls I didn't know kept glancing over at us, but they weren't the only ones. Josh's fierce expression met my own, and I quickly tore my gaze away.

'And this would be the perfect time for me to say something stupid to detract from the previous stupid thing,' I muttered.

'It wasn't stupid… So, you like me.'

'Yes, but I like Daniel, and we're—well, I thought we had a thing.'

'Maybe he has a good reason.'

'I really want to think that, but I feel really stupid.'

'Why?'

'Because I thought he could like me.'

'What's that supposed to mean?'

'People like him, like they like you, and I'm just… me.'

'Just you is just perfect, Andrea.'

I rolled my eyes as an annoying coat of tears stung them. 'I'm so angry and confused, and I have no idea why I'm telling you all of this.'

'Because we're friends,' he said simply. 'If he's ignoring you, he's stupid. But if there's a reason, then maybe you should give him a chance to explain.'

'He's had all weekend to explain. He's had all of Monday and Tuesday, too.'

'Maybe his phone died.'

I didn't think of that.

I turned on the small bench and caught sight of our hands together again. A niggling feeling of guilt crept up on me. I shouldn't be feeling bad. Daniel was the one who rejected me.

Julian shifted, positioning himself close beside me, and the hand that had previously been holding mine was brushing a strand of my hair behind my ear.

I held my breath.

'I want to see you. Outside of school and our walks home.'

'Why?' I heard myself say.

'Because I like you too, and I'd like to get to know you.' He searched my eyes. 'Come over after school.'

'What?'

'Yeah, meet my mum and my brother. Dad might be there too.'

My nerves tumbled into a hot mess.

'Come on, say yes,' he chuckled. 'We'll go out after. I want to take you out for dinner.'

'You have the game tonight,' I reminded him.

'It's not until later.'

'Won't you be stressed about not being ready?'

'Nah, I'm fine. I have other ways of releasing tension and nerves before games. Don't need a Zen break or anything.'

'Really?' *Dinner. Hanging out. With Julian Valesco?*

'Yeah, wouldn't say it if I didn't mean it.'

'I don't know, Julian.'

'Up to you. But I really do hope you come.'

The part of me desperate to push Daniel to the back of my mind and stop feeling so freaking hurt and rejected considered it. The other, more logical part told me to get up, call Daniel, go to class and then go home and study.

'This is my address.' Julian handed me a slip of paper with neat writing. 'I hope I'll see you.'

Before I could say anything I would regret, I gave him a tight smile, shoved the note into my pocket, and left.

~

While Benson was discussing the differences between books and movie adaptations, Hailey and I exchanged notes. I opened the tightly folded square and found her familiar pink scribble.

You and Julian looked suuuper cosy at lunch.

I supressed a smile.

He asked me to go and see him after school. I think I might!!!

I slid the note over. As soon as she opened it, she stiffened, then her hand shot up.

'Yes, Hailey?' Benson replied, keeping his eyes glued to the movie examples he was flicking through on his desk.

'I need to get some fresh air. Can I be excused?'

'Of course, take someone with you.'

'I'll take Andrea.'

He nodded, and I followed Hailey outside.

Once we were out of earshot from the classroom, Hailey whipped around, looking at me straight on, 'You're not seriously going to go, are you?'

I pulled my arm back and crossed it over my chest.

'I was considering it, why?'

'Because he's sketchy! He's a player. He knows how to talk the talk. You know this. You've seen the type of girls he goes for.'

'The *type?* What the hell does that mean? Hot? Rich?'

'Desperate.'

My brows shot up. 'I don't need this from you. I have a lot going on, and Daniel's being an asshole, and I just found someone who isn't treating me like shit, and you're getting mad at me for that.'

'Fine. Don't listen to me. But listen to yourself. You can feel that something is sus.'

'Why? Because he'd be interested in someone like me?'

'What does that mean?'

'I'm lame, Hailey. We both are. I don't want to be that girl anymore.'

'What are you on about?'

'We carry Buffy posters around like we're ten and pretend we're characters from the show. I have a *Matrix* coat at home. Hails, we're losers. I don't want to be a loser.'

Her eyes widened, and I immediately felt awful.

'You're a real bitch sometimes, you know that?' she muttered.

'Hails, I'm sorry—'

'No, you're not. You think you're the only one whose life is hard? You think you're the only one struggling at home and having to pretend to be normal and happy all the freaking time? My mum works stupid hours, and I don't even see her half the time. My sister and I run the household. I've been walking to school since I was like five because we can't afford the bus and you're having a bit of whine because your mum asks you to babysit?'

'Doesn't make my problems any less than yours!'

'No, but you're carrying on like a baby. You need to get over yourself and use your head. You're smart. You make sure everyone knows it, so *be* smart.'

Before I could say anything else, the bell rang, and she turned and left without saying another word. I sighed and waited until it was clear enough to make my way back to class to collect my things.

~

I'd fished out everything I needed from my locker and made my way to the back gate.

Logic had officially checked out.

I was actually doing this.

Despite the nagging feeling coiling around my heart, I

pushed it away and decided that it was just nerves and the result of the heated conversation with Hailey.

As I walked out of the school, I opened my phone and called Daniel.

It rang a couple of times before the line connected.

'I thought you were dead,' I said with a chuckle.

'I can't talk to you right now, so please stop calling,' he whispered in an unusually cold, quiet tone. And then he hung up.

As the shock of the phone call wore off, I ground my teeth, shoved the phone in my pocket and stormed down the gravel path toward the back gate, changing course.

That was it. I'd given him the opportunity to talk to me, to tell me that he'd changed his mind or explain himself about being MIA for four days, and his response was to hang up without any answers. I was reading him loud and clear.

CHAPTER NINE

Only Alleyways and Dark Roads

Taking the same route Julian and I took when we walked home together, I found myself weaving through a busy street lined with tall lampposts and gardens full of kids' toys.

Once I reached the end of the busy street, I stopped, checking the number written on the note and the one plastered on the quaint letterbox. The house was gorgeous, with navy blue accents around the windows and doors. Tall pines lined either side of the footpath. There was a white picket fence that spanned the entire front of the property and a little gate with a golden handle. There was a three-car garage revealing a small convertible in the drive and a cute *Welcome Home* sign on the door.

I quickly slung my bag to the front, pulled out my body spray and doused myself in coconut-scented fragrance. When I was satisfied that I smelled good and not like the musty halls of Deanell, I put it back in my bag, drew in a deep breath and pushed the gate open.

When I reached his door, I stopped for a moment, composing myself before I knocked. I heard loud, clumsy footsteps pounding on hardwood floors, and then the door was enthusiastically pulled open. A young boy who looked a lot like Julian grinned up at me. His hair was barely styled beyond a quick combing, and he clutched a PlayStation controller in one hand.

'Julian!' he yelled over his shoulder. 'Your girlfriend is here!'

Julian appeared from the living room with a wide grin. He was dressed in casual black pants and a really fitted T-shirt, and in his hand, he was gripping a guitar like Jelena's

'Not you too.' I rolled my eyes.

'I'm waiting to get the new one, but I have to wait until I get paid next week.'

'Apparently, my sister is giving lessons.'

'Oh yeah? We'll play when you're good.'

'Absolutely not.'

He ran his hand through his hair and looked down, shielding a smile. It was tousled like he always wore it at school. I giggled nervously and readjusted my bag on my shoulder. *Damn this bag. Why did I bring everything with me?*

'Let me get that.' He shoved his brother out of the way, handing him the guitar.

He took my bag and set it beside the door. I kicked my school shoes off and left them next to my bag.

'Thanks.' I rubbed my arms, ignoring the chill.

'Zach, this is Andrea. Andrea, this pain in the ass is my brother, Zach.' Julian's hand shot out to smooth the messy mop of hair, but Zach slapped him back. 'Be nice and say hi to Andrea.'

'Hi, Andrea.'

I grinned. 'Hi, Zach.'

'Mum, this is Andrea,' he said over his shoulder.

'Oh, hello!' she waved from the kitchen.

'So, this is it,' said Julian, gesturing to the house, which was literally a kitchen and living room in one, two bedrooms and a bathroom separated by a narrow hall, all of which I could see from the central point at the front door.

It was quaint but expensive and well-decorated. I could feel the love his mother put into making this a home for the three of them. Despite the narrowness of the closed-in walls, it felt light and airy.

'I'll show you my room.'

'Okay.' A flush of warmth coursed through me. 'Where are we going to eat?'

'You can choose.'

'I don't have a change of clothes. Hopefully, haute couture uniform is fine.'

'I'm sure it's okay, don't stress,' he chuckled. 'You make the uniform look good.'

'Yeah, the nun length does wonders for a girl's figure.'

He laughed and led me down the hall. Our footsteps sounded heavy, as though we were walking on a hollow floor even though a Persian runner, which felt unbelievable beneath my feet, softened our footfalls. We passed one room on the left, which had its door closed, and just next to it was another, which was open. Music filtered through, wrapping me up and welcoming me in.

He gestured inside.

I followed him in and looked around, taking in all the

artwork and photos hung haphazardly on the walls. There were childhood pictures, scenery from all over Europe and traditional tapestries that looked handmade.

Julian shut the door, the sound reverberated through the small space, making me straighten. Every sense was heightened as he walked around me, his gaze hot on my skin, almost like he was stalking me out in the wild. A chill travelled up my spine and caused me to shiver.

'Surely you can't be cold. The heater is blaring in here. Zach is mental with the thermostat.'

'No, just… never mind.' I pulled my jumper off, noting that it was, in fact, boiling.

'Sit?' he gestured to the bed.

'Aren't we going out?'

'I thought we could hang out here first. The restaurants are usually busy until about five.'

'Are they?' I had no idea.

'Trust me. There's an influx of primary school kids and their mums, basically, everyone who needs to get their groceries done before six.'

'Right.'

'Anyway, I wanted to talk, and I think it's better to talk in private than with dozens of prying eyes, especially considering half of Deanell High hangs out around the shops,' he said, his eyes seemingly darkening, 'if that's okay.'

'Talk? About what?'

'You, me,' he began, gently guiding me to the bed. 'I've had my eyes on you for a while, actually since the day you came to our school.'

What? Seriously? A little tumble of joy rolled through me. Then that tumble of joy turned to acid when I remembered that he'd dated Rachel Murdoch. Maybe it was petty jealousy. Rachel was one of the hot ones. They obviously weren't a thing anymore, but Jess was forever vying for his attention and the more time I spent with him, the bitchier they became toward me.

Suddenly, the space on the bed vanished, and he was beside me, so close I could practically feel the heat radiating off him, and I could tell he'd reapplied another spray of his cologne.

I drew in a deep breath and averted my gaze, looking at everything but him. The nearby desk had a lacrosse stick tucked underneath, a computer that was on and playing hip-hop music, art supplies, graffiti-style artwork, and the cologne I must have always smelled—it was Burberry. Beside the door, I saw his football gear ready and folded neatly atop his gym bag.

'You draw?' I asked quietly.

'Sometimes.' He leaned in closer, and thoughts of art vanished.

The bare skin on his right arm touched mine, sending shivers over my body. It was prickly and rough where the hair had started to grow back. He'd told me that his physio made him wear some hard-core tape to keep the muscles from hurting during practice, and he'd needed to constantly keep it shaved so the tape could stick. He moved again, the rough skin grazing mine, sending another hot flush coiling through me. It was a reminder of how I felt on Friday with Daniel. *Daniel.*

He never replied to me. Didn't even call back after that phone call. He just stopped talking to me altogether. *Who did he think he was?*

Julian's fingertips brushed my jaw, bringing my attention back to him.

There was a definite edge to his movements, something that made me feel excited and scared all at once. I'd never spent time with anyone like him, let alone outside of school and in such an *intimate* setting. But the latter vanished the second his hand cupped over my cheek again. The skin underneath my uniform broke out in goosebumps.

He traced his fingertips along the exposed skin on my arm, 'You really are cold?'

'I'm not...'

'Under the covers.'

My limbs weighed too much. He chuckled and helped me, and once we were both under the doona, I snuggled up against him and breathed him in.

He grabbed the mouse on his bedside table and changed the music. I recognised this song. It was frequently played on the radio. It was R&B, which I didn't really listen to, but it had a really good beat. Once he set the mouse back down, he pulled me closer to him.

'This doesn't seem much like talking to me.' I looked up at his face.

A corner of his lips quirked up. 'Well, I really like you, and I'm glad you're here. I was worried you wouldn't come.'

'I wasn't going to.'

'Because of Daniel?'

'Because of a lot of things.'

'But you did.'

'Yeah,' I sighed. 'And look I—I don't want to be a sleep-around kind of girl. I always told myself when I had sex it would be with a boyfriend.'

He smiled down at me. 'Sex and boyfriend, huh?'

A prickling along my neck sent a hot flush up my spine.

'Easy, I've wanted to be your boyfriend for a while. I really like you.'

Shock crossed with disbelief flooded me. Julian smiled easily. He was completely here with me, like I was the only person in space and time. It was so romantic. Just like in the cheesy books I swooned over.

'I still don't understand why you wanted me to come over.' My voice was small.

Julian didn't say anything. Instead, he leaned down and kissed me—gently at first and then fiercer. My body reacted; my hands moved on their own, resisting the urge to touch the skin underneath his shirt.

When he pulled back, resting his elbow beside my head, he smiled, tracing the line of my jaw with his free hand. 'When will you start seeing how hot you are?'

'Don't say things like that.'

'You are, though,' he countered. 'I want to hear why you think you're not.'

'Well, for starters, I'm not like Jess and Rachel. They're pretty and blonde and…'

'Boring,' he supplied. 'Why are you comparing yourself to them?'

'Because they're beautiful.'

'They're just clones. Like everyone else at school.'

'Was Elle Smith a clone too?'

His eyes widened slightly. 'Why are you asking about Elle?'

'You looked uncomfortable when you saw her locker beneath mine. I know you guys had a thing last year.'

'We did, and we also had a bad break up.'

'Really?'

'Where is this going?'

His clipped response made me shrink back but I needed answers. Josh and Hailey's pleas to stay away from Julian appeared in the back of my mind, and although I felt they were totally unfounded, I had to be sure.

'I want to know what happened. She left school so suddenly, and you looked like you freaked out seeing her name.'

He let out a long breath while he coiled a strand of my dark hair around his finger. 'We had a thing, yeah, she was hot, then she was cold. I thought she wanted more, and it turns out she didn't. We didn't see eye to eye after that, and then she just bailed. I don't know.'

'Wanted more?'

'It was a misunderstanding.'

'A misunderstanding? That's it?'

'What else would it be?'

I felt my cheeks flush. 'Nothing. Sorry.'

'Don't apologise, it's all good. Now, can we stop talking about my ex?'

He gave me a sharp look, the kind that made his brows knot in the middle and eyes narrow, then kissed me, and I kissed him back.

His free hand travelled down over my stomach, making every nerve light up and splutter. He gently tugged my top free from the waistband of my skirt, his fingertips brushing the bare skin on my stomach. Then he pulled my shirt up just enough to expose the hem of my cheap Kmart bra, which was light pink with darker pink spots all over it. I flinched.

'Relax,' he whispered into my ear. 'You're so sexy.'

I squeezed my eyes shut as his fingers traced the line of the bra until his hand was cupping my breast. I inhaled sharply and pressed my hand to his chest.

'Slow down, cowboy,' I gasped.

'Are you playing hard to get?'

'What?'

'Being a tease?' he chuckled, whispering against my lips. 'Because I thought you were here because you wanted to be my girlfriend?'

'I—I do…'

'Then?'

Was he really expecting *sex* right now? On the first date? Would I? Did I want to?

My breath stalled at desperate attempts to suck in air. I didn't know if I was ready for this. It was a lot. *He* was a lot.

'You look nervous,' he whispered, tracing a line across my jaw.

'I am.'

'Don't be.'

He brought his lips to mine again and lowered himself over me. His hand slipped under my skirt and coasted across my hip.

My eyes snapped open, and I reached down, wrapping my fingers around his wrist.

'Slow down, Julian.'

'Just relax. You'll enjoy it. I promise.'

A dark, sick feeling twisted through my stomach as he crushed his lips to mine. I pulled my face free from him and sucked in a breath.

'Julian… slow down.'

'You didn't think about slowing down when you came here,' he chuckled, sending a shudder through me.

My mind raced back to all the feelings that had warned me as he gripped the band of my underwear so tight I couldn't fight him and pulled them down over the curve of my hip and down to my knees.

I pulled one leg up, hoping to push against him and put some space between us. But he cupped his hand over my knee and pushed my leg to the side.

I reached down again, trying to pull his hand away.

'I thought you said you like me, right?'

'I did… I do…'

'Then relax. Stop pretending you don't want me.'

My body stiffened against his iron hold as he shoved two fingers inside me, tearing a startled gasp from my lips. I pressed my hand flat to his chest and tried to push him off me again.

But he was an immovable force.

'You really need to relax, or this will hurt,' he chuckled, turning my face into the pillow, forcing me to release the breath I'd been holding. 'That's it. Relax.'

Dinner. Stupid fucking dinner.

His fingers moved, and my brain shut down. The tension in my bones was so tight I thought I'd shatter like superheated glass suddenly exposed to extreme cold.

'It hurts…'

'Because you're not relaxed.'

I squeezed my eyes shut, releasing another small breath.

'That's it. You like me, remember?' he whispered, smoothing his hand over my hair. 'I like you a lot too.' He pulled my top up, exposing my bra.

My mind spiralled.

He kissed my neck and then my cheek, and eventually, his mouth was on my breast.

He slowed down. 'Touch me,' he ordered.

My voice was gone. I couldn't make my tongue move to form anything coherent. All I could do was lie there.

I did want this, didn't I? Maybe I just had to relax. Maybe I had to—

He brought his hand to my cheek again and kissed me, splaying his fingers at the base of my skull. Then, he lowered his body over mine and pulled his fingers out, and, for a dumb, fleeting moment, I thought it was over.

But I was wrong. He had just begun. He repositioned himself between my thighs.

'Relax, baby,' he ground out. 'This makes me so happy, doing this with you.' His hand dropped between us, and I could feel his hardness against my leg as he guided himself inside me.

'Touch me,' he ordered again.

I didn't. I couldn't.

I closed my eyes and kept my arms limp at my side. I didn't want to touch him or feel him. I didn't want to hear or see.

He reached down and took my hand, placing it on his body. My fingers were flat across his chest, but it wasn't in a sensual, carnal manner—everything was stiff, clammy.

Another gasp was stolen from me. *Why wasn't I reacting? Why wasn't I screaming?*

A hot sensation of tears stung the back of my eyes.

I wasn't here. I was floating away. I was back at school, reading books, planning my next essay and debate. I was building a table with Dad and getting ready to sand it before we stained the wood. *Natural Oak.* That's what Dad liked to use; it kept a good, natural look, he'd say before standing back and admiring our handy work. I was kicking Jelena's butt in that stupid game she wouldn't stop talking about. I was anywhere but here.

I looked outside the window catching sight of two colourful birds flying past the tall ferns swaying gently beside his window. How could something so beautiful exist in the same world where something so ugly was happening?

The deep rumbling bass of the speakers grumbled beneath the mattress, jerking me back to the present.

The smell of Julian's sweat mixed with my coconut body mist caused a vile taste to build in the back of my throat. He was saying something in my ear. I couldn't hear it over the whimpering coming out of my own mouth. I immediately clamped my jaw shut.

My body had grown numb.

He lowered his lips to mine and kissed me. A wave of confusion swept over me when I kissed him back.

Why was my body betraying me like this?

Because you like him, that's what people do when they like each other. They kiss, they cuddle, they have sex.

This wasn't…?

No. no. No!

That only happened in alleyways and dark roads at night when you weren't careful.

Not like this.

Not to me.

So why am I dying inside?

His hold around my waist tightened as he groaned against my mouth. Then he slowed, bringing his forehead to mine. His hair touched my skin, and I flinched as though the locks of golden hair I once adored were shards of glass laced with poison, cutting me wide open.

He said something my brain didn't register. Something hot covered my thigh and then he got up.

Is it over? I was too scared to move. Too frozen to make myself get up. Why wasn't I getting up?

'You did so good. Was that your first time?'

I nodded slowly. Everything was on autopilot.

I got up and dressed.

'I'm glad you trusted me with this,' he said.

I was numb. I managed a strained smile.

'And I'm glad you came over,' he said, getting dressed behind me. 'But you might want to go to the chemist, babe. We didn't use a condom.'

We didn't use a condom.

We.

We.

We.

Not we.

You.

You didn't use a condom when you forced yourself inside me.

He walked me to the door, our footsteps thumping on the thick red runner.

Julian stopped by the front door and picked up my bag, helping me put it on. I slid my feet into my shoes, forgetting to tie them. I half stumbled, half dragged the one that was barely on my foot and made it outside.

'Sorry we didn't get to dinner,' he said in my ear.

My brain shut down.

Home.

I wanted to go home.

CHAPTER TEN

The Morning After...

Icouldn't recall the rest of the night. All I knew was that I'd somehow made it to the chemist and bought the morning-after pill, stumbled up the stairs, and took it with trembling hands. Then I had a shower and sat on the floor for more than an hour. I knew because I was missing a rerun of Buffy. I'd been waiting for it all week; it was one of my favourite episodes, and I'd gone into the shower hoping to be out just before it started.

By the time I was seated on my bed, the credits were rolling and *Law and Order: SVU* was starting.

Ironic.

My phone vibrated beside me.

It was Daniel.

> *Hey Nekić, I'm so sorry I didn't reply! And I'm so sorry about that phone call. And for hanging up. I must have sounded like the biggest dick.*

I stared at the message.

> *Mum grounded me for coming home late that nite from urs. No regrets though. She literally took my phone off me.*

Grounded. That's why he didn't reply.

*I didn't have a chance to grab it until u called,
but she was coming, so I hung up! I had the
best time with u.*

The explanation continued.

*I really hope I didn't come across desperate.
The last thing I want is to scare u off. I mean,
I know ur tough. U watch shows about aliens!*

Tears welled in my eyes.

I hope ur not pissed at me.

I couldn't move.

*I was also really sick the last two days. U would
have laughed at how pathetic I was.
I miss u. Can u tell? I'm rambling now.*

The tears slipped down my cheeks. My stomach lurched,
and my vision hazed out in front of me. I'd been so, so stupid.

Andy?

Pls reply.

R u there?

Ur worrying me.

The messages kept coming through, one after the other.
His explanations making me feel worse than before.

*Shit. U must be asleep. Sorry. I'm clearly
delusional. It's all the medication, also I really
like u, so it's ur fault. U made me do it. HAHA.*

I breathed in deeply through my nose and exhaled.

*Can't wait to see u tomorrow. Oh, and that
dress is great. U look amazing in it. Can't wait
to hear u play!!!*

I set the phone on the bedside table and crawled under the

blankets. The weight of the night and of *his* hands on my body were impossible to differentiate. As the tears fell, the ache in my throat forced me to choke out a sob.

What happened?

Was that how these things were meant to go?

He was so nice… so kind...

But I didn't want that, did I?

The agony in my heart said no.

What was I meant to do now?

~

My eyes barely opened. My bones ached with every tiny movement, and my head pounded. It felt like I hadn't slept for days.

'Andrea?'

I tried to reply but my voice was as hoarse and rough as I felt.

'Andrea?' Mum tried again, sitting beside me on the bed, making me flinch. 'Ljubavi, it's late. You've missed your alarm.'

'I'm sick.'

'Oh?' She pressed the back of her hand to my forehead. A crease in her brow told me she knew I was lying, but I was certain my face told her to leave it.

Nausea welled in my stomach.

Yesterday wasn't real.

It hadn't happened.

But the pain down there said otherwise.

'The body needs to be lubricated before intercourse,' the sex ed lady had said. I hadn't planned on needing lubrication any time soon. My body recoiled and I curled into a tight ball and pulled the cover over my face, hoping the tears weren't visible.

'Andrea, what is wrong?'

'I just have a stomach ache.'

I felt her hand fold over my shoulder through the blanket.

'Okay. Do you want me to call the doctor?'

'No. I'm fine. I just want to sleep it off.'

It.

The nightmare I couldn't wake from.

I stifled a sob knowing I couldn't hide the pain from her. I was sure it was written all over my face. I was certain she would figure it out. Maybe she'd smell it on me, like I could still smell *him.*

'Get some rest. Call me if you need something.'

When she was gone, I turned onto my back and let out a long breath, quickly followed by a sob and more tears.

What was I thinking?

How had I put myself in that position?

Why didn't I fight back? Why did I pretend it was all okay? Why did I kiss him back?

I couldn't go back to school. I couldn't see him.

I cried, and I cried. Then I turned to my side, bringing my knees to my chest, and cried some more.

~

When my phone rang, I ignored it.

When it rang again, I groaned.

Then notification after notification came through. My heart raced faster and faster with each noise until I threw the cover off in anger and snatched up the phone.

Where r u, Nekić?

U bailed on me.

I know ur up. U never sleep in. Or miss school.

Did I do something wrong?

I ran my hand over my face and jerked back in response to how cold it was. My hands, my skin, my body—none of it felt like it belonged to me. And I guess after last night, it didn't. He'd taken it. Without my permission.

I sent a message. *I'm fine.*

Thank God. Andy, I was worried.

I sent back a quick reply. *Don't be.*

I threw the phone on my bed, snatched up some clean clothes and headed for the bathroom.

I turned the water on in the shower but found myself transfixed on my reflection. My eyes were dull and red. My skin was pale. The longer I stared at the face looking back at me, the more I started to question whether I was even looking at myself and if last night even happened.

Steam filled the bathroom and obstructed most of my view but there were enough clear patches on the mirror to catch glimpses of the dark purple bruises on my thighs and knees. Bile filled my throat, and I quickly turned around, dropping to my knees in front of the toilet.

Once I was sure I was done, I dragged my head up from the toilet bowl, catching sight of the undies I'd thrown in the hamper.

There was a red and white stain on them. I froze, staring at the crimson mark like I was expecting it to tell me last night was a messed-up dream. I dragged myself to my feet and snatched them up, throwing them into the sink and opening the tap full blast.

The water turned a dark pink.

I poured in a huge amount of hand soap and scrubbed them until the foam was pink too.

After draining all the water and examining the irrevocably ruined fabric, I tossed them in the bin.

My legs started to shake as the onset of a panic attack rolled through me. I took a deep breath and steadied my hands, reaching into the overhead vanity feeling around behind the assorted perfumes and skin care products until my fingertips brushed across a smooth, metallic surface.

I gripped the small pocket knife and pulled it out. I held it in my palm and looked down at the shiny red blade in my hand. I'd bought it years ago from a market stall. Told the guy I was shopping for my dad's birthday, that I wanted something small and discrete that would fit in his tackle box. I'd bought hooks and sinkers for good measure too.

I tripped over my own feet but somehow made it into the shower and clumsily lowered myself to the tiles.

As my vision was lost somewhere between the water pouring over me and my own tears blurring my eyes, I pressed my forehead to my bent knees and folded my arm in my lap. I flicked the knife open and lowered the blade to the soft skin above my wrist. High enough to be hidden under my school jumper, low enough to be able to wear a watch or thick bangle to hide it.

I screamed into my thighs and, in one quick move, cut.

Several small rivers of crimson slid down to my elbow and disappeared with the flow of water.

The physical pain sent a bolt of electricity through me and wiped out the mental ache. I leaned back against the wall, letting out a long, even breath. Then I reached up, turned the water off and sat in the shower until the bleeding slowed.

When I was certain I wouldn't ruin any towels, I dried myself off, dressed and wrapped a bandage around my wrist. I pulled my sleeves down and checked the mirror. The bandage was covered.

With another long breath, I gathered enough courage and left the bathroom.

~

When I heard my phone ring again, I ignored it and jogged down the stairs.

Just as I made my way to the coffee machine, a loud knock on the front door jolted me.

My heart leapt to full speed.

'Andy?' The muffled sound came through the door.

I exhaled when I recognised the voice.

'Can I come in?'

'I'm sick, Daniel,' I yelled back.

'I was sicker.'

I sighed and looked down at my clothes. I was a dishevelled mess.

'It's freezing out here!' he said. 'And I've been knocking and calling for twenty minutes.'

This was not how I wanted to see him. But if he kept banging on the door and yelling at me from outside, it'd be sure to raise some suspicion from the neighbours, which would result in them calling my parents, which would result in them seeing the way I looked, and I couldn't bullshit my way through this.

I opened the door and stood aside. His wide, goofy smile disappeared.

'Man, you really must be sick.'

'What are you doing here, Daniel?'

He continued to stare, and pressure clamped down on my chest.

'Can I come in?'

'No.'

'I didn't reject you if that's what you're mad about. I didn't have my phone. And I didn't mean to hang up like that. Mum was coming, and I didn't want to extend my phone ban.'

'I know, you said.'

'You didn't reply.'

'I was busy.'

'Doing what?'

'None of your business.'

'Okay, I'm used to you being snappy, but you've never been rude. What's going on?'

'Nothing is going on,' I said, throwing my hands up. 'Why does everyone think something is going on?'

'Well, for one, you never miss school, even when you are sick, and two, you've never spoken to anyone like that.'

I didn't have a response for that. He carefully stepped over the threshold of the front door, making me step back. He paused for a moment then placed his hands in his pockets. He didn't say anything, and I didn't say anything. We both just stared at each other.

'Andy, if something happened—'

'Nothing happened, anywhere, with anyone.'

His eyes narrowed, as if searching my face.

'Can you just go, please?'

'Not until you tell me what's going on.'

He stepped closer, and my heart lurched into my throat. I shook my head and closed my hand over my mouth to stifle a sob that was on the verge of escaping. As I did, Daniel's eyes shot down to my arm and before I could react, he reached for my hand and pulled my sleeve up.

'What is this?' he shot. 'Did you cut yourself again?'

Tears rushed to my eyes as I snatched my arm back and pulled down my sleeve.

'Andy, what happened?'

When he tried to take my hand again, I shoved him back, making him stumble and almost trip over the huge flowerpot by the door.

'Don't touch me!'

'Whoa! No touching, got it.'

'Go, Daniel.'

'Andy, I'm sorry if I've done something.'

'Get out of my house! Now!'

For a moment, he looked at me without saying a word or moving a muscle. Then the lines in his forehead deepened and he slowly walked to the door and left.

I rushed over to the door and slammed it shut after him,

securing the main lock, then the deadbolt, and finally the chain. My back hit the door and my legs gave way as I slid to the ground.

Today was going to be a write-off. How could I do anything outside these walls when I was crumbling inside my own?

I hauled myself to my room, found my phone and sent Hailey a message.

> *I'm sick. Won't be able to make it to your rehearsal. Sorry.*

She replied super quickly.

> *If ur bailing because ur seeing Julian, I'm going to kill u.*

I'm not seeing Julian. I replied.

> *Also, I'm sorry I was mean to you at school. Friends?*

Friends. Came her reply.

> *Btw, Deanell annihilated last nite. Ur bf kicked 3 goals, & the scouts saw!*

He went out to play after that…

He went out like nothing happened…

What did he say to me? He had other ways to release tension before games. My throat closed, and a sour taste filled my mouth.

I put my phone on silent and turned the TV on. Buffy always helped me when I was sick, but by the time the third episode started, I realised I wasn't feeling any better. Maybe Buffy couldn't fix this because I wasn't sick, was I?

This was the death of something innocent, something pure

that had been ripped away and discarded like it had never existed. This was soul death. The kind of rot that ate away at everything it came into contact with.

As the door opened downstairs and I heard my dad's familiar footsteps, my stomach twisted in on itself. He would have questions. He'd see the way I looked, and he would know something was up even before I said a single word. He and I had a bond like no one else I knew. He'd carried *my* photo around when he was running through the bloodied snow in the harsh Bosnian winters as the bombs fell from enemies that refused to retreat.

He knew all of me, and he would take one look at the paleness on my face and know something was wrong.

I made a beeline for the bathroom, slammed the door shut and turned the shower on full blast. While the steam filled the small space, I heard a few gentle taps on the door.

'Yeah, Dad?'

'Mum said you were sick, how are you?'

'I'm fine,' I called.

'You sure?'

'Yeah, Dad.'

He lingered for a moment. I could see the shadow just under the door pace for a few seconds.

'I brought home donuts to help.'

A small smile spread across my face before I could stop it. Then he left, and the tears came again.

Once I gathered enough courage to face my family, I splashed some cold water on my face and prepared myself. Just as I was coming out of the bathroom, Mum was coming up the stairs. Her concerned expression from earlier hadn't changed.

'Before you start, I'm fine. My guts just feel off.'

'Do you need something? I can help?'

'No, I spent most of the day in there.' I jerked my thumb over my shoulder.

'Vomiting?'

'Everything. So gross.'

Her lips formed a tight line before she turned from me and disappeared down the stairs. I used the opportunity to rush to my bedroom and quickly look around, making sure I'd disposed of any evidence. The morning after pill packet was gone, my stained underwear was gone. I sat down and pulled the covers up to my chin as she came back in with a tall glass of water, a thermometer, and some pills.

'What is all this?'

'Drink, check temperature.'

I took the water from her, gulped down the two pills, and tucked the thermometer under my arm. While the steady beeps continued for more than two deafening minutes, Mum and I remained in perfect silence. Her gaze scanned the room, no doubt searching for evidence of her daughter's sudden change in behaviour. Little did she know that evidence lay deep down inside me, in a sacred place that never should have been touched by undeserving hands.

Finally, the loud beeps signalling the completion of my wait sounded. I handed it to her.

'Is fine.'

'It's just a stomach bug,' I snapped before she could

challenge me.

Her mouth opened and then closed.

'Sorry, I just—I want to get some rest.'

'Okay, ljubavi. Sleep.' She kissed me on the forehead, giving me one more long look before she turned the light off and shut the door.

Just like that, I was left to my own thoughts, and that scared me more than anything else.

CHAPTER ELEVEN

The First Day of School

Mum and Dad were already at work by the time my alarm went off. I looked up at the ceiling and then at the phone. I couldn't do it. I couldn't go. What would he say? What would he do? Would he try to talk to me? Would he expect me to go over again?

As each thought came and went, my stomach tightened; that hot and cold feeling rushing through me signalled an imminent attack. But it was more than that. The physical pain was real this time. I pressed my hands over my stomach as another cramp made me grind my teeth. What was happening to me?

I exhaled through my nose, closed my eyes until the cramp passed, and then opened the calendar on my phone and counted the days. Today was the fourteenth, and my period wasn't due for two more weeks. Another wave shot through my stomach, making me almost double over.

Then it hit me.

The damn morning-after pill.

I rummaged through my drawer and pulled out the box. The instructions were squashed inside but still readable. I skimmed the first few lines and stopped when I read that the morning-after pill could make my period come earlier and it may be more painful.

Well, that was just great. I rummaged through the drawer again, pulled out a bunch of pads and tampons for good measure and shoved them in my school bag. Then I dressed, packed my books, and went to school.

~

As I approached the tall, looming front building, my heart started pounding. Every step brought me closer to seeing his friends, to seeing *him*. I could feel the hairs on my body standing tall, prickling against my clothes in the cool air.

Once I'd braved the front building, I was presented with my next challenge: people. Lots of them.

I walked past two couples making out and slipped behind a stream of foot traffic. Once I'd passed them, I stepped into the locker bay. A deep, heavy breath settled in my throat as I kept my eyes forward, my body rigid and ready to fight or run.

A loud laugh made me drop my bag; a loud shriek made me flinch. And when I finally packed everything away and I found what I needed, I was so jittery I could barely talk.

Hailey appeared beside me, and when she pressed her hand to my shoulder, I completely lost it, dropping everything.

'Uh, Andy,' she said quietly, 'You sure you should be here if you're still sick?'

'Can't miss more classes.'

Everything was so unbelievably loud, so bright. Everything flooded into me, making her voice and everything else come into intolerable focus, then fade out. I couldn't hold onto any thought longer than a second before panic quickly reminded me of his breath on my face, his hot skin against mine, his weight crushing me.

'You know I don't like to get deep and personal, but are you sure you're okay?' Hailey said, her eyes furrowed.

I shut the door, secured the lock, and ignored her question as I pushed past her.

'Andy?'

It was too much. I couldn't do it. I couldn't look into my friend's eyes and lie, or worse, admit she'd been right, and I was too stupid to see it.

~

First period came and went. I wrote down answers and handed in my essay.

Second period went a little slower. I started listening to the retelling of D-Day, then zoned out and started sketching little UFOs in my notebook. By the time the teacher was done, I'd drawn an entire recreation of the Rendlesham Forest incident. Once we were finally released from D-Day hell, I made my way to my next class.

Geography was always my least favourite subject but today in particular.

The cramps in my stomach were getting worse, and I was starting to feel like I was going to pass out.

As the teacher continued explaining the difference between the world's oceans, I found myself unable to focus. The writing on the board blurred, and the more I tried to read it, the worse it got. Every sound made my heart jump. By the time class was over and the bell had rung, I was so skittish I dropped my books three times before I got to the locker bay.

I stopped when I saw Jess by my locker with Rachel and Cara, who'd been on a family holiday to the Gold Coast and was back just in time to make my life hell.

Jess's eyes locked onto mine, and her tiny nose crinkled when she looked at me.

'You'll never be like us, no matter who you get into bed with. You'll still be a nobody.'

My tongue felt as though it had doubled in my mouth as I processed the ugly words she'd just spoken.

Rachel stepped in closer. 'Sleeping around makes you a slut, in case you missed the memo.'

'I don't know what you're talking about.'

'That's funny, because the whole school seems to know,' Cara muttered.

'What?'

I looked around. Several of the Year Twelves were watching the exchange, and down the back beside the rear entrance, Julian stood talking to a guy from the footy team, but his attention was solely on me. My fingers curled around the strap on my bag, instinctively clutching it to my chest.

Rachel stepped toward me. 'Guess you weren't even that much of a good root. He got with Jess anyway, luckily for you. Bet that's not what you expected after you got with him, is it?'

'I—I didn't…'

'Didn't what?' Rachel challenged. 'Didn't have sex with him, or didn't expect him to dump your ass?'

My cheeks burned with humiliation.

'Because we all know you had sex. Julian told us.' She looked me up and down, her eyes narrowing. 'What he saw in an emo like you is beyond me.'

Suddenly, she stepped into my space and grabbed my hand, forcing my sleeve up. I tried to pull my arm back but not before everyone saw the bandage.

'So cutting is the new thing sluts do,' Cara sniggered.

A short, sharp breath escaped as the edges around my vision seemed to dim. I tried to inhale deeper, only to fail when a pathetic little whimper came out.

I tore my eyes away, and down the hall, across the crowd, they landed on Daniel.

His bright emerald eyes locked onto mine. His jaw was set in a hard line, his expression cold, and the locks of his hair shielded half his face from me.

'I'd be pissed too,' Cara said with a snigger. 'Bet you feel super lame.'

My mind raced as panic set in.

'You're a real conniving snake, Andrea Nekić,' Jess said. 'Now piss off and stay away from him!'

Julian's friends were smirking as they fist-bumped him, all while Daniel stood still beside him.

My face burned as my public humiliation reached its crescendo.

Daniel was still watching me. There was a slight furrow in his brow and a tremor in his lip. Julian left, saying something to him before he did. Daniel's jaw squared, but his eyes remained on me.

Then it dawned on me, like a sick, twisted joke that I

wasn't in on. He thought I had moved on and had sex with Julian because I was over him. He thought that's why I'd ignored him and threw him out of my house.

Julian took away my dignity, my sense of self and parts of me I could never get back. But the look on Daniel's face broke what was left. He turned from me, which earned a series of cheers from everyone on *Team Daniel*.

When I tried to follow him, I was pushed back by some girl I didn't even know.

'Fuck off,' I spat and shoved her out of my way.

Everything was unravelling so quickly that I couldn't stop the shit show, no matter how much I clawed to hold onto the little control I had.

'Daniel, please wait!'

'Why?' he whipped around. 'Do you want to rub it in my face? Show me how popular you are now?'

'Popular?' I baulked. 'They're calling me a slut.'

His brow twitched.

'What happened between Julian and me wasn't meant to have happened.'

'You just slipped on his dick?'

I snapped my mouth shut. *Holy shit.* Julian had managed to turn *everyone* against me. Even Daniel.

I took a small step back, and Daniel threw his hand up, resting against the locker beside him.

'You want to talk, so talk. Tell me how it meant nothing. Tell me you just went over for some pizza or some other bullshit. Tell me how you got into his bed and then ignored all my texts when we were planning on hanging out again.'

'I'm sorry.'

'I'm sorry too. I'm sorry I didn't meet the Andrea Nekić popularity requirement.'

I couldn't say anything. Whenever the truth came up and pricked my tongue, the ridicule and the voices and their taunting came up instead and shut it all down.

No one would believe me. No one would believe a desperate girl wouldn't have wanted a boy like Julian.

Daniel's brows furrowed. He'd seen me hanging out with Julian before, swooning over him, and so did half the school. Julian knew it. He'd made sure that our *flirting* was public information. It's why he always made sure we were sat at the oval, where the boys played football, where Josh and Hailey and everyone else would see us.

Tears pooled and spilled over before I could even form another thought. I knew exactly how this looked. I wiped them with the cuff of my sleeve.

'You know, I spent the last few days trying to understand what I did,' Daniel said, shaking his head. 'And I have no idea. Does that make me stupid or what?'

'You didn't do anything.'

'Obviously, I did, because here we are,' he gestured around us, the now empty locker bay hauntingly silent. 'You have what you've always wanted now: the attention of the cool guy and the envy of the girls.'

I looked down at my hands.

'Seriously though, is it because I didn't want to have sex with you that night? Did you feel like I was rejecting you or something?'

'It's not like that.'

'Then what is it like? Because I'd really like to know. I want you to tell me, Andy, tell me that I'm wrong about all of this. Tell me he's lying. Tell me you didn't go to his house and sleep with him.'

The truth was screaming inside me. It was right there. I could tell him. I could have someone on my side. I could… I felt two hot tears leak onto my cheeks.

'I thought you were better than that, Nekić.' He shook his head. 'Valesco, though, of all people. Really?'

'Please—'

I didn't know what I was pleading for. For forgiveness? For him to see the truth? For him to stay, to keep asking the right questions, to give me a chance to be brave? I didn't know. My shoulders dropped, and Daniel turned from me.

He opened his locker, took out some books and shoved them in his bag. Behind a bunch of PlayStation games and books, I saw a folded-up sheet of the same paper he'd wrapped my gift in. More tears flowed.

Daniel shut his locker and turned back to me. For a moment, he didn't say anything, he just looked at me, chewing his bottom lip. Then he slung his bag over his shoulder and stepped closer to me.

'I liked you, Andy, a lot and—' He ran a hand over his hair. 'You know what, don't worry about it.'

By the time my brain caught up with what I wanted to say, Daniel was already gone, the door swinging shut behind him.

~

That night, I sat in my bed alone watching *Alias*. I had no energy for anything else. I hadn't done my laundry in days or put away my clean clothes. My brain wasn't really keeping up with anything. I didn't care, though. I couldn't let things with Daniel end the way they did.

I found my phone under the pile of clothes at the foot of my bed and found Daniel's name. I could have called Hailey. I could have called Josh. But I wanted to hear Daniel's voice. I pressed the call button, and slowly brought the phone to my ear, not expecting him to answer. But then he did.

'You answered,' I said quietly.

'I did.'

'Can we talk?'

'I don't know that there's really anything to talk about.'

I drew in a deep breath. 'It's been a really bad time for me.'

'I'm sorry,' he said. 'The girls at school are nasty.'

'It's not just about them.'

'Then what?'

My heart fractured when I recalled the way he looked at me in the locker bay when he heard Julian and I had slept together.

'I need you. I just really need a friend right now. Can you please come over?'

He was quiet for a while, and for a while, I'd allowed myself a moment to believe he would say yes, that he'd bring lollies and chips, and we'd watch movies together. This time, I would let him pick something.

'I'm sorry, Andy. I can't.'

'Can we maybe talk tomorrow?'

'I don't think that's a good idea.'

'Daniel, I really need a friend.'

'Isn't Valesco your friend?'

My fingers grew numb around the phone as tears slid down my cheeks.

'Okay, sorry I called late,' I said slowly as my mouth grew unbearably dry.

'Andy—'

Before I could hear what he was going to say, I hung up. I hugged my plush lamb to my chest and curled up under the covers. Before long, sleep claimed me and this time, Julian didn't make an appearance, but the girls at school did.

CHAPTER TWELVE

Different

'Andrea,' Mum called from the bottom of the stairs. 'If you hurry, I can take both of you to school now.'

'Don't worry, I'm walking!'

'Are you sure?'

'I'm sure,' I said, pulling the cover over my head.

The weather was finally starting to warm up, and school holidays were just around the corner, which meant my part-time job would be hiring some Christmas casuals and I'd be needed to help train them. It also meant it had been almost a month since Julian… a month since *it* happened and a month since I'd spoken to Daniel.

Time had gone fast on some days and painfully slow on others. One thing was consistent, though. I was numb, coasting through the days, trying to do the best I could to do my homework, go to piano, and be present at home.

But all I desperately wanted was some alone time.

As if to remind me why I wanted to be alone, Jelena stomped up the stairs to bang on my door. She did it every morning, and every morning I wanted to kill her.

'Come on!' She pounded her fist on the door.

'Go to school!'

Jelena pounded on the door again.

'I swear to God, I am going to punch you in the teeth,' I snapped.

She laughed and thumped on the door again. 'I'll see you tonight.'

'Yeah, you will,' I muttered.

Once her footsteps disappeared down the stairs, I threw the covers off and stumbled over to the dresser. I avoided the mirror, managed to throw my hair up into a simple bun, and ignored the make-up drawer staring up at me. I really needed some colour on my face, but no matter how much concealer, blush, or bronzer I slapped on, I still looked like a scared little girl.

A notification alerted me to a new message. I took a deep breath and opened it.

It was Josh.

> ***Man, Daniel is beside himself. You two can work this out. I know you can.***
>
> ***There's nothing to work out. He hates me.*** I replied.
>
> ***He doesn't hate you. He's just hurt.***
>
> ***Yeah, well, so am I.***

For a second, I wondered if I should have said something else, tried to explain the situation, and then decided against it. I didn't want his pity.

> ***Daniel is as stubborn as you. Please talk.***
>
> ***I can't.***

I put the phone on silent to avoid seeing if he wrote anything else and threw on my dress, my jumper, and finally, my blazer. It was meant to be warm today, but somehow, even the blaring heat of the sun couldn't warm through the ice that seemed to have swallowed me.

I locked up and began my slow walk to school. My brain was so scattered that I didn't trust myself to catch a bus anymore. I couldn't even be trusted with my straightener now. My hands were in a perpetual state of fine tremors that might affect my recital if I didn't learn to control the anxiety. But it was easier said than done. Every time I caught Daniel throwing quick glances at me or heard hushed sniggers from the girls around school, I felt the bile rise to the back of my throat. Why couldn't I have just said something to him?

Because you're ashamed. Because you're an idiot. Because it's your fault.

How could I have been so fucking stupid?

It was my fault. Plain and simple.

What else would Julian have wanted me for? Why had I allowed myself to believe that a guy like him could find any interest in someone like me? I should have known. *I was just a game to him.*

It didn't matter now. None of it did.

I just wanted to go home. I wanted to sleep. I wanted to forget.

But first, I had to get through the day and nail my recital.

~

Jelena ran in holding out my dress with a huge grin on her tiny face. 'Can I help you do your hair?'

'Only if you don't burn it off.'

'I promise I won't,' she said, brimming with excitement, then disappeared.

I heard her rummaging around my bathroom while I changed out of my uniform and jumped into the shower. Once I'd rinsed off, dried and dressed in the gorgeous dress Mum had bought me, I stood in front of the floor-length mirror and smiled. It was from Garfunkle, the coolest shop at Chadstone, and we'd usually never dare spend so much on clothes, but Mum said for this occasion, we could spare the money. I felt incredible in it, but the moment she appeared behind me and frowned I felt myself shrink back.

'You've lost so much weight,' she said quietly, tugging the dress around my waist.

The fit had been perfect when we bought it, but now it hung off my shoulders. I swallowed hard.

I turned and started rummaging through my dresser, 'There have to be some safety pins around...'

'Andrea, what's going on?' she asked sternly, sitting on the edge of my bed.

'She's probably throwing up to get skinny,' Jelena muttered.

'Get out!' Mum and I said in unison.

Jelena huffed and dropped the brush on my dresser.

'Andrea. I need you to talk to me. Now.' She looked down at the gaudy extra-thick diamante bracelet I'd bought to hide the new cut. 'What is this?'

When she reached for it, I snatched my arm back.

'Did you and Daniel break up?'

'No,' I said, pulling away from her.

'Did he do something?'

'No, Mum, of course not.'

'Then what is going on?' She tugged me toward her. 'Are you on drugs?'

'Oh my God, Mum. No!'

'Then what?'

'Nothing.' I snatched my arm back again. 'Can you just help me make this dress work?'

She didn't move, and for a second, I thought she would give up on me and my dress and everything else. Panic quickly made me reach for her hand.

'Please, it's just school and the end of the year. I'm stressed, and I don't know if I'll do well tonight—'

'Okay, okay, relax.' She dragged me over to the dresser and forced me to the mirror.

I'd never seen her disappointed; I didn't even know what that looked like on my mum. When I told her about the piano school, she was sad, but the look she gave me now, with a small crease in her brow and downturned expression, I knew this was it.

She took the safety pins from me without a word and turned me so my back was facing her. I could still see her in the mirror as she looked over my body. I hadn't noticed until now because I always hid under my school dress and avoided reflective surfaces at all other times.

My collarbone was pronounced, my cheeks hollowed, and my shoulders more visible than they'd ever been. The bruises and marks were gone, but if I looked really hard, I swore I could still see them. But the real sign that something was eating me up were my eyes. The green was sullen, dark, and devoid of that healthy gleam.

After fifteen minutes of "Frankensteining" my dress with a shit load of safety pins and fashion tape, I looked presentable.

Jelena came back in, her eyes meeting mine in the mirror. For once in her life, she kept her remarks to herself. Instead, she stood by the stool in front of my dresser and waited for me to sit down.

The moment I sat, she began styling my hair without a word. She should have been ecstatic to be using the straightener I rarely let her use, but she didn't even crack a smile. When Mum left to bring my shoes, Jelena shoved the door shut with her foot and reached for a hair tie.

'I don't know what's wrong, but I can see that something is. You're not alone, though. Just so you know.'

'Thanks.'

'No problem.'

The whole conversation felt so alien. We didn't hate each other, but we weren't close. She was seven years younger than me, annoying to the point where I considered murder, and always on my case.

But this moment changed everything.

I got up once she'd fastened the very pretty braid she'd created and hugged her. She tightened her hold around my waist and looked up at me.

'Promise me that if you're ever in trouble, you'll come to me,' I said.

'Okay,' she nodded. 'Promise me if things get worse, you'll tell me.'

I chuckled and shoved her out of that way.

'Andy?'

'Yeah?'

'You didn't say I promise.'

'That's coz I'm not a baby.' I stuck my tongue out, getting a smirk out of her.

'Let's go, ladies, we're going to be late!' Dad shouted from downstairs.

'You heard him,' I nudged her. 'Let's go.'

~

I stood at the wing with my sheet music gripped tightly in my fist.

I looked out over the audience, who were filing back in after intermission, and frowned. Daniel should have been here tonight. When I looked out at the front row where my family were seated, the empty spot beside them made me feel lonelier than I had in weeks.

'And now we have the talented Ms. Andrea Nekić, who will play us *Moonlight Sonata No. 14*.'

As the audience settled and the lights dimmed, the spotlight fell on the piano. I took a deep breath and walked ahead. When I sat, I kept my eyes locked on the shiny keys and away from the haunting look of the dark abyss where the audience sat.

The instant my fingers began to dance across the keys, my heart slowed, and I was transported into a starless sky, dancing to slow and solemn strokes of music.

Pain, real and raw burned through me, colliding with every note that resounded in the still auditorium, reminding me of the helplessness and sorrow that consumed me. It felt like an eternity that I was lost in the tune, gliding through the notes of the sheet music. In this moment I could pretend I was just me, devoid of the horrors Julian had imprinted on my mind and body, devoid of the shame and worthlessness.

When the final haunting note resonated through the still blackness, I closed my eyes and bowed my head. Applause exploded, yet I barely had the strength to look up and take my bow. I knew then that no matter what I did or told myself, that's all it would ever be. Just pretend. The loathing and nothingness would always return.

Helen knelt with a bouquet of roses.

'That was wonderful. I'm very proud of you.'

I gave her a tight smile and nodded, taking my bow. Everyone was standing, everyone was cheering me on, giving me the honour I didn't deserve. I rushed off the stage and out the back.

CHAPTER THIRTEEN

Thank You

The profound sense of emptiness far outweighed everything else.

Disappointment.

Failure.

Misery.

The recital was everything I hoped it would be—a perfect success, with endless offers from teachers to have me perform for their students. I gave them all the same answers: I'd think about it. The truth was, as soon as I left, I was never going to think about it again and I was never going to play again.

'You made every other student and their academy look like children,' Dad said proudly. 'You have natural talent.'

'Thanks, Dad,' I said without real conviction.

Once we'd pulled into the drive, I took my giant bouquets and made a line straight for the kitchen. I should have been elated, happy, something. But I wasn't feeling much of anything.

These *nothing* moments were the ones where I fumbled with my phone, willing myself to reach out to Daniel and tell him everything. I even considered telling Hailey when she kept pushing and prying. But I always changed my mind at the last minute.

Occasionally, I'd receive a message from the girls at school calling me a slut, and sometimes from the anonymous account telling me I deserved the bullying. I didn't know why they bothered anymore. The whole school heard how I'd gone from guy to guy.

Julian's name still hurt to say. I couldn't say it out loud. But if I ever had to tell anyone, God help me, I wouldn't be able to get the syllables out through the bile in my throat.

After putting the juice back in the fridge, I stopped at the counter.

'Ljubavi, I'm worried about you,' Mum said, her eyes narrowing.

'Stop worrying.'

'Well, as mother, that's not option.' She stepped closer to me, putting her arm on my shoulder.

I started sobbing.

Mum's arms were around me before I could take my next breath. I didn't hear what she said in my ear or notice that she'd walked me over to the couch.

'What's happening?' Dad asked, coming to kneel beside us.

'Give us space,' Mum said. 'I think it's a boy.'

Dad backed away. He was always super awkward about this stuff. He led Jelena away and soon after, I heard the strumming of guitars filtering through the walls.

'Andrea?' Mum coaxed my face up to hers. Tears stung my eyes as I watched my mother's green eyes search my face.

I didn't know what to tell her.

I didn't know where to begin.

With dread lacing my bones, I undid my braid, which seemed entirely too constrictive now, and let my hair fall around my shoulders.

'Please, Andrea.' Mum took my clammy hand in hers. 'What happened? You have changed.'

'I—'

She smiled, as if encouraging me to speak. I noticed the dark circles under her eyes. She hadn't been sleeping either.

'Mama...'

'I'm here.' She sat patiently.

I fantasised about how good it would feel to tell her. I imagined her loving arms around me, telling me that everything was going to be okay. She would make me coffee, and we'd sit on the couch together. I'd cry, and she'd comfort me. I'd tell her how sorry I was, and she'd tell me it wasn't my fault.

But I knew that was bullshit.

It *was* my fault. I was the complete moron who was butthurt when her not-even-boyfriend didn't reply for a few days, then found comfort in the only other boy who'd shown her attention.

Unfortunately, though, this boy happened to be a predator disguised behind perfect grades and a smile to die for. And I was the absolute fool who was in denial about it all.

He was a friend, I'd told myself repeatedly. That's why we hung out, not because I was secretly enjoying the dirty feeling of being envied by those bitches for one day in my sad life.

But he wasn't a friend, and I couldn't cry to Mum and tell her all these things because once it was all said and done, it was on me. I went there. I climbed into his bed and let him put the covers over me because I thought he was being *sweet*. Now, I had to live with that.

'I'm just tired, rundown. That's all,' I said.

'I don't think that's all.'

'Daniel stopped talking to me,' I said, knowing it would appease her enough to stop asking, and it was partially true.

'Oh, Andrea,' she said, wrapping her arms around me again. 'What happened?'

'I don't know,' I lied. 'I feel so alone. I hate school. I don't want to go anymore.'

'You know you have to be brave and face him.'

'I know.'

'You're smart and strong. You can do it.'

If only I could. If only that was all.

~

The next couple of days after that, I was back to my usual self—study, tennis, homework.

At least on the surface, that's what it looked like, and that's all that mattered.

Hailey walked beside me. 'So, I finished that painting and then started a new one. Not sure which I'll hand in now.'

'How come?' I asked, trying to be interested.

'Just had a new wave of inspo, so I didn't want to sell myself short, you know?'

'Yeah, guess that's good, though.'

'What about you?'

Before I could answer, I stopped at the door to the locker bay spotting a tiny, folded-up piece of paper peeking out the top of my locker.

'What the hell?' Hailey muttered, stalking over and yanking it out.

I read it while she held it open.

You should kill yourself. Cut deeper next time, emo.

Tears burned behind my eyes. I blinked them back and tried to put on a brave face, but my lip quivered, and the second Hailey looked at me, I scrunched the note into a ball and burst into tears.

'You were right,' I sobbed.

'Wait, what?'

'You were right. I was so, so stupid.'

'Andy, I don't know what you're talking about.'

The words wouldn't come out. She quickly pulled me into a hug while I cried into her shoulder.

'Andy?'

'He was… he was just using me, and you—you were right.'

'Oh my God, Andy, what happened?'

'I—I can't…' I shook my head. Everything around me started spinning. 'I—I'm going to be sick.'

I dropped to my knees and threw up.

Hailey quickly knelt, hiding the evidence from whoever might have been walking past. When I lifted my head to take a breath, I saw her wave someone over. Through the tears, I made out the blurry image of Mr. Benson.

'Andy's sick. Can you help me walk her to the sick bay?'

she said gently.

'Of course. Come on, Andy. Let's get you outside.'

I didn't hear a single word either of them said as they led me towards the sickbay. I swayed as I walked, stumbling over my own feet.

Neither Benson nor Hailey said anything, but the weight of what they were probably thinking crushed me into the ground.

Eventually, Mum came and took me home.

She asked questions, and I refused to answer them.

Mum checked in on me every hour on the hour until I fell asleep, thanks to some sleeping pills.

~

The next day at school, I sat by myself at lunch for the first half hour. I'd gotten through the first four periods without incident, and all I wanted to do was go home, but I knew I had to be strong and stay.

Eventually, Hailey joined me. She set down a bag of sour worms between us.

'Did he do something?'

I nodded. Keeping my eyes on the football posts. No one was playing today, but there were some Year Sevens kicking a soccer ball around.

'Crap, Andy, I don't know what to say. What can I do?'

I looked over at her. 'There's nothing you can do. I'll be fine.'

'This isn't right.'

No, it wasn't. I was beyond caring, though.

We sat in silence as the younger kids ran around

screaming and laughing.

A heavy feeling settled over me. I'd officially become the pariah I imagined I was. My shining star was condemned to the inky blackness of the vacuum-less sky, just biding its time until it lost all control and went supernova, and the cutting wasn't helping anymore. Those small steam holes I'd relied on failed me now. There was too much pressure, too much bubbling beneath the surface that I couldn't think around the constant intrusions in my mind.

Flashbacks to the words he'd spoken in my ear and the way I reacted didn't match up. I was violated. I knew it through and through, but my lack of response confused me. Maybe I'd just imagined it. Maybe that's how it was meant to be. Maybe I was too sensitive. Maybe I expected fairytales…

'Andy?'

My eyes travelled up to Hailey's.

'I've got Home Ec, but I can wag,' she said. 'Wanna go to the movies?'

'No, that's okay. I have to get ready for work.'

'You sure?'

'Yeah, I need to. Saving up to fix my car.'

'Andy…'

'Thank you for being you, Hails. I'll see you later.'

'You don't have to thank me for being your friend.'

'I do.' I collected my bag. 'And thank you for everything else. You're truly a gem, and don't ever forget it.'

'Andy, that doesn't sound…'

'See you next term,' I said quickly.

She frowned but hugged me.

~

I coasted through the rest of my classes, focusing only on breathing and getting through the day without a meltdown. I barely noted anything the teachers had said.

By the time the bell rang, I found myself walking to my locker alone. As I neared the building, I spotted Josh cutting through the quadrangle, heading over to me.

'Want to come hang after school?' he asked.

'Sorry, got work tonight.'

'After work?'

'Need to study.'

'It's the holidays,' he frowned. 'Surely you can take a night off.'

'Can't do that. I've fallen behind.'

He pressed his hand to my arm, and I stopped walking.

'Is it because you don't want to see Dan?'

'He doesn't want to see me,' I reminded him.

'Then come out with me and Hails. I'll tell him to stay home tonight.'

'No, it's okay. Don't do that.'

'I want to hang out with you. It's been so weird at school, and I'm worried about you.'

'Don't be, I'm fine.'

He dropped his gaze and scratched the back of his neck before our eyes met again. 'I've heard what the girls have been saying about your wrist.'

'Yeah, well, should've covered my arms better,' I laughed.

His jaw squared. 'Andy, this isn't funny.'

'It is to them,' I reminded him. 'Don't worry about it. I'm a big girl. I'll see you next term.'

Before he could say anything else, I gave him a faux smile and continued to my locker. There was another note. I sighed and opened it. There was a phone number at the bottom of this one too.

Call me for a quickie. I love girls who cut. Maybe we can cut each other.

My stomach twisted. I tossed the note into the bin beside my locker and shoved everything inside. My bag was empty for the first time in my life. I shut the door, secured the lock, and left for the front of the school.

~

The shift tonight was a quick one, four until close.

I dropped my stuff behind the counter, taking Chloe's list of lay-by orders. She had a hot date and begged me to start earlier and cover for her.

'Be careful tonight,' I said as she released her hair from her ponytail and checked her face in the reflective glass beside the front door.

'I'm always careful.'

'Everyone says that, but no one really thinks about it.'

'You sound grim.'

'I know,' I sighed, trying to force a smile to the surface.

'Don't worry. I'll be careful. Have a good shift.'

She left after giving me a quick hug, and I clocked in. I found myself unusually at peace.

The shift was easy. Most of the regulars in the shopping

centre came in to say hello, and some even bought some of the sale jewellery we had in the window, which meant less stuff for me to put away later.

I checked my phone just before my last break and saw a message from Mum.

I'm staying late at work to cover shift. Dad too.

No prob. I replied, glad they weren't going to be home. Jelena was at a school camp, which was perfect.

Mum sent another text.

I'm sorry. Soon, all four of us can go away camping. For your birthday.

Sounds awesome. I wrote back.

Maybe we can go to the mountains!

Whatever you want.

I felt my heart tighten.

When nine o'clock rolled around, I helped the other girls lock away the diamonds and secure the store.

My boss gave me and another girl a lift home like she did every Friday shift. I made small talk and joined in on the banter like I always did. Just like I played the dutiful daughter who'd done no wrong in the world.

When I was safe inside my house, I gently set everything down by the front door, making sure to be as neat as possible. I made my way to my room, changing into my comfy trackies and t-shirt, and then I sat.

For a few minutes, I didn't do anything. I gazed around the room, then over my desk and my bookshelves. They were filled with notepads outlining endless dreams and goals, none of which would ever be realised. Then I took a deep breath and picked up my phone.

Ignoring the unread messages, I searched for Daniel's name. He'd been bumped down all the way to the end of my list. With a deep breath, finding the courage I'd lacked until now, I opened up a new message.

> *I'm so grateful for you. From the first day at school when you said you liked my pencil case to the nights we watched UFO shows eating too much chocolate.*

I composed myself and continued.

> *I'm sorry I never let you pick anything to watch. You know I hate comedies. I loved that you played games with Jelena and let my dad teach you about woodwork.*

I ignored the burning of tears.

> *I loved that you wanted to watch me play the piano and that you drank my mum's coffee which was more sugar than coffee.*

Finally. I sent one last message.

> *I'm sorry for hurting you, Daniel. I didn't want it. I didn't want what he did. I'm sorry for it all. I wish things had been different.*

I waited a few seconds to make sure the messages went through, then I put the phone on silent and set it on the bedside table before swiping the blister pack of antidepressants I'd been taking, along with the sleeping pills Mum had given me. I opened the packets and held them for a moment.

I dropped one, then another, and another until they were

all in my hand. I stared at the deceptively small pills for a second before I put a few in my mouth and drank them down. I repeated that four more times until they were all gone.

Was this meant to be quick?

I didn't really know what to expect. I grabbed two of my favourite stuffed toys, a white beanbag lamb and a tiny brown teddy, which according to Target's Christmas catalogue ten years ago, was supposedly a reindeer, and I curled up on the bed, hugging them both to my chest.

My eyes became heavy. So did my limbs. Warmth spread through me...

I blinked and looked at my phone. It was ringing. Daniel's name popped up on the screen. Then, the call ended.

I closed my eyes again, and when I opened them, it felt like only moments had passed, but the screen said another sixteen calls had come through.

How did that happen?

My throat was so dry, and my sight was rapidly dimming. The dark edges circling my vision doubled. I blinked, trying to focus on the phone. The screen went dark but quickly lit up again.

Message after message came through. Tears pricked when I saw his name pop up again. I should have told him not to worry and not to call. But I knew that no matter what I said, he would have done the same thing because Daniel was a good, kind person.

Through blurry eyes and the weight bearing down on my chest, I curled onto my side, as the drowsiness fully kicked in. I watched the screen light up over and over, taunting me with Daniel's face until I couldn't keep my eyes open anymore.

My stomach recoiled, and my heart started thundering. Sweat broke out across my skin, and short, rapid bursts of breath left my lips.

Panic set in.

What have I done?

Why did I do it?

My heart cracked as my entire being was torn in two.

It was too late now. I'd made my decision.

Then, it all slowed.

It didn't take long for the feeling to leave my fingers. I dropped my teddy and felt my hands go next, then my arms and the rest of my body.

Then, there was darkness and warmth.

There was silence.

There was peace.

Then... nothing.

CHAPTER FOURTEEN

The Garden

My feet hit the soft grass outside. Dad had been tending this garden for more than twelve years; he was obsessed with the gardenias and pear trees. We never got to eat any of the fruit, though, because as soon as they ripened enough, the birds ate them. Dad would chase them around the yard, laughing and cursing. I smiled and trailed my fingers along the hedges lining the well-loved garden.

There were ferns, yuccas, roses, and cacti I couldn't name. They were all pretty in their own way and deadly in another. Every time I got too close to the edge, the yuccas stabbed me. Every time I leaned over to smell the roses, a bee would chase me away.

Everything in the garden knew how to defend itself despite its perceived fragility.

'Andrea?' I heard Dad calling me.

I looked around, stunned.

'Andrea, please come back.'

'I'm just out the back, Dad,' I called.

'Andrea, please, it's going to start raining soon. Come back.'

'What?' I muttered to myself. There was no rain; the sky

was bluer than blue, the clouds softer than they'd ever looked, and everything had a soft hue, like it was fluid and alive.

'Please, Andrea, please come back to us.'

My brow furrowed. *What an odd choice of words.*

'Andrea!' There was a desperate edge to the voice, but it wasn't Dad's anymore.

What the hell? I looked around again. The blue sky had turned dark, streaks of blood red tore through the blackened backdrop, and my body shook. I realised now it was getting colder, and a violent bolt of lightning cracked through the sky chased by roaring thunder.

But the thunder wasn't just outside, it was inside me. It burned through my heart like a million volts were being shot into my body, causing it to jolt into the air and crash to the ground.

'Andrea!' the voice called again. It was Daniel's this time. 'Come back!'

I spun on the spot and saw him standing by the sliding door, hand outstretched and eyes wide. 'Please come back!'

I glanced over my shoulder and saw a sheath of rain racing toward me. I'd never seen rain like that, so visibly present. Fear raced through me as I whipped around and started running.

The thunder came back; the lightning tore through me once again, sending so much electricity through my body I thought I would die.

'Come back.' Daniel's voice was still there, colliding with the roaring above me.

My heart raced as I ran, but the more space I put between me and the storm, the quicker it seemed to come.

Now, in the rush of the storm above me, I felt the violent ripples of pain in my chest I'd only caught glimmers of earlier. It felt like someone was squeezing my heart and then letting go. Finally, it stopped. A sharp, blunt hammering came instead.

I clutched my chest as I kept myself moving.

Then there was beeping, low and erratic, somewhere in the distance, too far for me to make out.

The closer I got to Daniel's outstretched hand, the harder the beating on my heart got. A startled gasp tore free as a much firmer thump hit me in the chest making me almost lose my footing.

The beeping was louder, clearer now. It was closing in, and the pain in my chest burned fiercer.

Tears streamed down my cheeks as the pain kept slowing me down, forcing me to stumble and trip. I screamed out when I finally reached the door. Daniel disappeared right before my eyes as I threw myself in, and instead of hitting the wooden floor, I fell into a pit of endless blackness.

~

There was a steady beeping followed by hushed whispers. Then a scratching of pen on paper. Then more silence.

My eyes fluttered open against the ache of doing so. They felt sandblasted and dry. I immediately shut them again. Someone was sitting beside me. They stilled when I tried to open my eyes again, and then there was a hand on mine that gently squeezed my fingers.

I faded out after that, slipping back into the comfortable darkness.

The next time I came to, I felt the hand around mine still and then drift up my arm, coming to stop at my elbow.

When I tried to open my eyes again, the sandblasted sensation had subsided. My limbs were heavy, too stiff to move, my throat raw and dry, and my brain felt entirely too scattered. *What happened? Where am I?*

Footsteps slapped against tiles somewhere outside, voices faded in and out, and the hand around my arm gently squeezed again.

I finally opened my eyes and looked up. Daniel's stricken face was hovering above me. His eyes were red and the skin under them was dark like he hadn't slept in days.

'Oh, my God,' he breathed out, running his free hand over his face. His usually clean-shaven jaw was speckled with dark hair.

'Why… why am I…' My voice trailed off as a splitting, piercing pain shot through my head, cutting my words off. I scrunched my eyes shut.

'Don't try to talk. You need to rest. You're in hospital. You've been in and out for a day.'

A whole day? What happened?

I managed to open my eyes again and search his face. There were no hints of sarcasm, no lightness at all. His eyes seemed unfocussed like he wasn't seeing me at all as his chest rose and fell with rapid breaths.

A dull ache throbbed in my chest, causing me to wince.

Daniel shifted, his hand tightening around mine. 'I'll get

the doctor.'

'No,' I whispered with every ounce of energy I had. 'Stay.'

'I'm not going anywhere.'

With those words, I closed my eyes again and felt the weightlessness take me.

~

There were more people in the room this time. I stayed still with my eyes closed, trying to listen to where they were and who was here.

I heard Mum's voice first. She spoke quietly but frantically. 'It's all the pressure we've put on her.'

'In school?' Dad asked.

'Yes. We shouldn't have been so hard.'

I wanted to tell them both that there was nothing they could have done. That they shouldn't blame themselves. But the truth was that I was a coward; I didn't want to face them or tell them what happened to me.

Mum sobbed, and it shattered my heart. I felt hot tears wet my cheeks, and then, when I finally braved opening my eyes, a rush of hideous nausea hit me, making bile rapidly rush to the back of my throat. Without warning, I vomited all over myself. A nurse appeared at my side, helping me to the pan she was holding beneath my chin.

'That's a girl. We've given you some charcoal to flush your stomach. You'll be a little sick for a few days.'

A little? My eyes instinctively rolled.

The nurse chuckled. 'Just keep breathing through it, sweetheart. You're nearly there.'

After I heaved for the third time, I sucked in a deep breath, averting my eyes from my parents. They both stood with hands closed over their hearts.

The nurse drew the curtains and helped me out of the stained gown into a clean one.

'Drink this.' She handed me a small plastic cup filled with cool water, which I eagerly gulped down.

She checked the clipboard at the foot of my bed and did something with the IV drip beside me, and then with a quick smile, she opened the curtain, nodding to Mum and Dad.

'Oh, ljubavi!' Mum sat, her slender frame fitting almost entirely beside me. Dad took my drip-free hand into his and lowered his forehead to it.

'I'm so sorry,' I said, bursting into tears.

'Don't you apologise.' Dad cupped my cheek in his hand. 'You have nothing to say sorry for.'

'Ljubavi, what happened?'

'Just tired, swear…'

She shook her head and let out a sob.

She didn't believe me.

Neither of them did.

'Andrea—'

'Don't, Mum, please.'

Every word was inconceivably difficult to get out. It was like my brain and body didn't want to play on the same team. My mind fired off commands, but my arms and legs sat still. The words that were sharp in my head barely came out in tangible English.

Mum cried again.

As she sobbed beside me, I felt the panic rising. Before I knew it, the heart rate monitor started keeping pace with my speeding pulse, getting louder and louder. Mum pulled back, her wide eyes darting from me to the machine before the same nurse rushed in and checked my pulse.

'Can you give us some space?' she asked.

'No, I stay, please,' Mum begged, but Dad gave me a knowing look and gently walked her out.

I exhaled and then inhaled, but each breath was shallow and empty. I couldn't settle the hammering of my heart, and I couldn't stop crying.

The nurse gently squeezed my hand. 'Breathe with me, okay?'

'Can't.'

'Yes, you can. Come on, one, two, three, breathe.' She did the motion, and I tried to keep up. 'One, two, three, breathe.'

After following her lead for a few minutes, the beeping stopped.

'See, you can do it,' she smiled.

Memories started to form a coherent picture in my mind. I remembered what happened with Julian, the girls at school, texting Daniel, and watching as he called over and over while my body shut down.

'Now I'll tell your parents that you need to get some rest. If it becomes too much, you press this button right here.' She nodded to a small, red button on the edge of the bedside table. 'Okay?'

'Thank you.'

'You're welcome, sweetheart. I'll come and check in on

you later.'

As the nurse left and shut the door with a gentle thud, I dropped my head back into the overly soft pillow and let out a long sigh.

God. How did I come back from this?

CHAPTER FIFTEEN

The Friend

Monday, September 19th

I spent three whole days in the hospital.

I was fed charcoal to make me throw up and flush my stomach, then extremely diluted orange juice to hydrate me. My stomach hurt from heaving, and my throat was raw from the acid coming up.

Mum stayed by my side as I repeated the charcoal and vomit process. I cried. I screamed for her to go away. She left, and Dad took over.

Eventually, Daniel was allowed in.

I learned that my school had been informed about my *accident* and had set several measures in place for when I went back after the break.

It was meant to be *suicide*. Nothing accidental about it.

But that's what people did, wasn't it? They covered shit up that was too hard to look at and turned the music up when someone said something they didn't want to hear.

The nurse came and went a few times until a lady I didn't know arrived and introduced herself.

'We're from the Critical Assessment Team, Andrea. Do you know what we do?'

'Sure, you deal with messed up people who try to kill

themselves.'

She didn't even bat an eye. Guess becoming jaded was part of the gig.

'We help people who are going through something painful.'

I frowned.

'Now, I would like to set up some time to come and see you when you get home.'

'It's not really a question, so why don't you just go ahead and set it up.'

'I'm not going to make you do something you don't want to.'

'I am really sick of hearing that,' I bit.

'Is that something you've experienced?'

I shut my mouth and averted my gaze.

'Andrea?'

'Forget it, I'm still delusional.'

'Nurses said your brain scans are looking clear.'

I flicked my eyes back to her. 'Brain scans?'

'You were found on the floor in your room. The paramedics didn't know if you fell off your bed and hit your head because you were unconscious when you were found. Tests were mandatory to make sure you hadn't suffered a head injury.'

I looked away.

'You don't have to talk to me now, but I would like your consent to come and talk to you another time, maybe this week once you're settled back in at home?'

Consent. What a load of shit. There was no choice here,

just like there was no choice in joining the math class or starting piano or at Julian's house.

'Andrea?'

'Sure, why not.'

She smiled and noted something down on her notepad.

'I'm Sarah, by the way. It's nice to meet you,' she said speaking slowly.

'I'm nauseous, not stupid.'

She smiled just the same and proceeded to offer me several options for when she would visit.

After the time and date were set, she left with express instructions handed to my parents in case I bailed.

Mum appeared at the door, a small bouquet in her hands. 'Hailey came before, but I said you were still resting. Do you want to see her later?'

'No.'

'I can tell her to come another time.'

'No,' I repeated without looking.

I heard her sigh, then leave after she'd stuffed the flowers into a glass jar.

~

Mum helped me into some fresh clothes the second the nurses discharged me, and Dad took my bag filled with the clothes I'd come in with and helped me to the car.

I sulked on the back seat the entire ride home. I avoided breathing too loudly to evade any attention. I avoided looking around at anything but the headrest in front of me in case I locked eyes with Mum.

Not that I thought I could focus anyway. The highway

lights and cars speeding by gave me a headache and made me feel like throwing up. I gripped the sick bag the nurse gave me and inhaled and exhaled, then closed my eyes and leaned back into the stiff leather seat.

Once the pounding in my head had subsided, I opened my eyes, instantly regretting it as we turned onto the road that led to my school. My heart slammed into my ribs from thumping so hard. I shifted, and the leather groaned under my butt.

'How're you doing there?' Dad asked.

'Fine.'

His gaze met mine in the mirror. 'Your sister misses you.'

'Where is she?'

'Sent her to Maya's house for few days.'

'Oh,' I replied.

Neither of them said anything else for the rest of the trip.

Shame reddened my cheeks. God. I could never tell them, especially not now.

'We're home,' he said a few minutes later, pulling into the driveway with a sigh.

Before either of them could say anything, I got out of the car and made a determined line for the stairs.

'Andrea, wait,' Mum said.

I stopped.

Dad's heavy footsteps told me he was walking through the house, away from the kitchen, leaving me and Mum alone.

'Daniel asked if he could come and see you.' She placed her hands on her hip, sighing. Her eyes were dull, red rings circled them. 'I don't want him here to be honest, not while you still so sick.'

'Your house, Mum. Do what you want.'

She frowned. 'I told him that he could come over if you okay with it. I want you to have friend. Someone to talk to because you won't talk to me.'

'Mum, I…'

'I do hope you trust me to talk one day.'

Stupid tears filled my eyes again.

She hugged me and held me tight, and I held onto her like I never had before. When she pulled back, she wiped my face with the back of her hand and kissed my cheek.

'Daniel said he will message to see if you want him to come.'

'Thanks.'

She opened her mouth to say something but then closed it, so I retreated to my room.

The walk up the steps was hard. I stopped twice, and when I couldn't make it up, Mum came up behind me.

We walked together side by side, one step after the other. When I reached my room, I stopped at the door, and Mum paused for a moment as if she wanted to say something but again, didn't. She gave me a small nod and left.

For what seemed like the longest time, I stood at the mouth of my room, staring at the floor. It felt off. None of it felt like it belonged to me. A deep, consuming sense of dread settled in the pit of my stomach, making my insides feel like they were made of stone. Nothing had really changed, but inside me, everything had been rewritten and rewired.

I held my breath and stepped over the threshold. Nothing

happened. No dramatic change. Nothing scary or horrible.

I sighed.

The room was tidy, not like I'd left it. The empty pill packets were in the small bin under my desk, and all my toys and cushions were neatly placed on my bed. The blinds were drawn halfway, and my empty school bag was by the door.

My phone vibrated loudly on my desk, startling me. Dad must have put it on the charger. I sighed again and reached for it with trembling hands. I looked at the screen and carefully keyed in my code, almost afraid to look at the messages.

But I had to do it eventually, so why not now? I was already numb from the medication and the vomiting and everything else.

The texts were mainly from Daniel and Josh, a whole lot from Hailey and some girls from class who shared practice essays for next term.

Then, there was a calendar reminder for tomorrow. Sarah, from the Critical Assessment Team, was coming over. I closed my hands over my face and hung my head.

My phone vibrated again. I peeked through the gap my fingers made. It was Daniel.

I'd like to come and c u. Ur mum said it was OK.

And then a millisecond later another message came through.

Only if u want. I know ur probably feeling really sick, and I know I'm not in the mood for company when I have the man flu.

There was a grinning emoticon at the end. It made my lips tug into a small smile.

You can come over. See you soon.

Ok, I'll bring snacks.

I took a deep breath and decided I might as well read the rest of the messages. One was from Kayla. When I opened it, I sighed with relief.

I hope you're feeling okay. If you need anything, please let me know. I've given Mr. Benson the drafts you've done. I know you'd want to stay on track. Kayla.

The next message was from Josh.

Jesus, Andy. What happened? Pls tell me it wasn't something to do wit Julian, and pls tell me I wasn't right about him.

I wish I could. I wish I could tell my parents. I wish I could tell the police and anyone who cared. I wish I could make him pay for what he did to me, and probably Elle, and who knows how many other girls. But boys like Julian Valesco were so exceptionally good at saying all the right things in all the right ways that their words erased your own. And somehow, even if you'd managed to see the truth of what happened and find the strength to confront them, they would turn it around so quickly that no one would believe you anyway.

Then I made my way down to the messages from Hailey. My soul was worn thin, and she'd seen right through it and into the hollowness inside me that day on the oval.

Why didn't u talk to me? U know I'm here for

*u. Always. I'm so, so sorry u felt like this was
ur only answer. I'm so sorry I wasn't there for
u more.*

Then the next.

I'm sorry I didn't keep pushing u to talk to me.

I just let u go home knowing you weren't good.

And then, there was one final one.

Love ur guts man.

I ran a clammy hand over my face. I wanted to shoot off a generic response but decided against it.

*Please don't blame yourself. Nothing anyone
did or said would have made a difference.*

A few seconds later, she replied.

Can I come and see u?

Maybe later. I messaged back.

K. Call me when I can come.

I dropped the phone on the bed and made my way into the bathroom. I stripped, turned the water to volcano-hot, and got in. I slid down against the tiles and sat with my own thoughts, the raging water silencing everything else. Even the usual vanilla fragrance from my shampoo bottles that travelled up through the steam did little to quell the sadness inside me.

Once I was ready to face the world again, I dried off and dressed and stopped by my door when I heard Daniel's voice carry up the stairs.

Mum was probably giving him the run-down of what to say and what not to say, or worse, probably prying information out of him. I pulled on a loose hoodie and a pair of old leggings and twisted my hair into a tight bun before I walked down the stairs, tightly holding onto the handrail.

'Hey,' I said, stopping at the landing.

Daniel's eyes shot up to mine, then skimmed over my face, which a second-long look in the mirror confirmed was a horrible sight: I was gaunt, pale, and sullen. It was amazing what vomiting for several days straight did to the human body.

'I brought some chips. I don't know if you—well, I didn't know if you'd want to eat.'

'Thanks.' I gestured up the stairs without looking at him.

Daniel followed. When we reached my room, I stood aside, letting him in. He sat on the edge of my bed, the same place he chose last time. A pang of regret shot through me.

As if he sensed what I was thinking, he shifted, moving a little closer to the middle, keeping his eyes locked on me. I looked away but I felt his gaze on me as I took my time slowly walking over to my desk and eased myself into the chair. I carefully held onto the edge of the table in case the vertigo returned.

When I finally looked up, Daniel's gaze was on the empty blister packs in the bin. Neither of us said a word. In silence, we sat, unmoving, until suddenly he got up. He knelt in front of me and gently moved the bin away and out of my line of sight.

'Dad and I decided to do this stupid hike from the base of Kosciuzko all the way to the top one time. It was meant to be like a peace offering after he and Mum broke up. We were meant to make it to the halfway mark by six, set up camp before nightfall, and then continue the next morning.'

He paused, looking up at me.

With a small sigh, he continued. 'We were the only campers there. We get in the tent, start piss farting around getting ready for bed, and then this group of guys came up the mountain. Dad shit himself. I'd never seen the man scared of anything in my life.'

His gaze dropped to the space between our feet.

'They were dickheads being stupid. I didn't think they meant any harm to us, but Dad started yelling at them to piss off and that got them started. I was fourteen. I wasn't big or anything like some kids are at that age. I got my muscles a bit later,' he chuckled. 'So, I couldn't help him when they got into it. Fortunately for us, Dad had registered our hike with the base, turns out they send people up to make sure no one's dead or whatever.

'The ranger sorted them out straight away. Dad got away with a few bruises and a tarnished reputation of being king of the mountain, but the point is, Andy, that was the scariest moment of my life. I thought I was going to lose my dad that day.'

'That sounds awful,' I whispered.

He looked up at me. The faint smile pulling at the corner of his lips was so far from happy that it broke my heart.

'It was,' he nodded. 'But that was nothing compared to what I felt when you sent me those messages.'

I stared down at the floor.

'I called, and I called, and every time the phone went to message bank, I thought of all the worst things possible. I came straight here, broke your damn window, which, by the way, your dad and I bonded over while we fixed. I had no idea whether you were alive or dead, and you know those fucking shows make checking for a pulse look so easy, but it really wasn't.'

'You found me?' My voice cracked.

'Yes.'

'Jesus!' I shot to my feet, ignoring the wave of nausea. 'Why did you come here?'

'You're joking, right?'

'No, I'm not. I'm so far from joking that it's actually pretty funny, ironically.' I spun on the spot and faced him. 'You shouldn't have come.'

'You would have died!'

'That was the fucking point, Daniel!'

'Andy…'

Tears filled my eyes and when he took a step toward me, my fight died down and I burst into tears. I didn't pull away when he wrapped his arms around me, and I didn't pull away when he pressed a soft kiss to my forehead and led me to my bed.

When I was comfortably seated, he handed me the huge ass teddy I'd won at Luna Park last summer and sat beside me, tucking me right up against him. The first thought that crossed my mind as my body instinctively tensed was fear, quickly followed by the memory of Julian's prickly skin against mine, followed by anger. I cried harder. Is this what it was going to be like? Forever afraid to be touched? To be close to someone?

Daniel's hold on me loosened. But I refused to be

controlled by my stupid emotions like that. I reached for him and buried my face in his chest.

He drew soothing circles on my back and moved my hair over my shoulder. Then, when he turned me toward him, I saw the moment I'd been waiting for. The universe had lined everything up perfectly. He was right here, sitting right beside me, waiting for me to tell him everything.

'I know what I did hurt you. I—'

'I know something terrible happened, and I'm so stupid for not seeing it, so, so stupid for thinking...'

'Daniel—'

'I was angry when I heard about you and Julian, but I had this feeling that there was more to the story, but I was too pissed to see it. I'm your best friend, I should have spoken to you.'

'Why didn't you?'

'I don't know, that's the damn truth. I'm so sorry.'

'Me too.' I ignored the stabbing pain in my stomach reminding me of all the vomiting in the hospital. If I ever saw orange juice again, I'd die.

'Why didn't you reach out to me?'

I tipped my chin up, meeting his eyes. 'You probably don't remember, but I did after we spoke at school that day in the locker bay. I called you that night. I wanted to talk to you... to tell you.'

His eyes widened.

'And you said Julian was my friend. I knew after that I couldn't. It's on me, though. I should have said something at school when you asked me, but I—when I saw how you looked at me, I couldn't.'

There was incomprehensible silence. I took a deep breath, and with some effort, I folded my hands in my lap.

'He—' I looked up at the ceiling, willing the words to just come out. 'I didn't want what he did. Like, I know I was there. I was in his bed, and it felt right and then it didn't. But I didn't try hard enough to stop him. It was like my brain just…'

The *r* word burned through my brain like acid. I couldn't say it out loud, like somehow if I said it, it would give it life, it would make *it* real.

'He told his friends I did and—' I took a deep breath, almost like I didn't believe the words coming out of my own mouth. 'And the whole school believed him. Even you.'

Daniel's gaze lowered as he let out a long breath.

'And truth be told, I was scared he would corner me in the toilets at school or on my way home or something and make me do it again. Stupid, I know, but that seems to be the word of the year for me, doesn't it? Stupid Andy, stupid girl who put herself in that position.'

'No,' he said. 'You didn't *put* yourself in that position. He did that to you. Do you understand me?' His words were sharp and clear.

'I went to his house. Got into his bed like you said. I kissed him, I let him touch me, but—'

'He had no right to do anything else if you didn't want it.'

'Yeah, well. I should have been clearer.'

'He should have read the goddamn signs!'

The conversation ended abruptly. Daniel let out another

long breath and shifted beside me. When I chanced a look at
him, he reached over and hugged me.

CHAPTER SIXTEEN

Andrea Nekić is Not Fine

It took ten minutes for what I'd told him to really register, and when it did, he wasn't calm like before. There was anger, muttered words in Romanian that I didn't understand, and pacing. Lots of it.

Occasionally, he would look at me and then grind his teeth so loudly I thought they might crack. Then, he finally walked over to me and knelt. He stayed there silently for a few moments, and then let out a low, breathless laugh, taking both of my hands in his.

'I'm going to kill him, Andy.'

'No, you won't.'

His eyes snapped up to mine.

'You think taking a life and going to jail is worth it?' I challenged.

'He raped you.'

'I know,' I said, flinching. 'But ruining your life is not okay.'

His shoulders slumped, and he sighed loudly. 'I feel so useless. I don't know what to do or…'

'You're here now.'

'It's not good enough.' His gaze met mine. 'You called me, I didn't…'

Tears pooled in his eyes, and for the first time, I was determined to fight this damn thing because I didn't want anyone else to feel the pain I did.

'Stop. It is good enough. You're here.'

'Fuck!' He sat next to me, resting his elbows on his knees.

Things were going to be different at school now. I had Daniel in my corner, and even if I couldn't tell him now, it meant everything to me.

Daniel shifted beside me, and I flinched again.

'I'm sorry.'

'It's fine, I'm just…' I contemplated what to say, how to bury the feelings, and then, when his eyes searched my face, I dropped the act. 'I'm just not fine at all.'

'Really? Andrea Nekić is *not* fine?'

I smirked when he tipped his head to the side, brushing my cheek with the back of his hand.

'Yeah, who would have thought,' I said lightly. 'I don't know if I can go back there, not after this. I mean, I could handle it all before and even seeing his face, but this…'

'Andrea Nekić, you're one tough girl. You can do it.'

'I don't feel so tough.'

'I know, you're hurting, and you probably feel shithouse from the crap the doctors gave you, but you are tough. I see the light in your eyes. There's still fire in there.'

'It must be the only thing, then, because in here,' I pressed my hand over my heart, 'there's nothing. I'm empty.'

For someone like Daniel who always had a comment or a sharp comeback, there was indescribable silence. Yep. People tended to act like that around me these days. Even the friendly bantering in Methods class seemed to have fizzled out. I'd gone from a nobody to the school slut in a matter of twenty-four hours and then a pariah. Nothing had changed and yet everything had. It was madness.

'I'm supposed to be seeing this woman tomorrow,' I said. 'Though I've been begging mum to let me reschedule.'

'You don't want to talk to her?'

'No, not yet. I can't. I just want to finish this year, leave and be done with it.'

'What about your family?'

'They don't know anything, and they never will.'

'I'm not going to tell you what to do, but you know your parents love you, Andy. They'd do anything for you, and they'd listen.'

'I know all of that, but I also know my mum is so highly strung that she'd probably have a heart attack if she found out, and I also know my dad has his own problems.'

He didn't say anything.

'I hear her in the shower, Daniel. She cries. She knows some shit went down. I mean, it's hard to miss. Change of personality, check; change of clothing, check; change of fucking everything else, check.'

His eyes lowered.

'I'm not doing that to them. They think I'm stressed about school, and that's it.'

'Andy...'

'Don't,' I warned. 'I'm not breathing a word, and if you betray me—'

'I would never betray you.'

'Good,' I said, and an unsteady breath came free when Daniel scooted closer.

'You're everything to me, Andrea Nekić. I'm so sorry I failed to show you that.'

All I had known and felt for the past two months was darkness, a bottomless, lightless chasm of hell that sucked everything in and let nothing out. But now, with Daniel sitting beside me, with so much compassion and care in his eyes, I realised I wasn't really empty. I wasn't dead inside; I was still here, and despite everything Julian had done to me, I was alive.

Daniel smiled, and I leaned in and kissed him, so hard that he kind of stumbled.

He didn't push me away, though. I was afraid he would. I was terrified he'd see the mess in front of him and run but instead, he returned the gesture, kissing me tenderly, both his hands gently sweeping through the mass of hair over my shoulders.

When we parted, he lowered his forehead to mine and cupped my cheek, tracing a line across my jaw.

'I'll help you get through this, whatever it takes, and I'll support whatever you decide to do, okay?'

I nodded.

'Good,' he smiled. 'What do you want to do now, though?'

'Uh…' I looked down at the bag of food he'd brought in and then the bed.

'Good choice,' he said, switching on the TV, unpacking a range of snacks, and plopping himself down on the bed beside me.

'I have to warn you, though, I still get sick. I might vomit.'

'Do you want a bag?' he asked.

'It's gross, I don't want you to see—'

'Come on, how many times have we thrown up around each other when we've been tanked?'

'True.'

'And how many times have I held your hair when your ass was parked in my driveway after one too many Cruisers?'

I laughed again. 'Can't believe my parents never found out.'

'About all the underage drinking or that it was at my house?'

'Both,' I laughed.

'Choose something,' he said with a chuckle before tossing over the remote.

'You should pick.'

'Not how this works,' he winked. 'Choose.'

I smirked and picked my favourite UFO documentary, which, admittedly, I'd seen fifteen times. I ignored the raging sense of dread of what school would bring and closed my eyes, feeling a sense of comfort in the steady heartbeat thrumming through my ear.

I fell asleep with strong arms around my shoulders, arms that didn't cause me stress or fear, arms that made me feel safe like I was *before*, innocent and hopeful, a normal girl with a normal life.

CHAPTER SEVENTEEN

Last Week's News

I heard voices outside. His brother and mum were talking, and a shriek reverberated through the thin walls. I noticed they were white and peeling in some places; they were watching some kind of cartoon. Overly cheery music carried through the vents, then more shrieking. I tried to picture what it was; the voices were familiar. Maybe it was Tarzan. *No, no, it was something else, maybe* Aladdin.

My eyes coasted across the room: posters of girls on bikes, some band I'd never heard of, a small desk overflowing with school textbooks and other stuff I couldn't make out, the candle…, and his cologne. It was all so normal. On the wall beside it was a polaroid of the three of them: his mum, Zach in the middle wearing a Ninja Turtles t-shirt, and Julian, smiling his brilliant, warm smile. It was all so pretty, so out of place in this ugly room belonging to a boy who I thought had been the most beautiful soul I'd ever met.

My body was jolted when a painful nip at my neck made my imaginary world fall to pieces around me.

'You're so sexy,' he grunted in my ear. 'So hot.'

Tears pooled in my eyes, but I didn't want to cry in front of him, not like this, not when he was…

My body trembled and arched; everything I was doing

was reactive. I had no idea why it was betraying me like this. I had no idea why I couldn't stop it. I had no idea why I kissed him back.

This couldn't be happening. This couldn't be real.

This was just a bad dream. A terrible nightmare.

I heard more shrieks of laughter through the door, a stark contrast to the dense, heavy air suffocating me. I was far away now, drifting from my body, my mind cocooned safely inside a shell that was spiky and prickly all around.

No one could get to me in here, not even...

'Yes, baby,' he whispered. 'You're doing so good.'

Maybe I was lucky, though. Lucky that I knew him, lucky that I knew he wouldn't kill me.

Maybe this wasn't so bad; he'd be done, and this would be over. I'd get to walk away with my life, whatever was left of it. Some girls never got that chance. They were strangled or stabbed to death and discarded in alleyways becoming one with the litter caught in the gutters. Funny, that's what we were always taught. Rapes were perpetrated by strangers in alleyways, not by people you knew and shared classes with and swooned over in the locker bay.

My shell was cracking now, though; I heard whispers break through the walls I'd built, his hot breath surging through my safe world and into the real one. He was tearing every part of me down.

Dad would be so disappointed. He'd be so disgusted with how stupid his perfect little girl had been.

'Yes, baby,' he ground out again, then he spasmed, grunted a little and then slowed.

The wetness between my legs dampened the sheets. I couldn't tell whether it was him or me. All I knew for certain was the shame and the emptiness of the hole that was left where he'd ripped something out of me that I'd never get back.

He reached for my cheek and for the first time since this happened, I flinched.

I raised my arm to fight back.

~

'Hey, it's okay, Andy, you're safe.' Daniel gently caught my raised arm, tugging me to him.

My eyes opened and darted around.

I was in my room. The TV was still on but the documentary we'd put on was long since finished.

Daniel's hand fell to the curve of my jaw and turned my face towards his. 'You were having a nightmare.'

'This sucks…'

Every loud pump of my heart echoed in my head, and the taste of blood in my mouth dragged me into lucidity. Before I could stop it, bile rose to the surface. Daniel shoved the sick bag into my hand, and I threw everything up.

Like the hum of powerlines across cascading fields, my brain buzzed and hummed as Daniel traced gentle lines across my back, occasionally stopping to pull my hair out of the way.

I heard my parents outside the door, pacing and arguing in hushed voices coming in and out of focus. I heard my own heart thundering against my rib cage. Everything felt so magnified and off-kilter.

A ragged breath came free when I finally pulled my head out of the bag and tied it off. I noticed then that I'd bitten down on my tongue. Tears surged through me.

'Please tell me this will all go away,' I begged.

'I promise, Andy, this will all go away. Really, it will.'

'Liar.'

After a while, I walked over to the adjoining bathroom and turned the tap on. I splashed water on my face and took a second to look at the reflection staring back at me. I caught Daniel's gaze in the mirror behind me. He ran his hand through his hair, reminding me to sort out the mess on my own head. Without much conviction, I reached for the brush on the counter and started pulling my hair into a somewhat presentable ponytail.

'What time is it?'

'Just after three,' Daniel muttered. 'Didn't want to leave you.'

'My parents didn't try to kick you out?'

'They tried.'

I stood still.

Daniel shifted. 'Do you want me to leave?' he asked.

'No.'

'Are you sure?'

'No.'

He expelled a breath. 'Andy, I don't know what to do.'

'Me neither.'

What was he thinking now? Was he unsure, wondering why he'd come, wondering what kind of crazy he was involved with?

After a painful minute, he came towards me, and without even thinking, I jerked back so hard I knocked myself in the back of the head on the vanity. His hand shot out to stabilise me.

'Don't,' I hissed.

'I'm sorry.' He frowned, taking a big step back.

'I think you should leave.'

'Andy, I—'

'Please. Go.'

'Okay,' he said, his shoulders dropping.

After packing up the food, tidying my bed, and giving me a nod goodbye, he left.

I heard voices downstairs, and then the front door opened. *Why were they even still awake?*

Outside, a car door opened, and then an engine roared to life. I dropped onto the bed and pulled the covers over my head.

Before I closed my eyes to try and get some sleep, a tap at my door drew my attention.

'Ljubavi, Ms. Richards agreed to reschedule. I'll give details tomorrow. Goodnight,' Mum said.

I blew out a relieved breath. At least there was some good news.

~

The next week passed much the same. I was sick most of the morning, started to feel better by the afternoon, and Daniel always came over in the evening. It would be a nightmare or being sick that would make me chase him away and send him home.

But just like that, the school holidays were over.

It meant I'd have to go back to school.

God, school. I was not ready for that shitshow.

What would it even be like? Would they know? Would there be new rumours about why I tried to kill myself?

'Andrea, are you up?' Mum's voice sounded outside my door.

'Yeah, Mum. I'm up.'

She came in and stood at the foot of my bed for a moment before sitting on the end of my mattress. 'I made breakfast if you're feeling like it.'

'Thanks. That would be good.'

She eyed me for a minute as if studying my face. I should have told her everything then, should have made sure she knew it wasn't her fault or Dad's. But the rapid onset of shallow breaths and sweaty palms, accompanied by a little voice in my head that kept reminding me that I was the idiot who'd brought this upon herself, made me shut my mouth.

She gently squeezed my foot through the blanket and smiled. It seemed forced, the kind you give a perfect stranger when you're being polite on the train. I mirrored her faux smile.

She left and when I heard her reach the bottom of the steps, I sat up. She was talking to Dad, and I wondered what about. Maybe me, maybe Daniel, maybe all the things they thought they'd done wrong.

How do I tell them that wasn't the case at all?

A light knock on my door drew my attention as it opened a crack.

'Can I come in?' Jelena's small frame peeked from around the corner.

'Sure,' I smiled.

She came in and stopped at the end of my bed, her long fingers delicately tracing the line of the wooden frame.

'How do you feel?'

'I'm okay.'

'Can I do anything?'

'No.'

'I can stay home today. We can watch cartoons.'

I chuckled. 'No, that's okay. You've got your excursion today. You've been waiting all month to go.'

'I'm sure Mum can take us both next month.'

'Don't be silly, go and have fun. I'm not feeling the best right now, and I want to watch cartoons when I feel a bit more alive.'

She smiled again, wider this time. 'Okay, next time we can watch whatever you want.'

'Oh really?' I tested. 'Anything I want?'

'Anything.'

'Okay, awesome.' I held my arms out, and worried that for a second that she didn't want to hug me, but then she rushed over.

'I love you, Andy.'

'I love you too.'

She left, her feet thumping loudly down the steps as she disappeared downstairs. I smiled to myself. What was I thinking leaving her behind? She needed me. She needed her big sister. A dull ache spread through my heart. I would do whatever it took to be strong for her.

But first, I had to get through today.

I dressed, ignored my face in the mirror and avoided any overbearing smells. No perfume, no hairspray or anything that would trigger another bout of nausea. I had no idea what set it off. One thing I knew for sure was that I couldn't wear my coconut body mist anymore. Whenever I smelt it, I felt Julian's weight crushing me into his mattress.

'You're ready,' Dad said smiling when I walked into the kitchen.

'I am,' I said evenly, trying to sound as confident as I was pretending to be.

'Do you want to go for a hike this weekend?' Dad asked, shaking the small container of snacks we always took.

'Not really, Dad. Sorry.'

I didn't miss the disappointment cross his face. He tipped his head down with a small nod and a painfully forced smile. It's what he always did when he disapproved of something but didn't want to say so.

I sighed and ran my hands over my cheeks. Mum wore that polite stranger smile again.

Breakfast was like pulling teeth. Small talk, chatter about English class and staying on top of assignments, like that was something I cared about anymore. While Mum spoke and Dad agreed with everything she said, my mind wandered away, feeling the coil of Julian's hold around my wrist, his hot breath, and then the cool water going down my throat as I downed the pills. Then I was back at the kitchen table, eating pancakes and drinking juice. A perfectly normal, happy family. Somewhere in the house, my little sister was playing video games; somewhere else, I was just a normal teenager about to finish high school.

'Thanks for breakfast, Mum.' I pushed the chair out, the loud screech the four legs made on the floorboards cutting through the awkward stillness.

'Daniel is coming.'

'What?' I barely contained the anger in my voice. 'Why?'

'I don't want you to be alone right now.'

'Why? Because you think I'll run out in front of a bus or something?'

'Andrea!'

'No, let's not hide behind anything right now. You don't trust me to be alone.'

'No, I don't,' she shot.

'This is bullshit!'

Dad shook his head. 'Watch your language, Andrea.'

'Or what?' I challenged. 'You'll ground me?'

Neither of them replied as I stalked out of the room and toward the front door.

I slammed the door shut, cementing my attitude. Probably a little dramatic. Definitely spoilt. My parents didn't believe in *grounding*. They said there were more civilised and adult ways to discipline, but here we were, one bad word away from being grounded until I was thirty.

Just as I was making a right at the end of the street, Daniel's car appeared around the corner.

I rolled my eyes.

'Whoa, Nekić,' he said, pulling up on the side of the kerb.

'I thought I was driving you in.'

'No, Mum and Dad thought you were driving me in.' I kept walking.

'Andrea, wait.'

He left the car and jogged over to me. 'Hey, what's going on?'

'I'm not a fucking snowflake. I'm not going to fall apart.'

'Okay, I didn't think you were, I just—'

'You just what? Signed on for being my bodyguard to make sure I don't find a razor and slit my wrists or something?'

His eyes narrowed taking on a dark hue. He straightened, folding his arms across his chest. 'No, Andrea, I signed on for being your damn friend like I should have been from the beginning.'

My mouth clamped shut.

'So, if you're done feeling sorry for yourself because people actually care about you, can we just go?'

Unable to think of anything else to say, I silently followed him to the car.

Daniel drove without saying a word to me; he didn't even complain when I changed the house song on the radio, and he didn't even bat an eye when I started eating my muesli bar. Normally, he would have made me place a napkin on my lap or something; he loved his car more than anything else.

When he turned down the road heading toward school, I found myself sinking into the seat, wondering what today would be like. Would anyone try to talk to me, or would I be discarded like last week's news?

CHAPTER EIGHTEEN

Milkshakes and Real Talk

Daniel parked a street away.

'What are you doing?' I asked, looking down the unfamiliar road.

'Parking here so you don't have to look at the school yet.'

I pursed my lips and looked across at him.

'Are you ready?' he asked.

Within seconds, my palms became sweaty. I gripped the wrapper of my muesli bar until I'd squashed it into a tiny ball.

'I don't think so.'

Daniel reached over and squeezed my hand.

'Let's leave then,' he said.

'We can't leave.'

'You're not well,' he trailed off. 'You can't even look at the road that leads to the school. What will you do when I actually drive us down there?'

The looming grey and white facade peeking through the old seventies roofs made a shudder roll all the way from my spine up to the back of my neck.

'I have to.'

'Not right now, you don't. There's time. You can go back tomorrow or the day after.'

'What about you?'

198

He shrugged, turning the radio on to my preferred station. 'I hate today's classes. I'd rather spend time with you.'

'Exams are just around the corner.'

'Don't care, Andy. I'm asking you if you want to leave.'

We looked at each other for a silent moment. He didn't falter or recant. He gave me a little smile, and really, it was all I needed. Not like I needed much convincing of anything right now.

'Let's go and get burgers,' I said.

'For breakfast?'

'Why not?' I shrugged, making Daniel chuckle.

Daniel drove for a few minutes until we reached the old burger place down behind his house. He'd been trying to convince me to come and eat with him there since I started at Deanell, but I was always busy. In hindsight, I realised it wasn't about the burgers or the milkshakes; it was about spending time together.

Why did it take a horrific ordeal and a near-death experience to make me realise all of this?

'The strawberry milkshake is amazing. Otherwise, if you're not feeling like something that sweet get the vanilla one.'

I smiled as he led me in. He was nervous; his hand missed the handle twice, and then he pushed when the sign saying "pull" was bigger than my head.

'Or you know, there's Coke, and uh, all sorts of other drinks, if that's what you prefer.'

'Thanks,' I chuckled, ducking under the plastic flaps behind the door. 'I'll have to take you to Soda Rock one day.'

'The diner in South Yarra?'

'Yeah, it's my favourite.'

He shielded a smile and a flush of red spread over his cheeks. 'That sounds good. We should go soon.'

'Can't wait.'

Daniel buried his face in the menu the second we were seated, only looking up once or twice, probably to make sure I was still sitting opposite him, and then again when the guy came back.

'What can I get you?' he asked me, tapping the end of his pen on a tiny pad.

'Cheeseburger, coke and curly fries.'

'You?' he looked at Daniel.

'Same, but lemonade.'

'Got it.' He took both menus, repeated back what we ordered in the most monotone voice I'd ever heard, and then dropped two wrapped-up sets of cutlery on the table with a huff.

'Thought *I* hated being at work,' Daniel muttered.

'The last time I saw you at work, you told Mr. Grier to piss off.'

He baulked like I'd caught him out.

'I was there. I witnessed the whole thing.'

'Well, I mean, he deserved it; he was being a dick.'

'He was asking for help with his car.'

'No, he was asking Carly for help with his car so he could look down her top.'

Anger flushed through me. 'You're serious?'

'Unfortunately.'

'What is wrong with men?'

There was a pause, I couldn't tell what was going through his mind but the turmoil in his eyes was hard to miss. He was grinding his molars so hard I could practically hear his teeth creaking. He didn't even look up when the guy brought our burgers over, or when I noticed that he'd brought Daniel a Fanta instead of a Lemonade.

'People who do what Valesco did are trash, *lower* than trash.'

My jaw locked as if it was the only thing that could stop me from crying.

'I can't even express the rage I have inside me every time I think about it, Andy. I want to fucking hunt him down and break his jaw. I want to hurt him.'

I blinked back tears and shrunk into the seat. Daniel shifted in front of me.

'I'll never betray your trust,' he added softly.

Unable to stop myself from crying, I threw both hands up and quickly swatted the tears away. Daniel handed me a few napkins and I scrunched them into a ball and wiped my eyes.

'I know it will take time for you to open up and trust again. But I will wait. I swear to God, I will be here. I won't let you down.'

'What do you think I should do?'

'That's a dangerous question.' His voice deepened.

'You think I should go to the police?'

'Yes,' he sighed, opening the Fanta which he still hadn't noticed wasn't the right drink. 'But you don't want to.'

'No, I don't. I don't think they'll be able to do anything.

There's no proof, nothing but his word and mine.'

He rubbed the back of his neck and expelled a long breath. 'This is bullshit. He needs to be held accountable.'

'If it's okay with you, I'd rather just forget all of this for today?'

'Of course, sorry.' He smiled and squeezed my hand over the table.

'Thank you.'

'Now eat, these are the best burgers you'll ever have.'

'I'll be the judge of that,' I grinned.

CHAPTER NINETEEN

Your Heart Knows the Truth

I managed to avoid going to school all week with a detailed sick note written by my GP under the proviso that I checked in with Ms. Richards. She had tried to reschedule with me three times but thanks to my persistence and begging, Mum convinced her to wait a few more days.

Sadly, I was out of excuses.

The world outside went by completely unaware, while everything inside these walls was different.

All I had to do was keeping moving forward.

One, then two. Breathe.

One, then two. Breathe.

It was just like following a metronome. Tick. Tick. Tick.

'You're up early,' Mum said when I made my way to the coffee machine.

'CAT lady is coming.'

'Ms. Richards,' she corrected.

'Whatever.' I set my coffee cup under the machine and waited for the coffee to fill to the top before stopping it. 'Where's Jelena?'

'She went to Maya's house. She's been relentless about this cartoon date you two have.'

'Yes, she promised me I could watch whatever I wanted,

so it's a pretty big deal.'

'*Little Mermaid*?' Dad asked.

'You know me too well. Though I might change it up this time.'

'Oh, *Anastasia* then?' Mum asked.

I feigned a gasp. Mum shielded a smile as I collected my coffee and took a long sip, enjoying the moment. Then the doorbell rang, and my pulse skyrocketed.

'She's here. We'll be just out there if you need,' Dad said.

'I'm sure I'll be safe with Ms. Richards.'

Before they got up to leave, I stepped forward. 'Mum, Dad.'

Both of them paused by the door.

'I'm really sorry. For everything.'

Dad walked over to me in two long strides and crushed me against his body before I could even take a breath. Then he whispered in my ear low enough for only me to hear, 'Whatever happened, mišu, whatever you're fighting, you aren't alone. Tajo is here.'

Not since I'd turned thirteen had I heard my dad use that word. It was kind of like a made-up, cutesy way of saying dad. I squeezed him harder than I'd ever hugged him before and let myself cry. Whether I told them now or in the future, it didn't matter.

When the doorbell rang again, Dad pulled away.

'Go, it's going to be okay,' he said gently.

When they left me, I remained in my spot for a moment, considering running upstairs and escaping on the downpipes. When it rang for a third time, my thoughts of espionage vanished. Instead, I walked over and let her in.

'Andrea, it's nice to see you up and about.'

'Mostly up, not really about.'

She smiled. 'It'll take time, but you'll get there. I was sorry we had to reschedule our first meeting until now.'

'Sorry I kept ditching.'

'I can understand needing time. I'm glad you've decided to go ahead with meeting with me.'

'Me too,' I lied.

'Tell me about your week. Did you return to school?'

'No.'

She nodded and followed me inside. She sat when I gestured to the couch. I'd chosen this room because it had two doors—both in my line of sight, both very secure and soundproof. The last thing I needed was Mum or Dad overhearing.

For the first few minutes, she observed the living room, noted down something in her book, and then gazed over the many sci-fi films stacked neatly along the TV unit. There were no family pictures, I realised, not like at Daniel's house or Hailey's or even Julian's. I shuddered.

'How have you been feeling since coming home?' she asked.

I shrugged, sipping my coffee, then placed the cup down and looked over at her. 'Still sick but I'm doing okay.'

'You said you didn't return to school yet. Do you want to tell me why?' she asked.

'I went with the intention of going, but I left.'

'Didn't feel well?'

'Emotionally, no.'

'Alone?'

'No, with my friend Daniel.'

'He's someone you can confide in?'

'Yes. The only one. At least in a way where I can be completely open.'

'Why do you think that is?'

'Well...' I considered the answer carefully, wondering how best to frame my response. But then I figured that she wasn't here for an oral presentation; she was here for my feelings, and feelings didn't need to be rehearsed. 'I trust him.'

'You don't trust your family? You don't think you could be open with them?'

'My family have their own issues, Ms. Richards. I don't think I could ever be open with them.'

'And you really don't think your parents want to hear about your concerns?'

'No, they're busy.'

'They're your parents.' She tipped her head to the side.

'And I take care of them more than I think is normal.'

'Is that because you put that pressure on yourself?'

'No,' I muttered. 'It's because that's how it is.'

'How so?'

'How much time have you got?'

'As long as it takes.'

I sighed and looked around the plain living room. 'I was expected to be the best, I was expected to learn three languages, I was expected to ace classes, learn the piano, play tennis, get a job and—' I added dramatically, 'I was expected to fit in, not be an ethnic but also not really an Australian because that would mean disowning my past, which is a no-no, and then there's normal stuff like *boys*...' The last part made me flinch.

'So, you've been under a great deal of pressure?'

'You could say that.'

She noted something down. I tried to crane my neck to make it out, but her handwriting was tiny, neat, and barely big enough to see even if I was right on top of her.

'Have you spoken to your parents about the pressure?'

'Well, they found out I was dropping piano.'

'How did they take it?'

'Mum cried. She made a fuss, but she was happy I spoke to her about it.'

'And were you happy you spoke to her?' she asked.

I suddenly felt conscious that she could see the sweat beading on my forehead. I looked away, shrugging.

'And your father?'

'What about him?'

'Were you happy telling him?'

'I didn't tell him. Mum did.'

'Do you think your dad just wants you to do something great with your life?'

'I know he does.'

She noted something down again. 'And what about the rest of your schooling and grades, how is that going?'

She flipped through her notepad; I saw a glimpse of the school logo on the top of one page and figured it was the current school report. I cringed.

'You've got the report there, you tell me.'

'Is that why you wanted to take your life?'

My eyes snapped up to hers. She didn't seem phased by the question she just asked.

'Andrea?'

'Yes. I was stressed about not getting into uni.'

'Is that really the reason?'

'You don't believe me?'

She took a deep breath and set her notepad down. 'Andrea, I've worked in youth counselling for ten years. It means that I have worked with many people who've experienced many things. It means I can see when something is deeply hurting someone.'

I folded my arms across my chest, pulling the jumper around me as tight as it would go.

'Andrea, I've seen the same look that's on your face before. I've seen your body language before. I know that what you're harbouring is not just school stuff. And I also know that what's hurting you deep inside is not easy to talk about. You must feel afraid and alone, but you aren't, and you need to know that.'

Tears burned in my eyes.

'Andrea?' she said gently. 'It's great that you're talking to your friend, Daniel, and I hope you continue to do so.'

'But?'

'No but. You aren't alone, and somewhere inside, where I'm sure it's hard to find things that make sense right now, your heart knows the truth.'

I didn't know what to say to that.

For another half an hour, Sarah continued to tell me all about the ways the mind and body reacted to trauma and how everything I was feeling, including the chills and fragmented thoughts, was normal. Somewhere, a part of me was relieved.

'I've made an appointment with your school nurse. I'm hoping you will speak to her willingly.'

'I don't really have a choice, do I?'

'Andrea, I'm not going to tell you what to do. I can only suggest what I think might help.'

'I'll think about it'

She smiled. 'I think that's probably enough for today. I'll be back on Thursday morning.'

I walked her to the door, and when she was gone, I slowly made my way back to my room. I sat on the computer chair, bringing both knees to my chest, resting my chin in the 'V' they made. I turned my computer on and opened a folder of photos from last year's camping trip.

A quiet tap on the door drew my eyes up from the screen.

'Can I come in?' Dad asked.

'Yeah.'

He poked his head from around the corner and stood by the door, resting against the wall. He was silent for a few moments, and then he cleared his throat, folding his arms over his chest.

'Can we have a talk?'

'You don't have to walk on eggshells around me, Dad.'

He looked away.

Both of them had been doing it for days. The last time I

saw them like this was when Jelena was born. They thought I'd have a mental breakdown or something. I wasn't far off it, to be honest. I'd been suddenly expected to drop everything for her, and I hated the change.

This situation was a bit different, though, and I realised now that neither of them had been given a magical handbook on this stuff.

'How do you feel?' he asked.

'I actually felt almost eighty per cent human.'

'What's the other twenty?'

'Alien,' I smirked.

He chuckled but then his smile disappeared. 'I don't want you to worry about school right now.'

'Why?'

He sat on the edge of my bed and smiled. 'If you want to go to uni, you will find other ways.'

'Do you think I've already failed?'

'No, mišu, I think I have.'

'Dad…'

'You needed me to support you. You needed your tajo to protect you, to see when you were in trouble. I am sorry I didn't.'

'You're wrong, Tajo. You didn't fail. You're my hero, always have been.'

He tipped his face down, shielding a smile.

I sat beside him and hugged him. We sat like that for a few moments before he looked up at my computer screen and craned his neck.

'What's that?'

I dragged the mouse over and started clicking through with a smile. 'It's Bright.'

'I didn't know you took those photos.'

'I took heaps, filled the whole SD card. I wanted to remember it all.'

'It was a great holiday, wasn't it?'

I chuckled when I found a bunch of photos of Dad and Jelena by the water. Mum had fallen in a rock pool only an hour after these were taken. We'd all laughed before we realised she actually might have been hurt. Luckily, she wasn't but she didn't let us live it down the rest of the trip.

'Remember when Mum fell in the hole?' he asked.

I laughed again.

He slapped my shoulder, snorting through a laugh, 'You know it's rude to laugh. She could have been hurt.'

'Pretty sure she lost a shoe too.'

We both burst out laughing again.

Together, we went through the rest of the album, laughing and teasing each other.

CHAPTER TWENTY

He Said, She Said

'Hey!' Daniel smiled broadly when I got into his car the next morning. 'You look happy.'

'I am,' I smiled, but frowned when I saw the coffee holder was empty.

'I was running late, so I thought we'd stop on the way.'

'Thank God.'

'How was the CAT lady?' he asked, pulling out of my street.

'Fine, she's actually pretty nice.'

He pulled into the drive-thru and waited for the car ahead to place their order.

'She said I should speak to the school nurse,' I added. 'Apparently she's expecting me this morning.'

'Will you?'

'I don't know.'

He glanced across at me but remained quiet until the car ahead of us moved. 'Two flat whites, please, no sugar.'

'Regular?' The girl replied through the scratchy, barely audible speaker.

'Yes, thanks.'

'Drive through, please.'

Once we'd driven out of the drive-thru, coffees in hand, I

immediately sipped mine. There were no expectations or uneasy gaps in conversation to fill. With Daniel, we could sit in complete silence, and I felt safe.

We reached school and Daniel parked at the end of the street.

'Okay, ready?' he said as we got out of the car.

'Yeah.'

I slung my bag over my shoulders, gripping the straps until my fingers grew numb. Every breath felt like dry ice burning through my lungs, every step made my legs feel heavier.

When we reached the grey building bustling with a sea of white and blue, I stopped abruptly and focused on deep breaths. I half expected everyone to come to a screeching halt and stare at me. I expected *it* to be visible to everyone. But nothing seemed to have changed; everyone continued doing what they were before, and I exhaled a breath of relief.

'I'll walk you to the office and then I've got to bail. I have a test first thing for History.'

'You go, I'm fine.'

'Where're you meant to meet the nurse?'

'Coordinator will take me.'

'Yeah cool,' he nodded. 'Sure you're going to be okay?'

'Yes. Go.'

One brow arched up as he looked at me like he didn't believe me at all. Finally, he nodded.

He pressed a kiss to my cheek before leaving. I watched, smiling, as he turned the corner before readjusting my bag and heading for the main building.

Once I reached the coordinators office, I found a corner to stand in and waited. It didn't take long for him to arrive.

'Ah, Miss Nekić, this way,' he said as he met me at the doors. 'I'm glad to see you back at school, and I'm sure your friends and teachers are too.'

I forced a tight smile. I didn't know if Sarah had shared her thoughts about what she imagined happened, but then I stopped my mindless worrying; she wouldn't have shared anything; she was bound to confidentiality.

He nodded to the school nurse's office, which was aptly labelled *Nurse*.

This was the last thing I wanted to be doing today.

The nurse, whom I'd never actually met, opened the door. I was stunned for a moment when I was met by young woman with a warm smile on her face. She wore a simple black skirt and matching blazer with a fun pink shirt. She looked the part for sure and made me feel a pinch of comfort.

'Thank you for coming in, Andrea. I'm glad you decided to see me.'

I wasn't sure whether I was supposed to thank her or just nod, so I did the latter and stood with my arms wrapped around my middle until she gestured for me to come in and sit in the chair opposite hers.

'Sarah gave me the details about your stay at the hospital. I know she's delving a little deeper into that with you, so I won't make you repeat yourself. What I would like to do is be your point of contact at the school, help you here however I can.'

My *stay*. Like I was at some fancy retreat?

'Okay,' I said instead.

She smiled and sat back in her chair. The dim lighting in the room was probably meant to evoke a sense of calm. Instead, I found myself struggling to focus. It was too similar to the lighting in *his* room with the blinds drawn.

Before she even started speaking, I knew I couldn't go through with this. The realisation dawned on me, punching the air from my lungs—I had no leg to stand on, just like in those awful *Law and Order* episodes. It was he said/she said. And no one would believe me when everyone saw us hanging out and flirting.

I shot to my feet, hugging my bag to my chest. 'Thank you for trying to help. Sorry for wasting your time.'

'Andrea?'

It happened.

I knew it did.

I felt the fear and the shame and the ache inside me every time I closed my eyes and tried to sleep. I should have been stronger and spoken up. I should have had the courage to say "no" and not worry about disappointing him.

But I'd been so conditioned to say "yes", to behave, to smile, to do whatever anyone asked of me that I was terrified of having my own opinion or voice and that's exactly what it came down to.

'Andrea?'

'I'm sorry,' I muttered and rushed out of her office.

I stormed through the corridor, ignoring the hushed and sometimes not-so-hushed comments. I knew now, as I walked through the common room, spotting Julian resting lazily against the window ledge at the back, that this wasn't going to go away.

A fallacious voice inside me whispered *you weren't clear. You gave him the wrong idea. You're making him look bad. You're lying.*

Around and around, the voices inside my head continued.

'Andy?' I heard my name out loud but couldn't tell where it was coming from. 'Andy!'

I heard it again but kept walking.

'Andy, wait!'

A hand wrapped around my wrist, and I whipped around, literally knocking whoever off balance, causing them to trip and fall into the lockers behind us.

Startled laughs broke out around us. I couldn't tell which way was left and which was right.

Josh looked up at me, his eyes wide, hands outstretched.

'Andy, I'm sorry. I just wanted to see how you were. You didn't reply to my messages.'

'Don't touch me,' I hissed and continued down the hall.

I didn't care anymore. About any of it. School. Piano. My *friends*.

I was well and truly done with it all.

CHAPTER TWENTY-ONE

New Me

Daniel's eyes locked onto mine from across the busy locker bay. He pushed through the sea of bodies until he finally reached me.

'Hey, Josh messaged me before. He said you freaked out,' Daniel said gently. 'What happened?'

'Nothing.'

'Bullshit,' he challenged. 'What happened? What did the nurse say?'

'Nothing. I didn't stay.'

'Maybe she could have helped?'

'She would have told me it was my fault.'

'You know that's not true—'

'Isn't it?' I stated. 'Because it's all so messy in my head, and I can't tell. Maybe I did give him mixed signals. I mean, I didn't say the word "no", I don't know and I—'

'Stop it. You're hurting. You're going to be having all sorts of thoughts, but you know what happened and how you felt after. You're not imagining that.'

My resolve broke, and tears quickly followed.

I was so sick of crying. My nose was raw from wiping it all the time.

'I'm so confused.'

'I'm sure this is all normal, Andy.'

Maybe he was right… the ache didn't lie. But I could have done more, maybe if I'd been clearer…

'Andrea, listen to me. You're having horrible thoughts about the whole thing, but you are not a liar. I *know* you.'

'Leave it, Daniel.'

'No way.'

'I'm done. I don't care.'

'Well I do…'

'Thank you,' I said, turning to him. 'For believing me. God, sometimes I don't believe myself. I can't believe that this could happen, you know. I don't want to believe that I put myself in such a stupid situation. It's my fault.'

'No. It isn't.'

'I went there. I stayed.'

'He took advantage of you.'

'I kissed him. We were in his bed.'

'I kissed you. We were in your bed. You told me to stop, and I did.'

I closed my mouth, letting the truth of those words settle in my heart. Daniel listened, he asked questions, he'd checked in on me and how I was feeling. Julian… Julian did not.

'Doesn't matter what you did or didn't do. It didn't make it okay for him to do what he did.'

'I want you to know how much I appreciate you, okay,' I said. 'Thank you.'

Daniel looked away and rubbed the back of his neck.

'Don't worry, this isn't a suicide thanks or anything. It's

just an—I don't know, the end of Andrea Nekić as you've known her, thanks.'

~

I walked with my head held high, Josh and Daniel by my side, and we went straight to the back of the classroom and sat.

'Page sixteen, people,' Mr. Benson said as soon as he walked in.

When his back was turned, a small, folded note appeared on top of my diary, and Josh sheepishly looked away.

I'm sorry about before.

I'm sorry. I was in a bad mood. I wrote back.

He gave me a small smile and then returned his attention to the abridged version of the play on his desk.

'Tell me what your take is on the existential crisis Romeo is facing in this chapter.' Mr. Benson looked over his shoulder, searching the faces of the disinterested students while his hand hovered over the board, ready to take notes. 'Andrea?'

'Sorry, haven't read it.'

He baulked, and I could have sworn his left hand twitched on the board. He lowered his hand, smudging the sentence he'd just written. 'That's okay. Take this week to catch up, and then we can work on the deadlines for the assignment when you're done.'

Of course, they'd all have been filled in on my suicide attempt, and of course, they'd all be tiptoeing around me now, hoping they didn't say something that would set me off and send me searching for a pointy object.

I dropped my gaze and zoned out. It was easier than I

cared to admit. I gazed out the window wondering what it would be like to disappear into the clouds, float away with the birds and be weightless, thoughtless and—

'Tomorrow we'll discuss what Juliet could have done differently to avoid—' He cleared his throat, and I could see he was avoiding looking over at me. 'To avoid…'

'To avoid killing herself,' I said firmly. 'You can say it. It's part of the text, isn't it?'

The room went silent despite the bell going off.

No one moved a muscle.

No one said a word.

'Suicide seems to be the word of the year,' someone muttered off to the side.

'McKenny, shut it,' Mr. Benson said.

'It's fine,' I snapped. 'Curious what a bunch of assholes and some nasty words can make a person do? Almost like they have power.' I turned and looked in their direction. They recoiled in their seats.

The trance was broken when Mr. Benson cleared his throat. Everyone finally snapped out of it and filed out.

Mr. Benson stood with his hands on his waist, waiting by his desk.

'Can you hang back for a moment?' he asked.

'We'll wait outside,' Josh said as he slipped past me.

Once Mr. Benson and I were alone, he sat in his chair and folded his hands neatly on the desk.

'The text has already been set for the final exam, but I can work something else out if this is going to be a problem.'

'No, it's fine,' I said. 'Starting something new would be

harder.'

'Alright then.'

I nodded curtly and left.

~

Lunch came, and I met Josh and Daniel first. The outburst in the hall outside the office was forgotten, much to my relief, and lunch felt kind of… normal. While we waited for Hailey to arrive, I kept scanning the oval. Julian was a no-show. Maybe the asshole had gotten the hint.

'How did the talk with Benson go?' Josh asked.

'Fine, I'm probably going to need an extension on *Romeo and Juliet,* though.'

'Damn, you and me both,' he sighed. 'What about you, Danny boy?'

He shrugged. 'I think I passed the History test this morning. And so far, so good on *Romeo and Juliet.*'

'At this point, I'm just happy not to fail,' Josh muttered.

'Yeah, I hear you,' I nodded, squinting up at the sun as I saw Hailey cut across the oval and join us.

'Sorry guys, I had to help Mum at home,' Hailey mumbled between bites of an abnormally large apple.

'Is that why you missed English?' I asked.

'Yep. I had to wait around for her physio to come past. Sorry.'

'It's fine. We were just about to kick some Year Eights off that bench there,' Josh said, nodding towards it.

'Nice one,' Daniel laughed, and the four of us began our journey with determined expressions.

As soon as the Year Eight boys saw us, they got up. Hailey

sat first and I took a spot on the grass in front of her, kicking my shoes and socks off, letting the cool grass weave between my toes.

Daniel sat behind me and pulled me against him, fitting me between his legs. I giggled when he pressed a wet kiss to my cheek.

'You two playing today?' I turned, looking at Daniel.

'Nah, we'll skip.'

'Don't be stupid. Go,' I said sternly.

Before either he or Josh could argue, Hailey threw her huge bag on the bench, stopping Josh from sitting.

'I see how it is,' Josh smirked.

'We're going to be talking about periods and tampons, so you're welcome to stay if you want.'

'No, thank you,' Josh smirked and excused himself. Daniel looked like he wanted to stay but changed his mind when Hailey wiggled her brows at him.

Daniel kissed my other cheek before getting up, leaving me and Hailey alone.

'Good move,' I laughed.

'I know. Always works.'

'How are you feeling now?' she asked.

'Still a bit sick.'

I saw her bite her lip. It meant she had more on the tip of her tongue. It's how all our hard conversations started.

'What do you want to know?' I caught her gaze.

'I'm sorry, I'm being nosy.'

'Hit me, ask whatever you want.'

She got comfortable in front of me. 'What happened to

you? Were you okay? I mean physically… I noticed you always looked sick, and Daniel did too—'

'I took the morning-after pill, so when my period came, it was really bad. It was like the worst period ever.'

'And what about now, after the…'

'Suicide attempt?' I offered.

She nodded, crossing her legs.

'I feel like I'm in that weird state of being half asleep but not able to wake up fully.'

'Like you're not really in your own body.'

'Yeah. I'm just here for the ride. I hate it.'

Her tongue darted out, wetting her bottom lip while she looked off into the distance at the boys kicking the ball on the oval.

'I'm so sorry you've dealt with all of this alone, Andy,' she whispered.

'I'm not alone now.'

'I'm here for you. Always, okay?'

I nodded.

'It's your birthday on Friday. We still on for bowling?'

'I don't think so.'

'It could be good for you.'

'I don't want to. I just want to focus on my license test.'

'Do you think you'll pass?'

'I think so,' I nodded, packing everything up.

When the bell sounded, Hailey and I collected our rubbish and tossed it into the bin on the edge of the oval.

'What have you got now?' Hailey asked.

'Double methods.'

'Gross,' she said, shuddering.

'Yep, all three of us,' Josh sighed, catching up.

'Well, no point hanging back then. I'll see you guys tomorrow. I'm going to head home and try to finish this other painting,' Hailey explained.

We said our goodbyes and parted ways at the boys' and girls' locker bays. Daniel and Josh went left to collect their things while I went right. When I was alone, I felt a sudden unease wash over me.

I quickly collected what I needed from my locker and then rushed to class. Unfortunately, everyone was rushing around like me which meant I was suddenly swarmed by too many people which sent my heart rate skyrocketing. My head was also starting to hurt.

Fishing out the small pack of carefully sectioned-off Panadol—I was only allowed four in a pack—I popped two into my mouth and downed them with some apple juice just as I reached class.

Daniel and Josh waved me over. We seated ourselves at the back again. When Proctor spotted me at the back, his hand stilled over the papers he was leafing through, but he quickly returned his attention to his work.

He got straight into the lesson without asking anyone for any input. Part of me thought it was by design. He was an intuitive man, someone who read between the lines and probably lived through a lot more than most of the other teachers.

I happily got stuck into chapter seventeen and the algebra module.

After the first period ended and we settled into the second half of the double, I found myself losing focus. The letters and numbers in front of me started to blur. The collective sickness, headache and anxiety seemed to have closed my throat, making every movement infinitely harder.

I looked up and stretched my neck out and then flinched when the stabbing pain in my head returned. The sickness came back twofold. I looked over and met Daniel's gaze. His brows were furrowed again.

'You okay?' Daniel mouthed.

'Sick.'

'Want to get some air?'

'No,' I said, closing my eyes for a moment. 'I'll be ok.'

He frowned but dropped it. I returned my gaze to my paper. All I had to do was remain somewhat focused, eyes down and pen moving.

Finally, the bell went. Daniel and I rushed out with the first few people and ditched the locker bay altogether. I didn't want to risk running into Julian or anyone else I didn't want to see.

Thankfully, I had already packed what I needed for tonight, and I could head home immediately. Daniel walked beside me, keeping his hands to himself.

He didn't say anything as we left the school grounds and headed toward his car. Every time I opened my mouth, I felt like I was going to be sick. When I breathed in through my nose, I felt like I couldn't get enough air.

Daniel stayed quiet. And when we pulled into my driveway, I threw the door open and rushed to my house, quickly fishing out my keys.

'Thanks for the lift,' I called back.

'Oh,' he said. 'I thought we were hanging out.'

I turned around as he reached the step, stepping back as he got closer. 'I just want to be alone right now. I need space and just...'

He stopped, rubbing the back of his neck. 'You're being serious right now, aren't you?'

'Yes.'

'Andy, I don't want to annoy you. I just don't want you to be alone.'

'I'm not going to do anything stupid, Daniel.'

'It's not about that.'

'Then what is it about?'

'I want to be here with you.' He paused. 'I just want to help.'

'Then help me by going home. Please.'

His eyes fell on the space between our feet.

'I just need space. Okay?' I said. 'You've been really nice, and kind, but it's a lot.'

'A lot?'

'I feel...' I paused, searching for the right words. 'I feel suffocated, okay?'

'Oh.'

'I'm sorry, it's just me,' I said, then added quickly, 'You're amazing, but I just need some Andrea time, just to try and find myself again. Please?'

'Okay,' he agreed. 'I'll see you in the morning, then.'

'Yeah, you will.' I smiled and waited until he was gone

before going inside.

Jelena was seated at the bench with a giant bowl of cereal.

'Why are you eating that?'

She shrugged.

'We playing or what?'

Her face broke into a smile, a dribble of milk escaping the corner of her mouth, making me burst out laughing. 'You're so gross. Come on.'

She hooked up two guitars, fed the game into the drive and handed one to me. When the first song started, I found my mind slipping and disappearing from the living room and travelling all the way back to Julian's little brother. Julian had suggested we play together.

I felt sick.

'Hey, Andy?'

'Yeah?'

'Did something bad happen?' she asked keeping her eyes ahead on the chords racing across the screen, hitting each note perfectly.

'Yeah,' I said softly.

She continued playing. I wondered whether she might decide to take up guitar instead of piano.

'Did you go to the police?'

'No.'

'Why not?'

'Because I'm scared.'

'I was scared when you were in the hospital.' She gave a little shake of her head and kept hitting the notes. She was focused and with nerves of steel.

But I heard the wavering in her voice.

'I'm really sorry,' I said.

'Don't do that again, okay?'

'Okay,' I said, mashing the keys on the guitar, not really seeing anything on the screen in front of me. 'I promise.'

And it was the complete and honest to God truth. I would never let her down again.

CHAPTER TWENTY-TWO

Many Ways to Say NO

Sarah sat in the same spot she did the last time she was here. I handed her a coffee and sat.

'Do you want to talk about it?'

'I'm not completely against it today.'

She smirked when I shielded a smile. 'Good, it's progress. Told you I'm alright when you get to know me.'

'Look, I wouldn't go that far.'

'Ah, I see the sense of humour is coming back.' She raised her eyebrow.

'Only just.'

She took a sip of coffee while I downed half my cup in one go, then opened her notepad and turned her attention to me. 'What are you feeling?'

'Lost,' I said honestly, meeting her gaze across the room. 'I feel like I'm not in my own body. I feel like none of that happened to me. I feel like I'm watching from the outside.'

She leaned back in her chair, tapping her fingertips across her notepad. 'Dissociation can be a way of protecting ourselves. When you've gone through something as stressful as you have, it can be a form of escape, to protect your mind.'

'It kind of felt like that then too. With him.'

She nodded slowly. 'Did you feel like you weren't there?'

'Yeah. It was like my brain shut down. I felt it all, obviously. But it felt like it wasn't really me. I didn't even try to fight or scream or anything... I don't... I don't understand.'

'Andrea, going through something like you have is very challenging and traumatic. We don't always respond in the way we think we might. Sometimes we freeze, sometimes we run, but sometimes we pretend like everything is okay and we just go with the flow until the conflict is over. Does that sound like something you've experienced?'

I nodded.

She smiled again. 'None of what happened to you is your fault.'

My eyes welled. 'I try to tell myself that.'

'Did you speak with the school nurse?'

'No.'

'Why is that?'

'I was scared she'd tell me I should have done more, that it was my fault.'

'Do you really believe that?'

'I don't know what I believe.'

'I believe that you experienced something that hurt you deeply.'

'When I close my eyes, I see it all. But it's different every time. Small details change, but the end result is still the same.'

'That can be very normal too, Andrea. We often hear of people recalling new details years after the fact: a smell, a sound, or something completely out of the blue can trigger it.

Even decades later.'

'What if I'm overreacting… what if it really wasn't that bad or…?'

'You walked out of there not liking what happened, not feeling like it was something you'd consented to, right?'

'Yes.'

'Then it shouldn't have happened.'

'But I wasn't clear enough.'

'Andrea, there's one thing I can tell you with absolute certainty; regardless of whether you whispered no or pushed him back or turned your face from a kiss without telling him to stop, if you didn't want it and it happened, it's not okay.'

'I flirted with him. People saw. He said he liked me too.'

'If he truly cared about your feelings, he would have made every effort to make sure you were on board. He would have checked in with you, read your verbal and non-verbal cues.'

'I was in his bed.'

'If you didn't want to take things further, you could have been naked on top of him, and he still shouldn't have done anything without your consent.'

'I never actually said the word "no".'

'It's going to take a while for you to learn to forgive yourself and accept what I'm telling you. But the most important thing you need to know is that what happened was not your fault. There are other ways we can say no. If it wasn't abundantly clear to him that you were or were not consenting, regardless of the words spoken, he shouldn't have continued.'

'He said really nice things to me. He was really sweet.'

'Did you feel like you *had* to continue?'

I nodded feeling hot tears burn through me. The fresh shame made my whole body erupt in cold flushes. 'I didn't say no. Or tell him to stop.'

'Andrea. That doesn't mean you wanted to continue. Do you understand?'

I shrugged, cradling my cup between my knees.

'I'm done with feeling like a worthless piece of garbage.'

She gave me a tight smile. 'Good, use that energy.'

'I want to get past this. I want you to help me.'

'I can do that.'

I relaxed, dropping my shoulders. 'How?'

'Let's start with getting you to a point where you're comfortable with finishing this school year. Breathing exercises, knowing your triggers, knowing how to react. Now, tell me about school, Daniel, and what you're looking forward to.'

'Looking forward to?' I baulked. 'I don't think I know what that means.'

She laughed and placed her cup on the table, 'There has to be something?'

'Maybe. I don't know.'

'What about spending time with Daniel?'

'I shut him out yesterday.'

'Why did you do that?'

'Because he was getting too close.'

'Physically?' she asked gently.

'No, God no. But even just talking, being together, it was too much.'

'Your trust was betrayed in the worst way possible, and it's understandable that you'd be cautious of any contact, whether it be physical or emotional.'

'I don't want to shut him out, though,' I explained.

'I know, but this will take time. You have to allow yourself the time.'

I groaned. 'Can we hurry it up somehow?'

'Unfortunately, there's no magic button that can do that,' she chuckled.

'It's my birthday tomorrow,' I blurted out.

Her eyes softened. 'Are you doing anything special, eighteen, right?'

'No. I'm not feeling in the partying mood.'

'What about a quiet dinner with your family?'

I shrugged. 'There's a party next weekend.'

'What do you think going to the party will help you do?'

'Start acting normal.'

'Ah, normal is a loaded word, Andrea.'

'Yeah, I know.'

'I'm glad. But if the party is something that will help you start feeling more like you, then I think that's a great idea. What about school?'

'School is school. I don't have the drive anymore, I don't think I'll get it back.'

'How do you feel about that?'

'Angry, sad. I was succeeding. I had plans, I was going to go to uni, knew what course I was going to do.' I looked up at her through the wetness in my lashes. 'And now, well, now I can't do that anymore.'

'Maybe not right now, maybe not next year, but if you want it badly enough, you will achieve everything you set out to do.'

'I get that. Doesn't make it hurt any less.'

She nodded. 'Being smart enough to understand all of this is a burden in itself. But you will pick up the pieces. You will make Plan B, C and D work.'

I looked down at my cold coffee. 'I shouldn't have to rearrange my whole life. I shouldn't have to make other plans and pick up the pieces while he gets to live his life like nothing happened.'

'No, you shouldn't, and you're right. None of this is fair.'

A tear slipped out onto my cheek and my throat tightened. 'I wonder if his friends are the same.'

'What do you mean?'

I shrugged. 'They all seem nice... like he did. I just wonder if they're like him too.'

'You know I can't answer that for you.'

'Yeah,' I mused. 'Anyway, it doesn't matter. It wouldn't change anything. I just hope if they're not, they'll see through his bullshit someday.'

'If they're not, then I'm sure they will.'

After a long pause, I hung my head, sighing.

'As hard as this is to hear now, Andrea, you have to *want* to accept that there will be dark days, months and years ahead, but if you allow this to consume you forever, you won't do any of the things you want to do. And that is when you will truly fail.'

I looked up at her. 'I hate him.'

'You're allowed to.'

Before she could say anything else, I decided there and then, 'I'm going to finish school. I'm going to do it on my terms, with my head held high.'

'I know you will. You don't know how to fail.'

~

When I put my cup away, I jogged upstairs, pulled my cupboard open, and found my hiking boots. I dressed, adjusted my favourite snowflake socks, and made my way downstairs in search of Dad. He was seated on the couch watching a replay of some basketball game I knew nothing about. He craned his neck when I peeked my head around the corner.

His eyes followed my hands, and when I jiggled the container of snacks, his face broke into a smile.

'Come on, it's perfect outside.'

'Give me ten minutes to get dressed.'

'I'll be outside.'

I packed a few more things and went outside to wait by the car.

Dad unlocked the doors. I jumped in and immediately dove into the CD wallet. He didn't say anything, but the smile adorning his face said it all.

I fed a Fleetwood Mac CD into the player and sat back, enjoying this normal and peaceful moment.

Andrea Nekić was making a comeback.

CHAPTER TWENTY-THREE

To Party or Not to Party

The next day, I felt refreshed. Alive. More so than I had in months. I didn't even have any bad dreams, and I couldn't wait to start the day. I picked up my phone and found Daniel's name.

I was mean. I'm sorry. Come over?

I set it on the table and quickly styled my hair into a low messy bun. Neat, like the old me, but not quite.

My phone vibrated.

Can't get rid of me that easily. I'll pick u up in 10.

And before I could put the phone down, another message came through from him.

Happy Birthday, beautiful Andy.

I grinned and jogged down the stairs, drank a glass of juice and locked up. Mum and Dad had another early day, and it would be another late night. Mum had left a note on the bench telling me to order pizza and check in on Jelena. She was at her friend's house again.

'Nekić!' Daniel yelled out the window. 'Looking more like yourself.'

'So are you!' I grinned, noticing the black eye.

'The game was bullshit, don't get me started.'

'Good thing you don't play any games where winning is the point.'

'Ouch, that one hurt.'

I laughed and got in. He waited for me to buckle up then handed me a cup of coffee.

'Happy birthday. You're a real girl now.'

'You're a loser.'

'You're the one who punctuates text messages.'

I smirked. 'Not the insult you hoped it would be.'

He laughed. 'Getting your license today?'

'Sure am.'

'We should send out a warning to the drivers of Victoria.'

'Keep talking, I dare you.'

He grinned but kept his eyes ahead.

'I'm really sorry about the other day.'

'You don't have to apologise to me, you know that.'

'So, I was thinking maybe you could come over and have pizza with me tonight.' I fiddled with the cuff of my sleeve. 'Mum and Dad told me to get pizza, so I'm not alone on my birthday like a loser. But you know—I mean we don't have to get that, there's Maccas or...' I looked up and flushed. 'I'm rambling, I'm sorry.'

'I'll be there.'

'Good.' I exhaled and buried my face behind the giant cup.

'We'll celebrate tonight.'

'We don't need to celebrate.'

'Not celebrate your eighteenth?' His brows shot into his hairline. 'Yeah, not happening.'

'Fine.'

He looked over at me a couple of times and then back at the road. He didn't say anything but gripped the wheel in a death grip.

Now it was starting to make sense to me. Suicide doesn't just affect the person ending their life; it affects everyone around us to varying degrees. No one said anything but it was obvious in the faraway looks or silent moments when the small talk ceased. It was in the way Dad barely made eye contact with me, or in the way Mum averted her gaze whenever she caught a glimpse of my sickly thin body. And the way Daniel's hands were perpetually tensed, like this burden of mine had woven its way around his core, hardening him from inside. He'd carried the weight of it too.

'I'm okay, Daniel,' I said, turning toward him. 'I promise, I'm okay.'

The smile he gave me was so forced it actually hurt to look at.

'Stop the car,' I whispered.

He looked over, frowning.

'Stop the car, Daniel.'

At the next street, he pulled over and turned to me. He opened his mouth as if he was about to say something but that inner voice that told me to do something kicked in. I leaned over the console and cupped my hand over his cheek. Then I kissed him.

His entire body froze.

For a minute, I felt like a complete moron.

Maybe he didn't like me like that anymore. Maybe he'd

moved on. Maybe all of this was just because he felt
obligated or—

He pulled away, and my heart kind of fell to pieces.

'I'm sorry, that was—'

'Stop talking, Andy. You're about to ruin the moment,'
he said, bringing his hand to my cheek, gently sweeping my
hair behind my ear.

His eyes found mine, and at that moment, I knew he meant
all the things he'd said to me. I felt it in the patience of his
touch; there was no urgency, nothing that made me think he
was saying all the right things because he expected
something in return.

That was the difference between him and Julian. He was
a man, and Julian was just a boy.

'You're so strong, Andrea Nekić, and you don't even
know it.'

Tears sprung to my eyes, kind of ruining the moment, but
he wiped them with his thumb before leaning over and
kissing me.

When he pulled back, he lowered his forehead to mine and
let out a low breath. 'It kills me knowing how much you've
been hurt, but I will do whatever it takes to prove to you I am
a man who will love and care for you.'

'Did you just say *love,* Daniel?'

'I did,' he said, deadpan. 'Don't repeat it, or I'll kill you.'

'No way you're getting out of it that easily.'

'Fine,' he grinned. 'You may repeat it.'

'You love me.'

'I do.'

Eighteen-year-old boys didn't dish that word out—maybe for a soccer player or whatever—but they barely even said the words *dating* or *girlfriend* because it was all too serious and quick. I knew then that Daniel never was one of them, and I was a complete idiot for ever thinking he was.

'I don't deserve you,' I said, turning away from him.

'Come on, don't say that.'

'I don't. I thought you'd rejected me after that night at my house.'

'I can't speak for what you thought, but I can speak for the fact that I should have tried harder to tell you how I felt. Maybe if I had you wouldn't have—'

'Don't do that. It wasn't your fault. I went there, I made that choice, and I paid for it.'

'Fuck,' he ground out, twisting his fingers through my hair. 'I want to hurt him so badly, Andrea, it scares me sometimes.'

'I think about it too,' I whispered, searching his eyes. 'I think about all the ways I could make him pay, tell the whole world, break him like he broke me.'

His jaw set into a hard line when he spoke. 'You're not broken.'

'My diary full of psychiatric appointments and house cleared out of sharp objects would say otherwise.'

'Your parents are worried about you.'

A deep crease cut across his brow just beneath the dark strands of hair that fell across his face. My heart stalled in my chest when he brought his hand to my cheek again in a single touch, making me feel safe.

This wasn't real life. It couldn't be.

Fairytales didn't happen. Or, if they did, I wasn't the main character I always imagined I was. Instead of being the princess, I was the witch. I'd already resigned myself to the stone cottage deep outside the dark woods, a lonely, untouched and barren place where no living creature dared wander because, if it did, the plague of my curse would suck them in and disintegrate their soul in a matter of seconds.

But maybe I wasn't the witch. Maybe I was the knight who rode into the forest to kill her.

'Where did you go just then?' he asked, tilting his head to find my gaze.

'Nowhere. I'm right here.'

'Good, don't you disappear on me. I'd be lost without you.'

'Only until Josh comes to save the day.'

'Well, you can't break up a good bromance.'

'No, no, you can't.'

Daniel pressed another featherlight kiss to my lips before he buckled back up, shifting the car into drive, and headed for school.

My phone vibrated.

I will pick you up at ten for your test! A message from Mum came through.

Can't wait. I replied.

I tucked my phone back in the backpack and smiled across at Daniel. Nothing could ruin today.

~

Mum and I stood outside the school after she'd let me drive

back with my brand-new P's. I hadn't stopped smiling the entire drive—even more so when I looked at the plastic card with my name and picture. I was so going to drive everywhere now.

When she drove off, I felt elated. I made my way through the gate and towards my class. When I reached it and saw that a note was stuck in the window, I groaned.

The day was, in fact, ruined.

Julian's History class has been cancelled, and in somebody's smart opinion, they decided that combining their class with mine was a good idea.

I walked into the rowdy classroom, slipped into the back, and sat. Julian noticed me, though. I could feel his eyes on me from the desk at the end of my row. People were talking, making jokes about something the teacher was writing on the board. The teacher was in on it, too.

All I wanted was some order, but it wasn't going to happen, as they all continued talking about something I couldn't make out thanks to the roaring of blood pumping through my ears. I turned my gaze down and focused on my hands.

I just had to make it through the next hour, and then this would be over.

A chair off to my left screeched, not loud enough to be noticeable but well and truly enough for me to hear. Oh God. Not him. Please, let it be anyone but him.

He sat himself down on the chair in front of mine and turned his whole body to face me.

All the hairs on the back of my neck stood on end. I could

feel the heat rising from underneath my collar up to my face. The churning of panic inside me threatened to erupt in a catastrophic display of vomit.

'You haven't spoken to me for months,' he said quietly. His voice made every nerve fire. I couldn't look up at him.

My hand trembled and I dropped the pen.

'When you came over, I thought you wanted to hang out,' he shifted again, making me flinch. 'You were into it. I mean, we were in my bed together. You said you wanted me to be your boyfriend.'

He couldn't be serious. I contained myself enough to lift my gaze and look at him. The second my eyes met his, my pulse skyrocketed making the blood rushing through my head unbearably loud. All I could see was the way he looked down on me when he was…

He reached out and grazed his fingers over my arm. I jerked back so quickly that the chair fell over, making a loud, ungodly noise that drew everyone's eyes over to me.

I couldn't think, I couldn't see, I couldn't… oh God, I couldn't breathe.

He stood. I thought he would step closer; I thought he would touch me, and I lost it. I shoved him so hard that he fell backwards over the table and crashed into the floor with a loud thump.

For a painfully silent second, the entire class remained motionless until Julian let out a stunned laugh.

'Crazy emo bitch!' Jess shouted, rushing over to him.

I snatched up my things and stormed out of the classroom. I heard steps rushing out after me. I slowed, thinking that it was the teacher but then when I turned and saw that it was Julian, I stepped backwards on shaky legs.

'Don't come closer,' I managed.

He didn't listen then. Why did I think he would now?

He stepped towards me and my entire body started to tremble. Tears poured out relentlessly. I didn't want to do this in front of him. I didn't want him to see how much he'd fractured me.

'If it was so bad, Andy, why didn't you say anything?'

I couldn't form a sentence that would have made any sense at this point. I couldn't even move. But I needed to. I needed to get myself out of here. Screw waiting around for the conflict to end. I needed to fight or run.

He took another step closer, and I felt my heart slam into my ribs. 'Why didn't you stop me? Why didn't you leave?' he challenged.

His voice was commanding, confident. It was the same tone he used when he told me he knew how to frame things the way he wanted them to be seen. Acid rose and licked the back of my throat.

'Are you acting like this because I cheated on you?' he asked coolly. 'Because you know, I didn't think you and I were going to work out and then you stopped replying to my messages anyway.'

Thankfully, the teacher seemed to have regained control of the class because he was striding down the hall toward us.

'Andrea Nekić!' he called over, saving me from this hellish conversation.

'It's okay, Mr. Garrison. Andy and I had a

misunderstanding. She was within her rights to knock me on my ass.'

I ground my jaw. A *misunderstanding?* The same kind he had with Elle Smith? I was going to be sick.

Mr. Garrison looked over at the two of us. 'My office now!' He ignored Julian and jerked his head to the office at the end of the hall.

Without taking my eyes off Julian, I picked up my bag and followed Mr. Garrison. I felt Julian's gaze on me until I was hidden behind the door.

'What was that?' Garrison said, closing the door behind him.

When he rounded the small desk in the room, walking too close to me, I jerked back, stumbling over the table leg. His hand shot out to steady me but as I pulled back and lost balance, I hit the ground hard. With a gasp, I backed into the corner.

'Holy hell, Andrea. Are you alright?'

Instead of Garrison's face hovering above me, it was Julian's all over again, and instead of a caring gesture to help me up, it was Julian's grip.

I held my hands up. I couldn't think around the fear roaring through my head or make sense of what was happening. The sounds around me clashed and collided. And then, I threw up. All over the carpet tile.

I heard a rapid intake of breath and my own racing pulse in my head. I couldn't snap myself out of it. I was stuck there, in *his* bed, with his hands on my body and smell of sweat and…

The familiar click of a handset being picked up jolted me to the office. Garrison's back was turned to me.

'Please don't call anyone,' I whispered.

His hand stilled as he turned his face to me. When I shook my head, he lowered the phone and opened a rickety drawer, retrieving a giant roll of paper towel and a plastic bag. He walked around the desk, kneeling in front of me, keeping a large gap between us as he started covering up the vomit on the floor.

'You need to tell me what happened, Andrea. I know you're a smart girl, and you know that I have to take everything seriously in my class, especially when one student assaults another.'

I laughed. I *actually* laughed. I didn't mean to, but it just came out. He didn't do anything; he didn't even tell me off. He did run a hand over his jaw and then exhale.

'Andrea, did Julian Valesco hurt you?'

His hand moved a little closer to get the last of the mess and every muscle locked inside my body making me freeze.

'Andrea?' he repeated, leaving the bag off to the side. 'Did he hurt you?'

'No,' I lied.

'Andrea.'

'I just want to finish Year Twelve.'

'Have you reported this?'

'There's nothing to report.'

'Jesus, give me strength,' he sighed, and looked up to the ceiling.

When he looked back down at me, he held his hand out.

Reluctantly, I took it and sat in the chair on the other side of his desk. He pulled out a wad of tissues and handed them to me.

'I have a daughter your age.'

My eyes landed on the framed picture on the side of his large desk. She was beautiful, with vibrant blue eyes and a pretty smile. She definitely looked smarter than me.

I bet she wouldn't fall for some stupid cheesy lines and a cosy snuggle in bed.

'I know these years are rough on you kids. I know all sorts of things go on in the schoolyard behind closed doors and at parties. But you have a right to feel safe.'

I scoffed.

'Can I do anything?' he asked when I remained silent.

'No.'

Before he said anything else, a knock on the door drew his attention.

'One second,' he said before he walked over to the door and cracked it slightly.

'Class is getting rowdy,' a voice said. I couldn't make out who it was.

'Tell the class to do some silent reading. I'll be there in a minute.'

'Okay, sir,' the voice mumbled, but I didn't hear them leave. 'Is Andrea okay?'

'She'll be fine, thank you Kayla,' he said softly and then closed the door.

I released a long breath and took a handful of tissues out of the box on the table.

'Have you spoken to anyone?' he asked.

'There's nothing to speak about.'

'Oh Andrea,' he rested his elbows on the desk, steepling his fingers in front of his face.

Garrison was one of those teachers you constantly questioned, not because he was weird or creepy but because he was so normal, so nice. He cared about his job and his students, and by the dozen or so framed pictures of his daughter and wife, I imagined that respect and care went beyond these walls.

'Can I call someone for you from the school? A friend?'

'Yes please.'

He nodded and gave me a tight smile. 'Name?'

'Daniel Mitrea, 12B.'

He picked up the phone and dialled. 'Yes, could you please tell Daniel to pack his things up for the day and come to my office.'

When he hung up, he folded his hands across his desk, his eyes coasting over his daughter's face before landing back on mine. *Stark contrast*, I thought. I felt ugly inside and out, so completely undone it was a wonder how I managed to exist and not just shrivel away into nothingness. So much for thinking I was on road to being me again.

'Andrea, I do have to ask.'

'Ask,' I sighed.

'Did Julian say anything to you in class to provoke you?'

'He was just being a dick.'

He kept a straight, professional face, but I saw him clench his fist and then grind his jaw when he looked away from me.

'Are you going to give me detention?'

'No, Andrea.' He shook his head. 'I think you've been through enough.'

Relaxing slightly, I leaned back in the chair and looked down at my hands. A few moments of silence passed before a knock on the door made my heart leap into my throat.

'Come in,' Garrison said.

The door slowly opened, and Daniel's eyes landed on me, then the mess of paper towels on the floor, then Garrison's serious expression.

'Please,' Garrison gestured to the chair.

Daniel pulled the chair beside me and sat.

'What's going on?' he asked looking from my face to Garrison's.

'There was an incident in my class, and Ms. Nekić asked to see you.'

'What happened?' he shot off.

'Julian provoked her, and she pushed him.'

'Did you break his fucking face?' he asked. 'Because I really hope you did.'

'Language, Mr. Mitrea, and no, fortunately.'

'Fortunately? That piece of shit—'

'Stop talking,' I snapped.

Daniel's eyes shot to mine.

Garrison wasn't an idiot. I'm sure he would have worked it out for himself, but I absolutely couldn't afford anyone knowing who had the power to contact the authorities. Once any of the teachers knew, they'd have to take this further, and it was the last thing I wanted.

'Mr. Mitrea, I called you here because I don't want Andrea to be alone right now.'

'Fuck me,' Daniel exhaled, ignoring the warning about language.

'I want you both to stay in here until school is finished. Is that clear?' Garrison added.

'Yes sir,' we both said.

'Good.'

He walked out, slammed the door shut, leaving me and Daniel in complete silence.

Daniel broke the silence. 'Are you okay? What did he say?'

'Said he didn't know I wasn't into it.' I lifted my head, finding the courage to look into his eyes. 'Asked why I stayed if it was so bad.'

Daniel's expression broke me. He ground his jaw and looked away.

'Some birthday,' I muttered.

Daniel bowed his head, taking my hand. We sat for the next half hour until the bell went. Even then, we stayed behind just to make sure that everyone was gone. We could deal with the fallout next week. Today, I just wanted to get out of here.

'I think we're good to go,' he said.

'I have to drop some stuff off at my locker.'

When we reached the bay, I stopped abruptly causing Daniel to plough into me.

'What the fuck?' he stormed forward, pushing past me.

My legs remained rooted to the ground.

Someone had used a giant sharpie to write *"kill yourself"* on my locker.

Daniel looked back at me, probably expecting me to cry, or break down, or do something other than stand completely motionless.

'Jesus.' He looked back at the locker. 'This is messed up, Andy, really fucking messed up. I'll get this cleaned up before Monday.'

'Don't worry about it.'

'We can't just leave it.'

'Sure we can.'

'This is wrong.'

'I'm tired. I don't want to play their stupid game anymore. This is pathetic and childish. You know it. I know it. I'm not giving in.'

'Okay, I get it.'

'Can we just go?'

He turned me from the locker and kept his arm around my shoulder as he led me out through the door.

CHAPTER TWENTY-FOUR

The Champion

'What do you want?' I called over from the kitchen while I waited on hold with the pizza shop.

'Aussie!'

'Yuck,' I muttered to myself as I scanned the menu.

'Aussie Boys Pizza, what can I get you?'

'Hi, can I place an order for delivery?'

'Sure, what can I get you?'

I panicked and chose the first thing I saw. 'Large Aussie and a large Margarita.'

'No worries, eighteen dollars and fifty cents. They should be there within the hour.'

'Thanks.'

I grabbed a beer from the fridge and brought one over to Daniel.

'Let's go to my room. We have blankets and pillows up there,' I said.

He nodded, following behind me. Together, we sat on my bed, scooted all the way until our backs were against the wall, and I turned the TV on. I was officially allowed to drink alcohol without my parents losing it. I grinned as I cradled the bottle in my hand. Small victories.

'Keen to drive?' he asked me with a grin.

'So keen. Obviously, I'll have to take Mum or Dad's car.'

'Where do you want to drive first?'

'Probably the mountains.'

'Yeah, cool,' he grinned, bumping his shoulder into mine. 'Where's your sister tonight?'

'Maya's again.'

Maya was the younger sister of a guy Daniel used to play football with years back. Occasionally, our old lives crossed paths and reminded me just how small the world really was. A part of me panicked at the prospect. What if I left here and ended up seeing Julian again? I didn't think I could deal with that now. There were too many what-ifs.

'UFOs again?' Daniel asked, bringing me back to the safety of my room.

'Not if you have something better?'

He chuckled and took the beer. 'You're so mean to me.'

'I know, I'm sorry.'

'I'm not,' he shrugged, snatching the remote from me. 'Just means it gives me leverage against you and your UFO shows later.'

I laughed and draped a blanket over myself. I probably should have put warmer clothes on, but the cute skirt I chose was too nice to banish to my wardrobe, and I wanted Daniel to see me in it. He didn't make any comments, and I wondered whether he thought I was being silly trying to dress pretty for him. But I wanted to for me because it was my choice to do this.

Daniel was completely oblivious, or maybe he wasn't.

Maybe he knew exactly how comfortable he made me but didn't want to draw attention to it. I kind of figured that was the case when he looked over at me, smiled, and turned back to the TV.

He scrolled through the menu and found a documentary I hadn't seen yet.

'Honestly, you don't have to put that on,' I said.

'I like it.'

'No, you don't,' I reminded him. 'But I appreciate it.'

His gaze lowered and his expression became more serious: a small frown, a tightening of his jaw. He turned the volume down and set his beer on the side table, turning his body so that we were face to face.

'Can I ask you something personal?' Daniel asked.

'I'm sure you know all the personal things there are to know about me, Daniel.'

'Maybe. You're right. I'm sorry.'

'I'm kidding. Ask me whatever you want.'

For a moment, he didn't say anything, but then he wet his lips and drew in a sharp breath.

'Spit it out. You're making me nervous waiting.'

'Were you a virgin before you went to his house?'

Shame heated my cheeks making my whole body feel uncomfortably warm. I drew my knees to my chest under the blanket and nodded.

Daniel let out a rapid chain of expletives under his breath.

'I'm so sorry, Andy.'

'Yeah, me too,' I said, chewing my bottom lip.

'Hailey said you looked sick for a long time.' He

scratched his head.

'You spoke to Hailey?'

'When you and I weren't talking. I asked her how you were doing almost every day. I think she suspected something, but she never said. Just told me you were sick.'

'You were checking up on me?'

'Always,' he sighed. 'Though it clearly didn't mean shit, you were still hurt and alone.'

'You were hurting too, Daniel.'

'I was being stupid.'

'A lot of stupid going around this year.'

He laughed harshly, the sound came out choked and rough, before running his hand over his face.

'Did he use a condom?'

'No. I took the morning-after pill.'

'Fuck.'

'Yep. He actually suggested it. Can you believe that? I wasn't even thinking. I probably would have just gone home and—' I couldn't even finish the sentence. 'That's why I was sick for a long time. The pill was awful.'

Daniel hunched his shoulders, shaking his head and releasing a long breath. When he looked up at me, his jaw was set in a hard line again.

'Are you okay now?'

'Guess so, period seems to be back to normal.'

He was silent again for a moment then he scooted closer to me, taking my hand. I held my breath as he carefully pulled my sleeve up. The bandage was gone, but there was a raised, angry-looking scab there now.

'I should've known something bad happened when I saw this. Should've stayed with you…'

'I threw you out of my house. You had no choice.'

'Doesn't make it better.'

'Daniel,' I nudged his shoulder with mine. 'You need to stop blaming yourself.'

He bolted upright like something incredibly urgent was on his mind.

'I want you to keep your phone with you and if he comes to talk to you, you message me, okay?'

'What? No. I'm not going to do that, Daniel.'

'Why?' he frowned. 'Because you don't need my help?'

'No, because I don't want you to get in trouble.'

'You know I don't care about that.'

'I know you don't, but I do. I will not be responsible for you missing out on the uni you want because you risked it for me. Just because my life is over, doesn't mean yours has to be.'

'Your life is not over.'

'Kind of feels like it is,' I said with a huff. 'I don't really know who I am anymore, you know? I look in the mirror, and I don't see me. I see hollow cheeks, red eyes, sadness…'

'I don't see any of that.'

'Oh really? Maybe you need to get your eyes checked.'

He cracked a smile. 'Got twenty/twenty vision. Actually, had an eye test last week. Mum dragged me there, they said—'

'Smart ass.'

'Smart definitely, ass—no.'

I shook my head, shielding a smile.

'In all seriousness, though, I see a beautiful, brave girl who doesn't even know how strong she is.'

'And do you see beyond Year Twelve? Do you see what my future holds?'

'I do. I see a smile on your face every day because you've beaten this shithole. You've come out on top, stronger than ever, with a degree in one hand and some kind of writing award in the other because I have no idea what writers actually win. And I see a woman who will be the champion of other women who've been silenced.'

Every single word was like aloe on burning flesh, soothing and healing, undoing a world of damage, sealing in the cracks that were left behind.

'You are not a normal Year Twelve guy, you know that?'

'I hope there's a compliment in there somewhere.'

'That is the compliment, smartass.'

I didn't let my overthinking brain stop me as I climbed into his lap. I didn't let it control me when I sat with my knees on either side of his hips or when I kissed him and thrust my fingers through his hair.

I didn't think when he kissed me back and brought both hands to my cheeks and held me, conveying how tomorrow and the rest of our lives would be better, how I would survive, how I would make it out and never look back.

He slipped his hand under the hem of my t-shirt, and his fingertips grazed my skin. I drew in a sharp breath and pulled back.

'Hey,' he whispered, dropping his hands to my hips. 'We

can stop everything right now. You just say the word.'

My heart slammed against my ribcage. Daniel stayed still beneath me, hands gently resting on my hips, waiting patiently. Shallow, rapid breaths made his chest rise and fall. Was he nervous?

'Andy, do you want to stop?'

I shook my head, biting my bottom lip as I slowly pulled my top off and watched as his eyes took me in.

'We don't have to do this,' he whispered.

'I want to.' I leaned in and kissed him again.

When he pulled back, he tipped my chin down, so we were eye to eye.

'Are you sure?'

'I want this with you. I want this to be my first time.'

A small frown appeared on his face. But when I leaned in and kissed him again, he wrapped his arms around me. He lifted me up and then gently laid me down on the bed, his elbow depressing the cushion beside my head.

'Is this okay?' he asked, brushing his lips across my cheek when my eyes squeezed shut.

'Yes.'

'Andrea.' My name was a whisper. 'Look at me.'

My eyes fluttered open. Daniel's head was tipped to the side, his lips parted slightly. I reached up and closed my hand over his cheek.

'Andy?'

'It's okay, I'm good.'

'You sure? This is too fast, maybe we should—'

'Kiss me.'

'Andy...'

'Daniel, kiss me.'

His soft lips landed on mine, and I felt my heart racing like it was trying to escape my chest. Every touch left a fiery trail in its wake, every deepened kiss set fire to the parts of me I thought were dead, and when his free hand trailed along the sensitive skin along my rib cage, I felt a new flame ignite within me, one that I was certain would never come back.

He carefully slid my skirt off, and I helped him out of his jeans and then his top, and finally, when we were naked, I felt every tiny piece of confusion and pain and fear and sadness leave me. The only thing left was hope, and I could see it clearly now.

This is what the first time should have been like. It was meant to be like floating on clouds, being nervous about the choice of daggy underwear or what your hands were doing, not filled with fear. Not pleading that it would be over soon.

'Condom?' he breathed. 'I don't have one, I mean I didn't think—'

'I have one in my bag.' My cheeks flushed.

His brows shot up, and a smile quickly pulled on the corner of his lips.

He disappeared for a moment, and when he came back, he gently lowered himself over my body and kissed me again.

I closed my eyes, listening to his rapid breaths as he brought our bodies together.

As the minutes disappeared from us and the careful caresses continued, I found myself exploring his body, embracing the way his soft skin felt beneath my fingertips. I couldn't get enough of him; I wanted more; I wanted him to know how much I needed this. How much I *wanted* it with him.

I kissed him clumsily, and he returned the gesture, and when his breathing sped up, meeting mine, I closed my eyes, burying my face in his chest.

A part of me might have been stolen, but in this moment, right now, I gained something else, something I never knew I could have again: power and control, and Daniel helped me find it.

CHAPTER TWENTY-FIVE

Progress is Progress

The doorbell sounded and made me jump off the bed. Oh God, pizza. Right.

Daniel chuckled as I rushed around searching for my skirt and top.

'I'll get it,' he said.

He disposed of the condom and the wrapper in the bin, pulled on his clothes and then disappeared down the stairs to collect our food.

When we were both seated on the round rug in the middle of my room, I drew my knees to my chest and watched as Daniel opened the box and took a slice.

His head lifted, catching me by surprise. A dark look floated across his features, and he dropped his slice into the box.

'I'm no expert, but usually there's more, joy... or talking...'

'I'm sorry,' I whispered. 'I'm just in shock.'

'Andy—'

'Not in a bad way,' I smiled, sweeping my fingers through his tousled hair and added quickly, 'I'm just enjoying the moment.'

'You're sure?'

'One hundred per cent.' I leaned over the food and drew his face to mine, pressing a soft kiss to his lips. 'Now eat, I won't be held responsible for cold pizza.'

He grinned and chowed down on his slice. For the first few moments, we ate in silence. After the fourth slice, I closed the box and placed it on the desk. Daniel did the same and then scooted over to me, wrapping his arm around my shoulder.

'I'm really glad you're here,' I said.

'Me too. And that skirt was gorgeous on you, by the way.'

I flushed to my roots again. 'It was something I bought a while ago.'

'Good buy.'

I grinned. 'Hey, I wanted to ask you. There's a party next weekend. Would you come with me?'

'Andrew's?'

I nodded.

He drew a hand over his mouth and looked sideways at me. 'You don't need me to tell you that he might be there.'

'I know, but I can't keep hiding. Today sucked, and I folded.'

'You know that no one would bat an eye at you for folding?'

'No one who knows. Everyone else just thinks I'm mental.'

'Fuck those people. Why do you think you have something to prove to them?'

'I don't know.'

'I'm telling you then, you don't have anything to prove.

To anyone.'

'I want to be stronger.'

He swivelled his body around so that we were face to face. 'You are strong, but if this is something you want to do, of course, I'll come.'

'Thank you.'

He pressed a quick kiss to my cheek and then helped me up when we both heard the sound of the downstairs door opening.

'Andrea, Daniel!' Mum called. 'I have cake.'

Smaller, more erratic footsteps followed.

'It appears I also have a small child that appeared in kitchen!' Dad laughed.

'You better come down before I eat it all!' Jelena yelled.

Daniel and I looked at each other again and I smirked.

'Your mother definitely knows how to win a man's heart.'

'No shit! My dad felt the same until he learned he had high cholesterol.'

'Lucky for me, I have excellent self-control.'

'Lucky indeed, however, the cakes she brings home are outrageous, and you'll quickly learn that no one has self-control.'

'Now I'm even more intrigued.'

We jogged down the stairs and met them both in the kitchen. Jelena rounded the corner and ran into me, hugging me tightly. 'We're still doing the cartoon nights, right?'

'Of course. Are they still my choice?'

'Damn, thought you'd have forgotten.'

'Never!' I nudged her and smiled.

'Hey, Daniel.'

'Hey, kid.'

She grinned and then ducked into the pantry while Mum opened the box with four slices of vanilla sponge. My mouth instantly watered.

'Is this from the store down the road?' I asked, handing out some forks while Jelena set out some plates.

'Yep, they were down to the last four slices, so I took them all.'

'So good,' Daniel dug in.

Mum watched him, smiling, and I found myself about a second from rolling my eyes.

As they all ate and joked about the time Dad ate an entire cake, I sunk back in the bar stool, watching them with fascination.

Mum set something else down, catching my eye.

My eyes met hers before she opened a small box. In it was a key.

'What is this?'

They looked at Daniel and then at me like he was in on something I wasn't privy to.

'Mum?'

'It's your car key. The engine is all done,' Dad said.

'No way.'

'I had to work really hard not to say something and spoil it,' Daniel added.

'Oh my God, you guys are the best!' I threw my arms around Mum and Dad and then Jelena for good measure.

Daniel hugged me last, handing me another package. It

was about the size of a shoe box but slightly lighter.

'It's not a black box to a secret UFO schematic or anything, but you might like it for your car.'

I ripped the paper off revealing a personalised travel mug and Buffy key chain. 'This is the best!'

'Matches the poster Hails got you.'

'These are so good, thank you, all of you.'

'You're very welcome. But it is late,' Daniel said sheepishly. 'I should go home. Don't want Mum to take my phone again.'

'I know, sorry,' I said. 'I'll walk you out.'

Mum and Dad said goodnight to him in a very obvious get-out-of-our-house-now way. It was somewhere between my mum physically escorting him out of the kitchen and narrowing her brow with a quick nod. I chuckled and led Daniel to the front of the house. Together we went outside. I closed the door, leaning back against it. He stepped up to me, and I wrapped my arms around his waist.

'I had a really good time with you, Andy,' he said softly, pressing a kiss to my lips.

'Me too and thank you for staying.'

'Like I said before, I'm around whenever you need me.'

'I'll hold you to it.'

'Please do,' he said, taking my hand in his and pressing a kiss to each knuckle. 'Wouldn't be much of a boyfriend if I wasn't accountable to you.'

'Boyfriend?' I cocked my head.

'Yeah, been meaning to ask you about that.'

'You're happy with the title?' I asked.

'I am. Are you?'

The ugly taste the 'b' word brought with it hurt. I'd been so stupid with Julian, so naïve. But this wasn't like before. To Julian, it meant nothing but a way to secure his way in. For Daniel, it was a way to secure my heart, to give me comfort and confidence.

I stepped closer to him and nodded.

'I'll see you in the morning?' he asked.

'Yeah, you will.'

He kissed me again and then made his way back to his car. I smiled as I waited until his car went around the bend.

Mum was still in the kitchen when I came back in.

'How was school today?' she asked.

'Fine.'

'How was Sarah?'

'Really good.'

'Oh?' Her eyebrows rose.

'Yeah, she has helped a lot, actually.'

'I'm glad.'

'Hey, Mum, do you think it would be okay if I went to this party next Saturday night?'

'Who is having party?' she asked.

'You know Josh?' I asked, trailing my fingers over the fruit basket. 'His friend, Andrew.'

'Is anyone else I know going?'

'Daniel.'

She seemed to relax the second I dropped his name. That was a definite win, though I kind of felt lame using him to coax her into letting me go out, but in hindsight, I should have been happy, considering she had literally packed away all the knives, sharp objects and even my razors…

'Okay. But you come home by midnight, and you don't drink.'

'I won't drink, trust me.'

For a moment, we looked at each other and a kind of heavy presence came to life between us like a bursting cloud, dark and grey, a raging storm so close you could almost smell it, but not quite, and I wondered what it would be like if I just told her. But when she hugged me and kissed me goodnight, the fantasy vanished.

'Goodnight, Mum.'

I watched as she slowly took the stairs, her body showing the tell-tale signs of how age and hard work had worn her down. This country gave us so much, but it took even more. She'd told me of the monsters in our home country who destroyed cities in the night, but she said the scariest monsters were the ones in the government buildings hiding behind orders and paperwork.

I knew that now. The monsters were real, hidden in plain sight, stalking wherever we turned, and we would be oblivious until the last moment when they struck.

Julian Valesco was that monster, and I'd be damned if I'd let him keep haunting me.

CHAPTER TWENTY-SIX

Dethrone the Villain!

The whole week passed without incident. I'd driven to school every day, hung out with Daniel a few times, and avoided running into Julian.

So when the weekend arrived, I was excited like I hadn't been in a long time.

When I woke up on the day that Julian did what he did, I was a different person, full of anxiety, full of fear that I'd fail this test or that. The girl who came home that evening, scrubbing off the blood and the shame, was fractured into tiny pieces and pulled apart thread by thread. Her perception of the world had been fully stripped down and blown wide open.

Everything in the past had been so... simple, childish even. Now, my grades were at the lowest possible they could be to still pass and gain my VCE, and I counted myself lucky to be able to graduate at all.

It must have been obvious to anyone who opened my school report that something happened. With nothing below A's to barely skimming D's and E's, it was a polarising reflection of an entire twelve years of schooling. But I refused to ask for leniency, and it had nothing to do with my pride. It was about taking charge. I didn't care about things the way I used to. The girl getting ready today *only* cared about surviving. Whatever the progress, it was monumental. I was even going to a party.

My phone vibrated, and I grinned when Daniel's name popped up on my screen.

> *Be there in 10. Wear comfortable shoes.*
>
> *Why?*
>
> *You'll see.*
>
> *There better not be a mountain involved.*
>
> *Just trust me, Nekić, wear something comfortable and bring water.*
>
> *I've already climbed a mountain this week.*
>
> *Sounds deep. HAHA.*
>
> *Well, it was literal and figurative, I guess.*

There was definitely going to be a mountain.

I ducked into my cupboard and found a pair of leggings, comfy runners and a hoodie. I threw on the outfit without really paying much attention to whether it all matched and tossed my hair into a high ponytail.

Mum gave me a grin when I walked past her. It still felt forced, but it was slowly getting better. A part of me thought she just didn't know how to ask the hard questions. I didn't envy her. Being a mum was hard work. Being *my* mum, even more so.

'I won't stay out long,' I said, stopping at the door.

'I just want you to be happy, Andrea.'

'I know, Mum.' I kept my eyes on Daniel through the glass pane in the door, but the nagging feeling in the pit of my stomach made me turn. 'I didn't try to kill myself because of anything you or Dad did.'

She set down the wet kitchen rag.

'I want you to know that. I want you to know that I appreciate everything you've done.'

Before she could make me spill every secret I'd ever carried, I rushed out the door and locked it behind me. When I was safe in Daniel's car, I let out the breath I'd been holding.

'Rough morning?' he asked, frowning.

'No, it's all good.'

Without further questioning, he pulled out of the driveway and before long, we were weaving through the estate and merging onto the freeway.

'So, we're really going to the party tonight?' he asked, keeping his eyes dead ahead.

'If you want to.'

'You know I don't, but I'll come because there's no way you're going alone.'

'You don't need to be my chaperone. I can handle myself.'

'I know that. But I want to be there with you.'

'So you can watch me?'

'Not in a creepy, stalker way.'

'I'm glad you clarified that part,' I muttered. 'Are you going to tell me where we're going that required comfy shoes?'

'We're going on a hike.'

'No fair! My legs are still jelly from the walk with Dad the other day.'

'Not my problem. Work your legs out more.'

I baulked.

He grinned.

'You'll like this walk, I promise,' he added.

'I'm sure I will, just not sure I'll make it.'

'When have I ever given you reason to doubt me?' he said and then held his hand up. 'Don't answer that.'

'Fine, but you owe me coffee.'

'Happily.'

I leaned back in the seat, letting the wind from the slightly open window cool the air in the car. Daniel reached over and threaded his fingers through mine as he drove, only letting go to shift gears. Somehow, we'd found each other's light through the chaotic mess of darkness and somehow, we were both stronger and better for it.

Not that I wouldn't take a magic pill the second someone offered it to me to erase the last two months from existence, but I realised now it wasn't just Julian or what he did that I was trying to vanquish into the abyss. It was fear. Fear of being a nobody, fear of disappointing people who expected so much of me, fear of not being able to live up to impossible expectations. Fear of letting myself down.

But now, most of that fear was gone, and there was just me. A raw, untouched journal ready to mark the lines of a new story in. It was almost like a clean slate, and I was excited to start.

If only it didn't come at the cost of what it did.

~

'Here it is!' Daniel announced, holding his hands out.

It took a few seconds for my eyes to register what they were seeing. There were mountains in every direction, down below, the bluest lake I'd ever seen, all around, vibrant green trees and colourful flowers.

'Do you like it?'

'Daniel, it's amazing.'

'I came across this path when I was hiking with Dad a few months ago. He said there's a nice place to sit down at the end, too.'

'You're something special, you know that?'

'Not as special as you. Come on, I've packed some lunch for us. We can have a picnic by the water.'

I threw on my backpack and followed him down toward the gravel path.

When we got onto the lower ground that was unobstructed by overgrown shrubbery and roots, I found a nice spot to sit and then spread out the blanket he'd brought.

'Hungry?' He held out a small cooler bag.

'You're the hugest dork ever, Daniel. Did anyone ever tell you that?'

'Mum tells me daily,' he mused for a moment and then laughed, leaning over the picnic to kiss me, 'Plus, you tell me all the time. Does that count?'

'I think it does.'

'Did you want me to pick you up later?' he asked.

'Yeah, if you don't mind. I mean if you want to drink, I can drive your car home.'

'I don't think I'll drink.'

'Me neither.'

For a few minutes, we both kept ourselves occupied with the food. I smiled to myself when I caught Daniel looking up at the sun, momentarily closing his eyes. When I was done, I carefully cleared enough space around me to lie down.

'Thank you,' I said, looking up at him.

Daniel tipped his face down, using his hand to shield his eyes from the sun. 'For what?'

'For saving my life.'

It wasn't one of those dramatic statements the girls in those teen dramas said. I meant it in the most literal sense. He'd driven to my house, smashed my window, called the ambulance, and kept me breathing while he waited. I knew that image would haunt him for the rest of his life, and I felt so guilty for it. But the truth remained: he came, and he was there when it mattered most.

'You don't have to thank me for that, ever.'

'I'll always be thankful to you for that.'

He was serious for a moment and then scooted over to me. Using one elbow to prop himself up beside me, he turned my face towards his with his free hand.

'There's one thing I never told you.'

'About?'

'You know how we were doing our movie essays?'

'Yeah?'

'I'd never actually seen *Mean Girls,* and I nailed that assignment.'

I snorted. 'How did you manage that?'

'I watched the plastics in our classes and wrote about them.'

I burst out laughing. 'Wow, I don't even know what to say.'

'I'd say that it's pretty genius.'

'I'd say so too.'

'But I brought that up for a reason, not just to gloat.'

'Oh yeah?'

He turned his face back to the sun. 'I saw the way Jess always watched him and then the way she reacted to you after what he'd told his mates. She was jealous.'

'Do you think she sent the messages to me?'

'Maybe not her. But I'd bet Rachel was involved. Trying to scare you off so her bestie could have him.'

'I don't know if I should feel sorry for Jess or be happy.'

'Got him in the end. Good riddance to them both. They're just as twisted and as disturbed as each other.'

'Yeah.'

He turned his face to me. 'In a few years when we're all living our own lives away from this hole, those girls, men like Julian, they won't have a good life. I'm not talking about karma or any mystic bullshit like that, but it's because of who they are. Deep down inside. They may grow up and have families, get decent jobs or whatever, but they'll still be rotten inside. Still narcissistic. Still only protecting their own asses and anyone with a brain will see right through it.'

'You reckon?'

He nodded and looked up at the birds on the horizon, 'They'll be exactly who they are now but older. Making excuses for shitty behaviour and blaming everyone else but themselves.'

'Thanks for saying that.' I smiled to myself, and we settled into a quiet moment.

'We should get going soon,' Daniel said after a while, 'I know I need like an hour to get ready. Can't even imagine how long you'd need.'

He snuck a quick kiss on the tip of my nose before I could argue and started packing everything up.

Days like these were going to make all the difference in my life.

~

Daniel chatted to Mum downstairs while I applied the red lipstick I bought two months ago. I exhaled at my reflection, finally convincing myself that I was brave enough to do this.

The jeans I chose were slightly too loose now; they didn't sit right on my hips, and the brown velvet singlet I'd found was also a little baggy. I draped a denim jacket over my shoulders and tucked the top in my pants, ruffling it a little so it looked intentionally big. It would have to do.

I gave myself one last look in the mirror, packed the lipstick, my phone, and a spare hair tie into a small black clutch and made my way downstairs.

Daniel's eyes shot up to me, a smile tugged at the corner of his lips, and I felt the same smile come over me. Mum stood motionless as if she were shocked that I was actually going through with this.

'Where's Dad?' I asked, kind of disappointed that he wasn't here to see me out on my maiden voyage post all the fuckery.

'He had a headache, ljubavi, but he's very happy that

you're going out.'

'Oh, I hope he's okay.'

'He will be when I make him soup,' she smiled, then walked around the bench and hugged me, 'Have a good night.' She looked over my shoulder at Daniel, 'Home by midnight and no drinking.'

'Midnight and most definitely no drinking,' Daniel agreed.

Once my mother released us into the night, I linked my arm through Daniel's and let him lead me outside. He ran around to the passenger side and opened the door for me.

'Loser,' I teased.

'Get in, you ungrateful brat.'

I stuck my middle finger up at him and laughed.

Before long, we reached the street on which Andrew lived.

The driveway was packed with cars parked on either side all the way to the street, though Daniel found a spot close to the front, stopping behind a huge Ford I recognised from the school parking lot.

Chances were low that Julian would come here, but I'd kind of gone behind Daniel's back, contacted Andrew, and made sure. He swore to me that Julian was barred from his house. His mother hated him on account of a stupid fight the two boys had gotten into during an inter-school football game when Julian was at his old school. It made me feel a little better. But I was lying to myself when I said I would be totally fine.

As soon as I opened the car door and the deep bass

rumbled beneath my feet, my muscles tightened. The twinkling fairy lights all around us were suddenly too bright. The citronella permeating the air made my stomach recoil.

I backed up and pressed my body against the car, trying desperately to convince myself that I was okay. When Daniel took my hand, I flinched.

'Too much?' he asked, looking at Josh and his small crew approaching.

'No.'

'Andy, we can go home.'

'No, I want to stay.'

As Josh approached, ducking under a strategically placed curtain of string lights, Daniel walked over and pulled him aside. While they spoke in hushed voices, I took a deep breath, counted to three and then exhaled, looking around, scoping out the surroundings.

My gaze followed a path of tiki torches lining a cobblestone footpath that led to a pool. There were girls swimming and boys throwing bugs at them. I rolled my eyes.

A few seconds later, Daniel and Josh both walked back over.

'I'm glad you came,' Josh said, carefully wrapping his arms around my shoulder.

'Me too.' I looked up at the house. 'I think.'

'We can hang out here for a while.'

'No, we came to have fun. I'll be fine,' I said, linking my arm through Daniel's, dragging Josh along.

As the thumping bass got louder and the beat reverberated through the ground, I found myself gripping Daniel's arm tighter and grinding my teeth harder. Maybe I wasn't going to be fine after all.

'Is Hailey coming?' Josh asked, dragging my attention back to him.

'No. She hates parties.'

'Yeah, fair.'

Daniel pulled his arm free, wrapping it tightly around my shoulder. Then he leaned in closer and whispered, 'I've got you; you're safe with me.'

Forcing a tight smile, I tried to nod, but I was certain that all that came out was a tiny jerk of the head.

'Have fun. I'll be over there if you need me,' Josh grinned, swiping a bottle of beer from a guy who was too tanked to notice.

He broke off and joined a group of girls I didn't know. They were all blonde, wearing the same kind of off-the-shoulder dresses and Converses. I was suddenly aware of how underdressed I was.

I dodged another blonde girl who was trying to shove a Cruiser into my hand. Daniel politely told her to piss off, but she was so drunk she barely heard him. She continued past us and started drinking from the bottle as she stumbled over an ice bucket.

'Nekić, you made it!'

My eyes shot up to the balcony and landed on Andrew. He waved at us with a huge smile.

'Stay there, I'll come down and say hi!'

I nodded with a smile. Daniel left me for a quick second before returning with two cans of soft drink. I took the Fanta from him.

'Josh is having a good time,' he nodded across the yard, and I choked on the drink in my mouth. On either side, Josh had one of the blondes sitting on a large bench seat taking turns drinking from a large bottle of vodka.

'Wow, didn't think he was a two-for-one kind of guy.'

'He's a whatever is going at the time kind of guy.' Daniel shook his head.

'Who are they?'

'Girls from Valesco's old school.'

'You're kidding.'

'Nope.'

I peeled my eyes away and looked around at the other people. Andrew appeared from around the corner and walked right up to us. I stepped into his hug and smiled when he held me close.

'You can chill inside if it gets too hectic out here,' he said, shaking Daniel's hand beside me. 'My parents are home, but they're watching movies in the theatre room.'

'I'll be fine,' I said. 'I think I need to start living again.'

'You know where the door is. Don't be shy if you need it.'

'Thanks, man,' Daniel said. 'Sick party, by the way.'

Andrew grinned, saluting him.

He gave me another quick hug before clapping Daniel on the back and jogging off to greet more of his guests. Most were engaged in private conversations, some yelling at each other over the loud music, and some, like me and Daniel, were standing close, intimately speaking, touching.

A huge guy who was built like a brick wall came over and sheepishly smiled at me before dipping into a conversation with Daniel. I zoned out and looked around at everyone else having fun.

Daniel, although lost in conversation, never let go of me. He pulled me close, and I felt my skin flush where his body was pressed against mine. When the guy who was built like a wall gave me a polite smile and left, Daniel turned me in his arms, so we were standing toe to toe. I tipped my head back to look up at him and looped my arms around his neck.

'You look like you're more relaxed.'

'I am, good observation.'

'You know me, I'm Mr. Observant.'

He took my drink from me and set it on the windowsill we'd commandeered as our own personal bench. 'I'm proud of you for doing this.'

'Not many guys are proud of their girlfriends for attending parties.'

'Not many girlfriends have been through what you have,' he said seriously.

Before I could answer him, he lowered his lips to mine and kissed me. My heart swelled and ricocheted against my ribs as Daniel held me tight.

When he pulled back, I couldn't help the grin on my face.

'You look happy now,' he chuckled.

'So observant.'

'Like I said—'

'Yeah, yeah,' I laughed, resting my forehead against his chest.

I let out a long breath and wrapped my arms around his waist, turning my face to look out over the partygoers. Everyone was lost in the music and their conversations, probably about completely normal teenage things. Everyone's world had continued while mine had stalled.

'Now I'm observing that you're drifting.'

'I'm not. I'm here,' I said.

His hands closed over my cheeks and angled my face up to his.

'Talk to me, what's going on?'

'Nothing. I'm good. I—'

Suddenly, I heard his voice behind us.

My spine straightened, and every hair on my arms stood on end like a blast of cold air had torn through the musky backyard.

Daniel's gaze lifted, travelling over my shoulder. His jaw squared and his shoulders tensed, and I felt the heat radiate off him in a split second. I gripped his arms, hoping to God that he wouldn't react. I couldn't do this. I didn't want him to see me. I didn't want the attention.

But all of that went to shit the moment I heard his voice and that of his friend's get closer. They were coming this way. Why were they even here?

Andrew stormed around the corner, some of his rugby friends in tow. His mouth was set in a hard line.

'What are you doing here, Valesco?' Andrew shouted.

'Thought this was an open invite.'

'You thought wrong.'

Julian laughed, and my skin turned to ice. The sound used

to remind me of cascading waves, cool and inviting. Now, it was more like the terrifying rumble you heard from a storm building on the horizon. You knew you were safe for the time being, but soon, the cracks ripping through the sky would get closer, and if you weren't careful, you'd be struck down.

When I turned to face him, still gripping Daniel like a lifeline, I shrunk back, seeing that both Illya and Nick were standing with him.

'Glad Garrison didn't give you detention,' he said lightly as if it were all in jest.

My mouth dried up, and Daniel's bicep hardened beneath my death grip.

Then everything kind of blew up. Daniel reacted so quickly I had no idea who moved first. His fist connected with Julian's face and from the corner of my eye, I saw Josh bolt from across the yard with three of his friends running behind him.

Julian rushed back to his feet. Josh grabbed Nick as he tried to jump Daniel, but Illya pulled him off, leaving himself open. Before I could scream for him to watch out, Julian rushed at him with an animalistic scowl on his face.

There were fists everywhere. People screaming and yelling. I was fighting off whoever was pulling me back, but I couldn't move an inch because it was the huge-ass dude who'd been chatting to Daniel earlier, holding me.

'Stop!' a girl behind us screamed.

But no one did.

My breath came out in useless whimpers, and my heart pounded against my ribs. My eyes darted around, and just as

Daniel regained the upper hand in the fight, Julian hit him right in the jaw, throwing him backwards. But as quickly as he went down, he was back on his feet, rushing Julian. Nick grabbed Daniel's arm, dragging him back, leaving him open for Illya to strike.

'No!' I heard myself scream. 'Stop!'

Josh's friends tried to help, but Julian threw one guy down, clearing the way for Nick to knock another one out. As Daniel rushed them both, Illya ran forward body slamming him to the ground. The grunt that came from him made my heart lurch through my stomach. This was now a three-on-one fight, and Daniel was hurt badly. Before I could scream again, another group of guys I recognised from Andrew's rugby team, turned up, ending the fight.

Daniel dragged himself to his feet, facing Julian down. In the second it took for my brain and eyes to catch up, Daniel was rushing forward again, and so was Julian. But before either of them could throw another punch, Andrew ran forward, pulling Daniel away.

'Enough,' Andrew snapped, turning his attention to Julian, 'You might have everyone else kissing your ass, Valesco, but not us. So, I'm going to tell you politely to get the fuck off my property before we call the police.'

Julian shook Nick off him and straightened his blood-stained polo. His eyes coasted across the few people standing guard, ready to jump in at Andrew's command.

'You're all a bunch of faggots.'

'Get the fuck off my property NOW,' Andrew repeated.

Julian shook his head. I knew that look. He was biding his

time, waiting for something... then he moved so quickly, surprising everyone, even Daniel, who'd turned back to me.

I saw what was about to happen. Daniel was already hurt; blood was flowing from his split lip and along the side of his right eye. If he took another hit, it would knock him out. It could kill him. I acted before I'd even thought it through.

As Julian swung, I lunged forward, pushing Daniel out of the way. Julian's fist missed the intended target and slammed into my shoulder instead. The force knocked me straight into Josh's arms.

My surprised shriek launched Daniel back into action. The guttural sound that came from his throat stunned me.

The fight exploded again; the music continued pounding in the background, vibrating through the ground and into my body. Screams got lost in the rush of the partygoers on the other side of the property, completely oblivious to what was happening here.

I found myself struggling to pull free from Josh. He dragged me back, away from the fight and away from Daniel.

'Andy! We have to go!' Josh was pulling me toward the back of the house.

'No!'

'Daniel will be fine.'

'How do you know?'

'Half the rugby team is there, he's good. Trust me.'

I opened my mouth to argue but promptly closed it when we entered Andrew's parents' house. He took my hand again and led me up the stairs to what I assumed was Andrew's room.

We stopped, meeting a guy who looked a few years older than Andrew but shared the same dusty blonde hair and blue eyes.

'Blain,' Josh said, shaking his hand. 'This is Andy.'

'Hey, nice to meet you.' He shook my hand before looking at Josh. 'You two good?'

'Yeah, just getting her away from the action,' Josh muttered.

'Good thinking,' Blain nodded. 'Feel free to chill out here.'

'We should be helping Daniel,' I shot.

'Daniel's got all the help he needs out there,' Blain said. 'Andrew loves this shit. He's in his element. I think he's been waiting for a reason to break Valesco's face.'

'What?'

Blain nodded. 'If you ask me, he's getting everything he deserves.'

'I don't want anyone to get hurt,' I whispered.

'Don't worry, my brother will rough him up enough to make him think twice about showing his face where he's not welcome, and Daniel will be fine; that boy can handle himself. Believe me.'

'Thanks, man,' Josh said when I failed to.

'No worries. Stay here, and I'll make sure they're all good.' Blain closed the door and left me and Josh alone.

I walked straight to the window and peered through the blind. I'd been to parties that turned feral, but this was different, more violent. Then again, maybe it just looked that way to me because it was personal, and it seemed so much more than the trivial shit people usually had punch-ons over.

I dropped the blind and walked over to the computer desk.

'You okay? How's your shoulder?' Josh asked.

'I'm fine, just a bit tender.' I rolled my shoulder to make sure.

Josh pulled the blind back slightly and peered outside. 'Blain's broken it up, but it looks like Daniel's going with Andrew.'

'Where?'

'Probably to get stitched up or something.'

'Did Daniel tell you what happened to me?'

'No,' he said and kept looking outside the widow. 'But I don't need a master's degree to work out that something did.'

I folded my hands in my lap.

Finally, he dropped the blind back into place and sat on the edge of Andrew's bed, his gaze travelling over my body and then my face, 'Are you sure you're not hurt?'

'I'm fine. I'm glad you were there to use as a shield.'

He cracked a smile, but then it was gone and he was serious again.

'Valesco shouldn't have been here tonight. Andrew told him he wasn't welcome, so I don't know his deal.'

'He's an asshole, that's his deal.'

His eyes flicked away momentarily. 'Exactly what I've told you already.'

'You tried to tell me that he'd use me, not...'

Josh turned his whole body and looked at me, and for a moment, I didn't know if he'd understand what had really happened. Then, as the pieces seemed to click in his head that he hadn't just come onto me, his eyes widened, and he thrust his hand into his hair.

'Andy… did he?'

'I should have listened to you, Josh.'

This time, he looked up with a serious and stern expression. 'It wasn't just me, was it? Hailey told you not to talk to him, so did Daniel. And it didn't change shit because you knew what you wanted long before any of us said anything.'

'And what was that?'

'To be anything other than who you are.'

A useless tear spilled out onto my cheek as the truth in his words burned me through to my core. I swatted it away with the heel of my palm.

'I shouldn't have been so fucking stupid. It's my fault.'

'Christ no, Andy.'

'He used me, and then he got with Jess straight after. Go figure.'

'Andy—'

'Forget it.' A breath rattled through me before I collected myself and stood. I straightened out my jeans and peeked through the blind.

'I'm going home,' I said.

'I'll walk you.'

'I've messaged my mum. She's outside.'

I left him and thanked Andrew's parents before meeting Mum down the road. I could be angry all I wanted, but he was right. He, Hailey, and Daniel warned me countless times, and not once did I listen because I didn't want to.

CHAPTER TWENTY-SEVEN

About Last Night

I woke up and panicked when I realised that I'd slept through my alarm, and when I barely made it out of bed without stumbling, I stopped, remembering that it was Sunday.

I sat back on the bed, snatched my phone off the side table and checked the messages. Shit. There was nothing from Daniel.

> *Please tell me you're okay. I'm worried.*

Nothing.

> *Daniel, I'm so sorry. We shouldn't have gone*
> *to the party. I shouldn't have made you come*
> *with me.*

Nothing.

I scrolled through messages and found Josh's name.

> *Any word from Daniel? I'm worried.*

He replied lightning fast.

> *No, nothing yet. I'll let u know as soon as I*
> *know.*

I sighed and sent off another.

> *I'm sorry about last night too. I was a bitch.*

For a moment, I thought he wouldn't reply.

> *U weren't & I'm sorry, I should've said more.*

***I should have been clearer & not beaten
around the damn bush. I'm sorry, Andy.***

My heart slowed. I didn't know how to feel. I didn't know what to say. So, I opted for the only thing that was acceptable. The only thing I could make myself write.

And I should have listened.

When no more messages came through, I dropped my phone on the bed and changed, making my way downstairs for breakfast.

Mum smiled as she set the table and gave me a cup of coffee. Dad and Jelena joined us just as the pancakes were set down.

'How was the party?' Dad asked.

'Uneventful,' I lied. 'Is your headache gone?'

'It's fine. I think I needed sleep.'

'Are you feeling better?'

'Yeah, Dad, I am. I'm fine.'

'Really?'

'Yes, really,' I nodded. 'I feel a lot better. Almost ninety per cent human.'

He grinned. 'Good. I was wondering if the alien was still here.'

Jelena kept her eyes on the food, inhaling pancake after pancake, making me wonder whether a changeling had replaced my sister. She was less annoying, less messy, less intrusive.

I raised a brow at her and then smiled to myself. She was growing up, learning how to read people and situations. Maybe I should have taken a page out of her book.

'I see you're spending more time with Daniel,' Dad said, keeping his eyes on the pancakes he was slicing into a dozen tiny pieces.

'I am.'

'You're happy?'

'Yeah.'

'And that other boy?' Mum asked.

My heart lurched. 'What other boy?'

'I don't know his name. The other one you walked home with… Julian?'

I couldn't control the shaking in my voice when I spoke next. 'He's no one.'

'You seemed close.'

'He turned out to be a bad person.'

Mum's eyes snapped up from her coffee. Dad's too.

'Did something happen?' Dad asked.

This was it. That the moment was right here. I couldn't lie. But at the same time, I didn't want to say anything either. I didn't think I had to. It must have been all over my face.

Mum shifted, the chair made an obnoxious sound, and I felt their eyes on me. Even Jelena looked up now. Her innocent, wide eyes beckoned to me. *Be brave.*

'Andrea?' Mum's voice was small. 'Did something happen?'

'Yeah, Mum. Something happened, but it's okay now.'

She looked away before releasing a chain of very lewd expletives reserved only for the mother tongue.

'Miš—' Dad began, but I cut him off.

'Everything was a mess, and I didn't handle things the

way I should have. But I'm better now. Things are better. I promise.'

A quiet unlike any I'd ever known in this family filled the kitchen. I took it as my opportunity to collect my plate and take it to the sink.

'I have to go; I'm picking Daniel up.'

Neither of them said anything else. They'd seen a part of me I couldn't take back and nothing else I said after this point would be believable. I could have masked everything, but I couldn't mask the way I reacted when they brought *him* up.

Dad met me by the fridge, stopping my escape. 'Did that Julian boy do something you didn't want him to?'

I nodded.

He cursed under his breath in Croatian using a few creatively pieced-together adjectives, followed by a loud sigh, followed by a hug only a father could give. He was safe, warm, and all-consuming, saying everything words couldn't.

'Please don't say anything to Mum. I know how she worries. I don't want her to worry about me too.'

'We both worry whether you tell us to or not.'

'I know,' I said, smiling sadly. 'Please don't say anything.'

'You can trust me.'

I hugged him again. 'Thanks, Dad. I'll be home later.'

I kissed him on the cheek and took my bag, giving him a quick look. His body was rigid, knuckles white. I sighed and left, making my way to my car.

It wasn't a Kodak moment where I bared my soul to my family on some spectacular, momentous occasion, but it was enough. It lifted some of the weight that had been making it impossible to breathe.

I opened the door and slipped inside. Before I turned the engine on, my phone vibrated.

> *I'm home. I'm so sorry about last night. Holy shit, I just lost it. I wanted to kill him. I probably would have if Andrew and his mates didn't stop me.*

My knees weakened as I sunk into my seat.

> *I'm glad you didn't. I wouldn't have been able to live with myself if you were in jail because of it.*
>
> *U know I would. No question.*
>
> *I do. That's what scares me.* I sent back.

A tremor rolled up my spine.

> *I'm coming over. Are you home?* I added.
>
> *For u, always.*

I grinned, stashed my phone in my bag, and turned the car on. I took a deep breath and pulled out into the street.

Daniel's house was only fifteen minutes away, and as I took the last turn and pulled into his driveway, I frowned.

He was sitting alone on the front step. A dark purple bruise covered the better part of his face, and the cuts in his lip and around his eye were stitched up and taped over. I barely turned the car off before I threw my door open and got out, getting yanked back by the seatbelt, twice.

'Holy shit!' I rushed over to him, tenderly covering the bruise with my palm. The skin was hot to the touch, and even though he didn't flinch, I saw the glimmer of pain in his eye.

'I'm fine,' he said, closing his hand over mine. 'Are you?'

'I'm okay.'

'Jesus, when I saw you get hit.' He ground his teeth. 'Josh told me he stayed with you.'

'Yeah, I left when you and Andrew bailed.'

'Sorry about that. Had to sort out some stitches from a non-legal source.'

'You could have been hurt badly.'

'I didn't want you to see that.'

'But I did, and I was mortified, Daniel. I never want to see that again.'

'When I saw how you reacted, I couldn't think around the rage.'

'Oh, Andrea, lovely to see you.' A woman's voice cut off what I was about to say next. I looked up and smiled when I saw Daniel's mum, Simona, coming down the stairs. She was two full heads shorter than her son, with hair big and curly enough to make Fran Dresher envious.

'Glad you get to see the mess this kid got himself into,' she said, a slight accent colouring her soft voice.

'He doesn't look that bad,' I lied.

She scoffed, looking at Daniel in mock disgust and led me to the kitchen. 'Coffee?'

'Yeah, thank you.'

Daniel kissed me on the cheek and then his mother. 'I have to get changed, then we're going for a walk. I'll be back.'

'No stress,' I nodded.

Simona led me to the bench and set out a small plate with

peach cookies.

'I didn't know Romanians made these too.' I picked one up and devoured it. Mum made these every Easter as part of our huge spread.

She turned to the coffee machine and set out two glasses. 'Hope the Fursecuri Piersicuţe are okay. It's been a while since I baked.'

'They're perfect, just like my mum's.'

'You're Croatian, yes?'

'Bosnian, technically.' It was hard to explain the dynamics of Yugoslavia and how each country existed post-separation. But she got it.

'Daniel said you're back at school?'

'Yeah.'

'Are you feeling better?'

'I am.'

'Daniel called me,' she said quietly like she was checking that no one else would hear. 'I waited with him at the hospital until your parents came.'

'Oh.' I felt my cheeks heat up.

Had Daniel told her everything? Maybe she knew what Julian did. Maybe that's why she wasn't chewing Daniel out about getting into a fight and grounding him, which seemed like a much bigger offence to reprimand someone over than missing curfew.

She brought our coffees over. 'I know Daniel is very happy you're home, and that makes me happy.'

Daniel's smiling face appeared around the corner. He snuck a peach cookie from the table and smirked when his mum scowled at him.

'Are you two going to go to the beach?' his mum asked.

I looked across at Daniel. 'Are we?'

He shrugged. 'Do you want to?'

'Yeah, sure.'

'Cool, we'll get some lunch on the way then,' he suggested.

'Oh, you should take her to the small one on the coast. What's it called?' She looked away like she was trying to recall a memory just out of reach.

'Dom's?' Daniel supplied.

'Yes, Dom's,' she beamed. 'Daniel and I love burgers. This place is amazing.'

I chuckled at the excited happy dance she did. Daniel shook his head like he was embarrassed. When she hugged him, making him shrink back in disgust, she laughed and tousled his hair. I found myself smiling like an idiot at the exchange.

While they bantered about which route was best to take for our road trip, I watched them and wondered what it would have been like growing up in a house where I didn't get to see my dad every day. The thought made me sad. Sure, my parents were a lot sometimes and expected loads of me, but they were my parents; they loved me more than someone could ever love another person; they skipped continents, left behind everything, and survived a war for me.

'Good to go?' Daniel's voice jarred me.

'Ah…' I looked down at the glass. 'Yeah, two seconds.'

I finished the rest of my coffee and made a beeline for the

sink. When she tried to pry the sponge out of my hand, I fought her off with a wet rag. When I finally surrendered the sponge, after washing everything in the sink, Daniel took my bag and laughed while I dried my hands off.

'You really didn't have to do that. Mum would have just put it in the dishwasher.'

'I know, but it was right there.'

'And so were all our breakfast dishes.'

'Well, it was a quick job.'

He laughed again. 'You're a catch, Andrea, don't let anyone tell you otherwise.'

'I don't,' I winked as he unlocked the car.

'Oh, I see how it is.'

'You should know, you're the one constantly dying to see me.'

'Always,' he chuckled.

~

After about two hours of driving, Daniel turned through the last of the winding roads, and we finally ended up at a car park that overlooked the ocean. The cliff face was a massive drop dipping right into the raging sea. Off to the side, giant structures peeked out of the waves every time the tide pulled the cover of the water back.

'This is amazing, Daniel.'

'You've never been here?'

'No, Dad is all about the other side of the bay.'

'Port Phillip is nice, but this has something different about it.'

'Yeah, I can see that.'

'The burger joint is just there,' he pointed over the bushes behind the carpark.

Sure enough, just over the sand dune covered in prickly native plants, the bustling street we'd come from opened onto a tourist strip. Dom's Burger Bar was nestled along the backdrop of a pastel blue sky. I followed him to the burger bar and then sat when he went up to the front to grab some menus.

'Have you tried everything here?' I asked, looking around at the food other people had on their tables.

'Yeah, I've had almost everything on the menu.'

'Of course you have. I think I'll grab a cheeseburger and some curly fries.'

'I'll grab it,' he said as he reached for my menu, but I quickly snatched it back. 'You paid last time, let me.'

'I insist.'

'Your mother insisted I leave the dishes; how did that work out again?'

His lips quirked into a smile. 'Fine.'

After he gave me his order, I took both menus to the front, ordered and paid, then took a bottle of water with a couple of glasses back to our table.

'So, about last night.'

'About last night.'

'I had to tell my mum about the hospital. I'm sorry she brought it up. I shouldn't have said anything.'

'It's okay.'

'She's been worried about you, and I kept telling her that you were getting better, you know?' he explained. 'Then last night happened, and she instinctively knew it had something to do with you.'

'What did you tell her?'

'Everything.'

I looked away.

'I'm sorry, Andy, I don't like lying to the woman. She can see right through it.'

'It's fine. I don't want you to lie to your mum.'

A chill settled over me, which seemed oddly out of place in the humid warmth of Torquay. We sat quietly until the food came, and then we ate without a word on last night's events or anything else that was shit.

'Are you ready for your exams?' I asked.

'I guess. School has been the last thing on my mind for a while.'

'I know the feeling.'

'If you don't get the results you want, you know there are other pathways to do the things you want to.'

'I know, it's okay. I've come to terms with it.'

'You make it sound so definitive.'

'I know I'm not going to get into uni, but it's okay, you know? It still makes me angry, but that's life, right? It doesn't always go to plan. I'm still here, and that counts for something.'

'It counts for everything.'

'I've gone over that night a hundred times in my head,' I said, 'and you know what keeps replaying over and over?'

He shook his head.

'I keep thinking how lucky I am that he wasn't some

unhinged psycho who might have killed me.'

Daniel sighed and balled his fists on the table in front of him.

'I'm *lucky* that I got to walk away with my life. Some girls are not that lucky.'

Daniel pushed around the chips on his plate with his fork before setting it down and reaching over, squeezing my hand.

'You don't have to say anything,' I smiled, closing my other hand over his. 'It's just an observation I made.'

Daniel's eyes took on that same stormy quality I knew meant he was battling serious inner demons. I knew a little about that.

'Eat,' I said gently.

He didn't. I guess neither of us had an appetite anymore.

'I'm sorry,' I said.

'For what?' He looked up, frowning.

'For ruining the day.'

'You didn't ruin anything.'

'Really? Because you look like you want to throw up.'

'I never want you to feel like you have to keep this from me, understand?'

I nodded.

'Good.' He continued to pick at a few chips. 'I'm not upset you told me. I'm just fucking angry about the whole situation. But don't ever apologise to me for telling me what's going on in your head.'

I released a long breath and picked up a chip. We ate in silence. I couldn't stomach much, anyway, and it wasn't just because of the conversation. The doctor said the aftereffects of the drugs I'd taken would linger for a few months.

'Sit on the beach?' Daniel asked.

'Absolutely.'

The walk over was short, and I was stopped twice by a bunch of tourists from out of state to take pictures of them by the iconic *Welcome to Torquay* sign.

We took the wooden steps down to the shore and walked a few meters down the sandy bank until we found a quiet spot to lay our towels.

'This is heaven!' I looked up at the sun and then over the picturesque water.

'Such a great beach.'

'You know something?'

'What?'

I got up and sat on his lap with my knees on either side of his hips, sinking into the soft sand beneath us.

'I'm looking forward to spending a lot of time with you visiting all these beautiful places you seem to know,' I said.

For a moment, his face was serious, and it made me question whether this was all a bit too much for him. Then he brought one hand to the base of my skull and kissed me. When he pulled back, he smiled up at me.

'Me too, Andy. More than you know.'

CHAPTER TWENTY-EIGHT

Final Days

'Andrea!'

My eyes snapped open, panic coursing as I threw my hand out, fumbling for my phone. *What the hell, Mum?* It must have been at least half an hour before my alarm.

'What?' I yelled from under the covers.

'Breakfast is ready.'

I kicked the covers off, checked the time, and confirmed that it was, in fact, early. But the smell of freshly made pancakes, maple syrup, and Nutella was enough to wake the dead. I considered going downstairs like I did every other morning, half asleep, still in PJs and mismatched socks, but then I stopped myself. No. Today was going to be different.

I got up, collected my uniform, and made a beeline for the shower.

Once I was done, I dressed and made my way to the dresser. I took out a tinted moisturiser and some mascara before braiding my hair and setting it with hairspray.

Downstairs, Jelena was already chowing down on a bowl of berries neatly set in the middle, no doubt meant to have been some sort of centrepiece. Mum and Dad grinned when they saw me. They both walked over, crushing me in a bear hug until I couldn't breathe.

'I think we squashed her,' Mum laughed, making me giggle.

'I'm a fragile little flower,' I laughed, readjusting my hair and finding my seat at the table.

'You are not fragile,' Dad said, suddenly serious.

He held my gaze. I felt stupid and weak. I felt like I'd betrayed them. They both thought so highly of me, and I'd done the most cowardly thing of all. I averted my gaze and sat at the table.

Mum called my name, but I couldn't turn away from a spot on the floor. After all of this, they still loved me; I could hardly believe there could be love and peace after all the carnage.

'Are you okay?' she said, gently squeezing my hand.

When I finally tore my eyes from the floor, I met her gaze and smiled.

'I will be.' And for once, it was the truth.

My heart swelled with elation. I decided then that if something was going well, I wouldn't be waiting for it to end. I wouldn't be waiting for the next bad thing or the next disappointment to take away the moments of happiness.

And as I ate my fourth pancake, I knew I'd found something I never had before: inner peace. It was an undeniably profound sense of acceptance, a calm unlike any I'd ever known.

I couldn't control everything. Sometimes, things went badly. Sometimes, they went well. And there was no rhyme or reason to it. I only wish it hadn't taken me almost dying to finally figure that out.

'She's daydreaming again, probably about Daniel,' Jelena teased.

'Nah, just daydreaming about *all* the games I'm going to get so good at so I can kick your ass when I finish school.'

Before she could say anything else, Mum reached over and hugged me again. 'I'm so happy seeing my two girls laughing again,' she said.

'Yeah, me too, Mum.'

I had one week left of exams, and then it was over. I would be free of school, free of the year that was, and finally, I'd be able to breathe without the constraints of Julian Valesco tightening around my throat every time I inhaled.

'You ready?' Dad asked.

Before I answered, I thought about what Sarah had said. She was right; we couldn't count on Plan A being the only one that would work. We had to have contingencies. Up until this point, I was certain my life would have gone a certain way, and when it hadn't, it crushed me.

Not anymore, though. I was going to make Plan C my bitch.

'Absolutely.'

~

Daniel's car pulled into my driveway, and he beeped, alerting me to his arrival.

'You look happy,' he said when I dropped my bag into the back seat. 'You know we're actually going to school today, no wagging.'

'I know, just happy to be finishing this week off. Feels

good.'

'Damn straight! We'll get through the week, and then it's over. We're free.'

'That sounds so good.'

One more week. One more week and we were out of there.

Monday

The math exam was up first. I looked at the rows of students nervously fiddling around with their pens and water bottles.

A small sliver of sadness crept through me. I'd lost too many hours of this class to make up with the little time I had left. So, I focused on the material I knew and hoped it would be enough to pass. Even with all that, I was certain I'd barely scrape a D.

'Two hours,' Proctor said from the doorway before the examiners ushered him out.

'Good luck,' Josh mouthed.

'You too,' I whispered back to him.

Daniel simply gave me a smile, which I returned.

When the examiners gave us the go-ahead, I turned my attention to the paper and began reading while furious scribbling began around me.

I watched for a few minutes. I considered writing my name and leaving, but that wasn't my style. I'd try my best, and I'd be comfortable with that.

Where this would have given me so much anxiety in the past, I felt oddly at ease.

When the time was finally called, I set my pen down, kept my eyes ahead, and left when everyone else did.

I followed Daniel outside with a huge grin on my face.

Outside in the hall, everyone was catching up on their exams. Some people seemed confident, others, like me, were a little carefree. Some, though, looked depressed, like no matter what they did, they'd never be good enough.

'Andy?' I looked up and smiled when Josh walked over, his bag slung lazily over his left shoulder. 'How'd you go?'

'Oh look, I don't think it was a complete fail.'

Hailey emerged and looped her arm around Josh's neck. 'How're you guys feeling?'

'When this fucked up year is over, we're all going away,' Josh muttered.

'Agreed,' Hailey mused as the bell rang, reminding us that the next exam was ready.

'Come on, guys. English. We've got this.' As Hailey led the way, I linked my arm through Josh's and Daniel's.

'I'm going to flunk this so hard I almost feel bad wasting their time,' Josh muttered.

'No way, I've taught you well. Remember all the points we made about *Alibrandi* in book club. You've got this.'

Josh grimaced but nodded. Book club was another thing that triggered a sour coating inside my stomach. Damn Julian for taking so much.

'Good luck, guys!' Hailey chuckled, shaking me from those thoughts.

'See you on the other side!' I waved as she rushed off to her seat and Josh, Daniel and I searched for ours.

As each student came in, silently taking their spots, my eyes met Julian's briefly. He didn't smirk or grin. He looked tired, his eyes dull, and the skin around his jaw was covered with blotchy black and blue bruises—I knew it wasn't just from the fight at the party. It extended out to the field, too. People were starting to see him for what he was. Julian Valesco's shining star was dimming.

'Andy?' Daniel's voice sounded beside me.

'I'm okay.'

He looked over to where Julian sat and scowled. I exhaled a long, shaky breath, reminding myself that this would be over soon.

'Two hours, people,' the examiner announced, dragging my attention to the front. Mr. Benson was there, greeting the last few students as they came in. When his eyes landed on me, he gave me a small nod, making me smile.

'You may start,' the examiner called as Mr. Benson left the hall.

I opened the exam paper and got to work. Once the first analytical essay was done, I took a deep breath and started writing my life essay, a journal entry into my soul telling the entire school, the teachers and those who should have been in my corner exactly what it felt like to be betrayed and discarded. That we couldn't be forsaken to the bedrooms of overcrowded, drink-fuelled parties with unattended glasses, or the shadows of underpasses hidden from security cameras and streetlights. We were right here, in the light, in the bedrooms of those who wore their school uniforms with pride, gleaming smiles and straight 'A' report cards.

But it wouldn't always be like this. One day, when the drugs left my system and the scars he'd left on my mind and soul were gone, I'd be the one to tell them all. I'd be the champion I never had.

Because I was a warrior, a survivor, and I wouldn't be silenced.

With each sentence that spilled out onto the page, I wondered how many girls and women feared speaking up and forever asked themselves why they stayed quiet or didn't fight back.

The same question always came up and kept repeating. I now realise what the answer to that question is.

Survival.

It was all about survival.

My mind and body knew what it needed to do to survive.

It knew what I needed to get through it.

And it knew exactly what I was capable of.

In the weeks following my rape, I couldn't see through the unfairness of it all. I couldn't see a way past it. I didn't know it then, but I knew it now. Life was just starting.

Tuesday

I had one exam, which was for Health Ed. I smashed out the questions about the risk of drinking while pregnant and even found some creative responses for the short essay questions.

Once it was all done, I found my way back outside and met Hailey.

'How'd you go on that one?' she asked.

'Better than I thought I would, you?'

'Not too bad. I think the question about the muscles really got me.'

'Yeah, I think I totally guessed all of those,' I admitted.

She laughed, heading to the locker bay. When we reached the steps, she stopped, and I ploughed into her.

'What the hell, Hails?' I grabbed my nose. I'd smashed my face right into her backpack, and it was a wonder I wasn't bleeding all over my white school socks. When I pushed her forward and stepped onto the step she was standing on, I saw what she was glaring at. Rachel and Jess were standing by my locker, very clearly writing something in black paint.

'Hails, don't,' I warned.

But she rushed forward, catching both the girls by surprise.

'You think that's funny?' she spat, looking at the very poorly half-written word "SLUT" on the door.

'It's kind of funny,' Rachel giggled.

When I walked over to them, she turned up her bitch game.

'Need your friends sticking up for you now?'

I barely opened my mouth before Hailey shoved her forward into the locker. Jess retaliated by slapping Hailey so hard I heard it reverberate to my core.

For a moment, I thought Hailey might just calmly back off. I was wrong.

'I'm going to rip your hair out!' Hailey screamed.

'Hails, Stop!'

It was no use, though. If she wanted to take all three of them out, she probably could have.

'Get your hands off me!' Jess shrieked when Hailey grabbed her hair, yanking her back. Several strands of blonde extensions came loose, and Hailey tossed them aside, making Jess scream like a feral cat.

The commotion in the locker bay drew the attention of a few others who ran in to help.

Cara grabbed Rachel and pulled her away as Jess went in for another slap.

I rushed in and pushed her back. I didn't even realise how hard I'd pushed her until her back slammed into the locker behind her, the half-wet "SLU" smearing as she sunk to the floor.

'You're a fucking psycho,' she spat.

'And you're a pathetic bitch.'

'What the fuck did you say to me?'

'Are you deaf too?'

She snapped her mouth shut.

'And while we're talking, you're also selfish,' I stepped closer. 'You don't know what it is to suffer a day in your life, do you?'

Her mouth hung open.

'You don't know what it is to be so afraid to come to school and wonder whether you'd make it home that day. You don't know what it means to work extra hard in every single aspect of your life because the second you came here as an immigrant, you were already two steps behind because people like you treat us like lesser humans.'

Behind me, I heard Daniel's voice, and when I turned, I saw that Julian had joined my audience.

This time when I spoke, I looked Jess dead in the eye. 'You don't know what it is to lose who you are because people like you,' I said, turning from her to Rachel and Cara and finally, to Julian, 'ruin people for fun.'

His jaw twitched.

I looked away and turned back to Jess.

'You're an attention whore. Y—you just want people to like you...' Jess stammered.

'And you are a scared little girl who thinks bullying is the answer to fixing your life. Maybe one day you'll grow up enough to see how fucked up that really is,' I added, and turned back to Julian. 'And maybe you'll realise what a pathetic little boy he is.'

Without another word, I walked over to Hailey and helped her straighten her bag.

I gave my locker and the smeared "SLU" one last look before I met Josh and Daniel at the door and left.

Wednesday

I finished the Geography and Politics exams and strode out of the school with my head held high.

'Hey! How did you go?' Hailey caught up to me.

'Good, I think.'

'Yeah?'

'Yeah, I think I'll pass.'

'That's great news.'

Daniel appeared beside me, throwing one arm around my shoulder and the other over Hailey's. 'You two look so relieved to be done.'

'Aren't you?' Hailey asked.

'So happy,' said Daniel.

'Nekić!' Josh clapped me on the back, appearing on my other side. 'You did it.'

Andrew and his best mate, James, joined us. I recognised him as one of the guys who'd helped break the fight up with Blain.

'We did it, guys!' I said. 'Like, really did it, it's finally over.'

'*You* did it,' Josh said.

Andrew nodded beside him. 'You are one sick chick.'

Together, the six of us continued toward the front of the school, the last ever walk out of there as students.

Daniel slowed when a bunch of faces I really didn't want to see emerged from their exam and started walking in our direction. More Julian Valesco fans.

'You've got to be shitting me,' Daniel muttered under his breath, stiffening beside me.

The group of three guys and two tiny brunettes strode toward us and stopped. An irate feeling sizzled to life within me. *What now?*

'What do you want, Kyle?' Josh shot.

'Wanted to say sorry for the shit Valesco put you through.' The guy Josh spoke to looked at me.

'Little late for that, mate,' Daniel snapped.

Kyle stuffed his hands into his pockets, and the rest of his crew looked down. 'I know. But I wanted to say it. You deserve to hear it.'

'Yeah, thanks,' I muttered.

'Come on, Andy,' Andrew gently touched my shoulder.

I turned and started for the exit.

'You okay?' Daniel asked, looping his arm around my waist.

'Yeah, all good.'

'Ah crap,' Josh muttered. 'Can't we just get a clear shot out of this bloody school.'

'Seriously,' Andrew ground out, stalking forward so he was flanking the group.

I looked up and flinched when I saw what they were talking about.

Julian, Illya, and Nick were standing by the gate. He briefly met my gaze before looking down at the ground.

Julian didn't press charges against Daniel because doing so would mean admitting why they were fighting in the first place. Guess the tables had turned on him.

Daniel kept our group moving, and I was thankful for it. I didn't want to falter or show Julian what his presence had done to me. I finally knew what it was to have control and power back, and it felt incredible.

Together, we all left Deanell with hopes and dreams and a smile wider than I ever thought I'd have again.

We were done. Really done.

CHAPTER TWENTY-NINE

Only the Brave

Mum and Dad threw me a party on the weekend. They invited Hailey, Daniel, and Josh, who were allowed to invite one friend each, so Andrew and James, along with my parents and some of their friends like Željko and Ruźa, sat around the garden drinking beer, eating sausages fresh off the barbeque, and listening to terrible songs from the nineties.

'I have to go, guys. Mum's outside,' Hailey said, throwing her arms around mine and Daniel's necks, 'I'll see you at graduation!'

'Yes, girl! Can't wait!'

I walked her out and waited until she was safely inside the taxi with her mum before returning to the party. I snuggled against Daniel and laid my head against his chest, smiling at his heartbeat thundering steadily in my ear. Every time someone had a drunken recollection of something that made them cry, Daniel tightened his hold on me and kissed the top of my head.

We all had something buried deep inside us that made us cry.

As the night drew to a melancholic close, Josh and the boys said their goodbyes and walked themselves out. The adults dipped into a low and emotional conversation as they recalled escaping Yugoslavia.

Daniel pulled me tighter. 'You know what's on the thirteenth?'

'No… am I forgetting something important?'

'It's our one-month anniversary.'

'Really?' I straightened.

'Yep.'

'Well, Daniel, not sure how to break it to you but anniversaries are usually a year thing—'

'Monthserrie, then.'

'Monthserrie? I like that.'

He nodded. 'Me too. And I want to celebrate everything with you.'

'You're super corny, you know that?'

'I think I do.'

I chuckled and then kissed him.

'I think I'm ready for bed. You?' I asked him.

Daniel nodded.

We walked up to my parents, giving them each a hug. Mum didn't even give me the look, warning me about boys staying the night.

Dad held me at arm's length, one hand on either shoulder. 'Do you know that your picture in my bag was the only thing that got me home to you?'

'I know, Tajo.'

'Surviving that war and surviving what you did, it's the same, mišu. Only the brave can do it.'

I threw my arms around his waist and buried my face in

his chest. His deep belly laugh made me cry tears of happiness.

'You're my best friend,' he said.

'And you're mine, Tajo.'

He finally released us, and Daniel and I made our way up to my room.

Together, we snuggled under my fluffy doona. With the comfortable buzz of alcohol and happiness coursing through our veins, I felt myself drift off as Daniel's gentle caress eased me to sleep.

~

When I woke up, Daniel was gone, and a small handwritten note was on the bedside table.

I'm sorry I'm not here when you wake up, but I had to help Mum with some stuff. I'll be over after for that dinner date you promised me. Love, Daniel.

I grinned at the small, terribly drawn love heart he added to the end of his name and carefully stashed the note in my underwear drawer. I'd promised to take him to my favourite diner when we finished school, and now that the time was here, I was so excited. I could kill a man for some onion rings right now. I quickly showered, changed, and made my way down the stairs. Mum and Dad were watching TV.

'You're alive,' I grinned, watching them both down coffees larger than my forearm.

'Don't feel alive,' Mum groaned.

'I'm glad I didn't drink too much,' I teased.

'Smart,' Mum chuckled, 'What are you and Daniel doing?'

'I said I'd take him to Soda Rock.'

'Can I come?' Jelena jumped up and down.

'Not today,' I laughed. 'Next time, I promise.'

'You better.'

Once I'd helped them tidy up the coffee cups, I went upstairs and searched for my sports bag. I found it tucked deep inside my closet, hidden with all the things I swore I'd never wear again. As I grabbed the strap and pulled a small, square-shaped parcel fell out.

Daniel's gift.

My heart sank. I'd never opened it.

The clumsy wrapping was adorned with way too much tape and ribbon. I gave up trying to tear it open and reached for my scissors. When I finally pried the paper off, I grinned when I saw what it was—a CD. He'd drawn a cute teddy along with a small note tucked neatly inside.

Andrea, this CD comes from the heart. Not really because there are techno songs on here. But they're all my favourite songs, things I listen to when I drive or work out. And as cheesy as this sounds, I really hope that one day soon, u and I can listen to these songs together and maybe go for long drives. Ur friend, partner in crime, and all-around nice guy, Daniel.

There was no doubt in my mind that Daniel was, and always had been, the one anomaly I could never read or quite understand.

I knew how lucky we both had been to find each other. Now that I had him, I was never letting go.

~

Daniel arrived within the hour.

He pulled out onto the highway, and when he wasn't looking, I fed the CD into the stereo.

As the first song started, I burst out laughing. 'I'm so glad we can finally listen to these songs from the heart.'

'You finally opened it. I thought it ended up in the bin months ago.'

'Not in the bin, the back of my wardrobe.'

'So, same, same then.'

'You ass.'

He grinned and twisted his fingers through mine. I would never tire of this. I would never forget the way he made my heart flutter, and I would never forget what he'd done for me.

Daniel and I sang, sometimes well, sometimes butchering the song, but mostly we laughed. *Every day was going to be like this now*, I thought. *Fun, safe, hopeful.*

He turned off the freeway and continued down the road until we reached our destination on the corner of Chapel Street.

'You really love this place, don't you?' Daniel said with a smile.

'I really do. Mum, Jelena, and I accidentally found it once when we were out in the city on a day trip and got hungry. And it's been my favourite place since.'

'I can't wait to see it.'

I felt my cheeks burn with the intensity of his gaze. I found myself falling in love.

The second the thought formed, it hit me like a storm on a summer night. I slowed on the footpath and moved aside, letting another couple overtake us.

'You okay? I thought the diner was further up.'

'No, sorry, I'm fine.'

'Andy?' he turned me toward him, 'What's going on?'

'Nothing, I'm fine.'

'You just froze, you're not fine.'

'I'm in love with you,' I blurted out.

He took a step back, and I found myself about to start backtracking, but then he took both my hands in his and smiled. 'Well, good, I thought you were going to tell me you weren't sure about wanting to eat here tonight and I just paid for parking.'

My mouth hung open like those clowns at Luna Park, shocked and a little ugly.

'I love you, too.'

'You do?'

He wrapped his arms around me and kissed my forehead. 'Yeah, I do, and I think I remember saying so once before.'

'Yeah, you did. I just didn't know if it was real.'

'It was. It is. Come on, I'm starving,' he chuckled, nudging me along.

With a bounce in my step, we walked through the doors and were welcomed by a guy my age rolling around on skates. I grinned as he led us to a small booth.

'I'll give you a few minutes to look at the menu, and I'll come back to take your order.' He dropped off a couple of menus and skated away.

Posters of a bygone era lined the walls, and giant pin-up girls advertising Coca-Cola were carefully placed around the booths. Small jukeboxes were fitted on each table, which Daniel eagerly utilised. He smirked and fished out two one-dollar coins.

'What do you want to listen to?'

'You choose. I always make you watch my shows.'

'I don't mind your shows, just between you and me.'

I laughed. 'Oh, really?'

'Really.'

'Well, anyway. I think it's only fair if you get to choose something.'

'Okay.' He fed a coin into the machine, 'Shake it like a Tail Feather, it is.'

I smirked. 'Oh, you'll love what comes next, then.'

As soon as the song came on, the waiters rolled out to the front, and when the music started, began dancing.

Once the song ended, we gave our order to the waiter on skates. Soon after our food arrived, Daniel reached across the table and took my hand.

'I'm really happy you told me the thing before.'

'The thing where I said I loved you?' I teased.

'Yeah, that little thing,' he said, his smile widening.

'Oh, you know, thought it might be important to mention.'

'Yeah, glad you did. It's a kind of a big deal.'

'Is it?' I teased again. 'I thought it was just a passing comment, you know, before you go to dinner?'

He laughed.

Once we were done, Daniel paid for everything and insisted that I could get it next time. I grinned all the way home and then grinned even more when I realised my parents and Jelena were asleep, which meant I insisted Daniel come upstairs.

I closed the door with a gentle thud and gently pushed him towards my bed.

'Andy…'

'Sit,' I said as my hands drifted over his arms, gently pushing him down.

I kissed him with everything in me, and when his hands slipped under my shirt and grazed over my bra, I buried my face in the crook of his shoulder.

'I love you,' I whispered.

Daniel drew my face back to his and kissed me harder before pulling back to look at me. 'I love you more.'

As he slipped my shirt off and I helped him out of his, I stopped his mumbling by pushing him down into my bed and under my sheets.

'Kiss me,' I whispered.

And he did.

CHAPTER THIRTY

The End of an Era

It wasn't just the end of high school that today signalled, or the end of almost thirteen years of schooling, which resulted in a single sheet of paper telling you how smart you were, irrespective of the mountains in your way over the years, or the ditches you found yourself climbing out of.

The piece of paper signalled the end of an era, a transition from having your whole world planned out to suddenly having no more structure.

For me, though, it signalled the beginning of something new and exciting, the next step in my life as an adult, no longer constrained to the horrors of four walls and a glass ceiling deceptively telling me to aim higher.

For me, this piece of paper was my gold star, a testament to the strength and survival I never knew I had in me. It was my ticket to a life I'd earned, proof that I was as worthy as anyone else here, and it didn't matter where I'd come from or what my name was. I made it. I survived.

'Sign it!' Josh nudged me in the rib, dropping his little *autograph* book on the table in front of me.

The teachers and students who'd organised the valedictory dinner spent all year planning the perfect time to present us all with one of the small leather-bound books, a memento to take with us to the next part of our lives.

Mine was gone, making the rounds, probably missing every second person because no one knew who I was. Josh's was full. I smirked at the overly cheery promises of catching up and very forward proposals of hookups.

Josh disappeared, leaving his book on our table as Daniel plopped down beside me. He scoffed down two croissants while I flicked through Josh's book, looking for a blank page.

'Have you signed some?' I asked him.

'Yeah, I managed to do a few, but they're all over the tables,' he said over the loud music.

I glanced around the dim room lit only by the flashing lights dancing in sync with the music. Everyone was so alive, leaving behind any previous grievances about boyfriends or lost grades. If only things that plagued my heart and weighed on my mind could have been so easily forgotten.

It will be. One day. Maybe in a few years, maybe in a decade. And that's okay.

Finally, I found a blank page. I clicked my pen and began to write:

Josh, my best guy friend (don't tell Daniel), you've stood by my side, fought even when I didn't want to, and surrendered when I needed you to. Above all else, you taught me who I was. Thank you, Andy.

I looked over the note and smiled again.

Daniel took Josh's book and flicked to the next page, scribbling something in himself. I couldn't make it out but laughed when I spotted the giant poo he drew.

'So mature,' I said, shaking my head.

'He'll appreciate it, trust me.'

'Oh, I'm sure.'

'Got any more there?' He craned his neck, searching the table.

I saw two more and snatched them up.

'Students!' The principal announced, 'or should I say ladies and gents, you're not my students anymore.'

A few jeers and hoorahs exploded around the room.

'We'll be wrapping up in the next fifteen minutes, and while I know this party signals the end of one life and the beginning of a new one, I know that every one of you will be brilliant wherever you go, whatever you decide to do. So, as your principal, one final time, thank you for a wonderful, sometimes challenging, memorable year. Good luck!'

As he continued his stern warnings about not slacking off at uni or work, I grinned and opened Hailey's book.

You are the bestest friend a girl could ever hope for. You're the Willow to my Buffy, and I know you were always there, even when we didn't speak, even when I was too tired. Thank you for everything. Andy X

I smiled at the message and then closed it, taking a few moments to tune back into the speech.

'Congratulations, Class of 2006, you've done it!' he shouted to erupting cheers and celebrations.

Everyone at my table, aside from Daniel, jumped up and started dancing. I shook my head with a grin and reached for the final book. When I opened it, my hand stilled over the deceptively innocent text staring at me.

Daniel closed his hand over mine, glancing over the book.

'Leave it, I'll take it over.'

'No, it's fine,' I smiled.

'You don't have to write anything.'

'I want to.'

His fists balled on the table as I carefully opened the book and found a blank page. There, I wrote one simple sentence. Then I got up, packed my phone and shoes, and twisted my fingers through Daniel's.

'Let's get out of here,' I said.

Daniel and I walked hand in hand. I took a deep breath and walked ahead, stopping just short of Julian's table. Jess immediately closed her mouth and shot me a scowl.

Julian slowly turned. When his eyes found mine, I saw something I never thought I would before: remorse, *regret*.

I dropped the book in front of him, 'What you did to me was unforgivable, and nothing you say to try and justify it will ever make it better, and nothing you say to me will ever make this my fault. You're not the victim here. You're not the one whose life was ruined, you're not the one who suffered, and whatever you tell yourself to sleep at night is a lie. I know the truth.'

His gaze lowered.

'I hope that one day you truly understand,' I added. 'Though I doubt a guy like you ever could.'

Before I could let him hear the shaking in my voice, I turned and let Daniel wrap his arm around my shoulder and guide me out. Together, we walked out of the school gymnasium for the last time ever.

He pressed a kiss to my cheek as we walked through the

gate. 'What did you write?'

What did I write in his book? How did I articulate in one sentence all that I had endured, all that I had faced and overcome?

I smiled and kept walking. When we were free of the gates, I stopped and looked back over the looming building one last time.

'Julian Valesco, you didn't break me.'

A MESSAGE TO MY READERS...

Dear Reader,

I never imagined what Year Twelve would have in store for me. Amidst the monumental task of making new friends–*yet again*–remaining a perfect student, dutiful daughter and sister, I didn't see that my greatest battle was about to unfold.

As the years crawled on, so much about that period came into a strange new focus. PTSD and depression from the war in Yugoslavia, leaving Dad behind, and migrating to three countries–all before I was six, left an indelible mark on me, one I wish I'd known about earlier.

Part of me wonders whether the pain of those days shaped me, creating an almost perfect storm of vulnerability and naivete. A part of me wonders whether that's why Julian Valesco so easily subdued me. Another part still blames myself.

But as the years go on and the conversation around consent and coercion grows, so too do the discussions and support systems. We know now and understand with each passing day as the conversation becomes one of necessity and not of taboo, that these monsters don't just lurk in the dark; they hide behind kind smiles and respectable positions. It is never the victim's fault. Knowing all I do now, I would have perhaps had the courage to stand up to Julian and fight back, go to the police or at the very least, seek justice.

But like so many women, I didn't get my closure. I've had to live with the knowledge that he never admitted fault, never apologised, never acknowledged what he'd done. He took parts of me I could never get back, and so many years later, I still think about him. Did he ever feel bad? Did he ever regret his actions? Does he even know what he did was wrong? Part of me wonders, and another doesn't care.

But this story isn't a tragedy. It's a tale of love—the love of my friends, my family, and those who supported me.

Hailey and I are still close, and she still supports me on my healing journey to this day. We still talk about *Buffy* and *Alias* and Josh became a sports star like we all knew he would. We watch his games and cheer from the sidelines.

And after spending every single day together during my final summer as a student, I realised Daniel was the love of my life. We travelled the world together, made dreams together and married soon after. He still holds my hand when he drives, he still holds me after nightmares of that night chase sleep from me but most importantly of all, he shows me every day what love should be like.

I have the best relationship I could have ever hoped for with my family. Jelena became an artist and a musician. And I became an author, just like I'd always dreamed. It took a while to heal and to find a way to make it happen, but I did it.

I now help women who, like me, were betrayed and victimised. I shout for them when their voices have been taken.

I may have been attacked and betrayed, but I refuse to be a victim any longer.

So here this book sits in your hand, my faithful reader; a story I'd committed to the darkness of my mind, finally brought into the light so many years later.

Some days are still hard. Some weeks catch me

completely off guard. But I stand tall, weather the storm, and fight like hell to get through it, and I'm forever thankful I didn't die.

Because even though there will always be Julian Valescos out there, I know there will also be Daniels, Joshs, and Haileys. And no matter how hopeless, how dark, and how uncertain life can get, we–*all of us*–can be warriors.

Stand tall because silence will not win.

Silence has no place where only the brave walk.

Love,

Andrea Nekić

ACKNOWLEDGEMENTS

Mum & Dad, you had your hands full with a teenager like me. I didn't thank you as often as I should have, if at all. I apologize for young Vikica but present Viki appreciates you. You gave everything up to come to Australia, you fought in a war that had no winners, to come to a country that made us feel alienated. But even when we had close to nothing, I was the richest kid in the world. Your love and your compassion were more important than the things you wish you could have given me. Thank you.

My Vanessa, you endured much more than any kid should have because you had to live in the shadows of my chaos. Your fierce, determined personality saved me more often than I can count and you helped in more ways than one. You were just a kid, but you were far beyond your years. I'm eternally grateful for your support, offers to play Nintendo, watch Anastasia and Swan Princess. Whenever I need you, I know you're just a message away. Hvala, Seko.

Sorin, you quite literally saved my life. How do you top that? I don't even know where to begin but to say that you were brave enough to stand beside me, generous enough to care for me, and fierce enough to love me. Without you and your steadfast love, I'm certain I wouldn't have survived that year and, more recently, when everything came to light. You were my rock then and forever will be. I love you, what you do for us, how you make me feel about myself, and what we are together. We are the ultimate love story; Ace and Illarion got nothing on us.

Adele, you were the first friend I openly talked to about

what happened. I still remember our drunken walk to the station from JCDecaux (I know you said it the same way I did!) when I burst into tears, recalling the event. You stood with me at Richmond station, telling me I was strong and brave. I didn't believe it then, but I do now, and you have been right there beside me every step of the way, watching my journey, cheering me on and supporting me. You're always there, always listening, always patient. I love you and I cherish you. Nine-Nine!

Angeline & Daniel (Daniel, you and I go way back; you were always a gentle and caring soul in school, and I'll never forget your kindness). Ange, you came into my life in a series of weird, cosmic coincidences. When we met, I presented my world to you in a bag full of tiny, shattered pieces and *so* many tears (did I cry every session? Probably). Girl, not only did you put those pieces back together, but you did so with cement, superglue and pure magic. You gave me the validation my heart so desperately needed, and I can never thank you enough for giving me my voice back.

Tegan, my dear friend. Since I was eleven years old, I looked up to you as the rising star at school. You were always kind, always encouraging and when I was too scared to take on my first big role (a Grade Six play) you refused to let me quit! And now with Andrea, with all the things I fought through, you reminded me like you did then that I could do it, and that I would. You read the first version of this book, helped me navigate the feelings and process the emotion. Our morning walks and early coffees have saved me countless times. I am eternally grateful to you.

Sifu Damien, the universe has a funny way of bringing people into your life when you need them most. We've known each other for close to two decades now, but when I needed help the most, you were there to walk with me and guide me. You taught me to find my strength.

My beta team: Tara, Crystal, Louise, Lana, Cat, Diana, Richard, and Rena. You've all read the very first versions of this book so many years ago and without your constant commentary and updates as you read, I wouldn't have been as confident with this book as I am today. You helped bring something powerful to life. Thank you.

My incredible team at Dragonfly Publishing, Lisa and Rebekah. What can I say that will suffice? You took on a massive project, which was hard enough to begin with. Your job was to edit and perfect this story, but you went above and beyond. You approached each conversation and edit with such care and empathy, making me feel safe and heard every time we met. That is a testament to your values and who you are as people and what DP stands for. I cannot thank you enough for taking a chance on me and Andrea and bringing this book to life.

Finally, to you, the reader. You embarked on Andrea's journey, which would have been hard at times, wonderful at others, but most importantly, honest and raw. Just as Andrea's pain and suffering are reflected in the eyes of countless women around the world, so too is her strength and resilience. Too often, stories like Andrea's—like mine—are censored to make people comfortable, but I'm not here to make you comfortable; I'm here to make you think.

So, while Andrea's story is not a carbon copy of mine; it is a glimpse into the journey I overcame. I didn't get the closure I sought; I didn't receive the apology I hoped for, yet I did gain something far more important: belief in myself.

ABOUT THE AUTHOR

Violeta Bagia is an author, speaker, writing coach and advocate. Armed with a Master of Arts, a Graduate Certificate, and a Diploma in Professional Writing, she's basically a wizard of words with the credentials to prove it!

Having authored eighteen books and published eight—both traditionally and independently—Violeta brings her fearless prowess to the literary world. The mission? To spark meaningful conversations about consent, bullying, and mental health awareness. The method? Using the power of story and the magic of words to shine a light on the issues that matter most in ways that are palatable to all.

When she's not crafting her next wild and wonderful narrative, coaching aspiring writers, or speaking on the topics closest to her heart, Violeta can be found baking, wandering the great outdoors, or playing Barbies with her daughter.

She is currently represented by Dragonfly Publishing and Vulpine Press.

NEED TO TALK?

Lifeline provides 24-hour crisis counselling, support groups and suicide prevention services. Call **13 11 14**, text 0477 13 11 14 or visit lifeline.org.au.

Suicide Call Back Service provides 24/7 support if you or someone you know is feeling suicidal. Call **1300 659 467**.

Beyond Blue aims to increase awareness of depression and anxiety and reduce stigma. If you or a loved one need help, call **1300 22 4636**, 24 hours/7 days a week or go to beyondblue.org.au.

MindSpot is a free telephone and online service for people with anxiety, stress, low mood, or depression and provides online assessment and treatment for anxiety and depression. MindSpot is not an emergency or instant response service. Call **1800 61 44 34**.

Kids Helpline is a free 24/7 confidential and private counselling service specifically for children and young people aged 5–25. Call **1800 55 1800** or visit kidshelpline.com.au.

headspace provides free online and telephone support and counselling to young people aged 12–25 and their families and friends. Call **1800 650 890** or visit headspace.org.au.

DP *Fiction* is an imprint of Dragonfly Publishing.

Dragonfly Publishing books can be purchased via the website: www.dragonflypublishing.com.au/dp-books, from major online retailers, and in Australian bookstores.

9 781763 552593